Bel Barker: Psychic Detective

Book One

SHADOW

by

T. Loker

Tuesday 18th June 2019
12:18
Day Five

Bel Barker stood in front of the huge smoked-glass door to the police station, one hand gripping the metal handle as she absent-mindedly did that thing she did with her bottom lip, biting at it nervously with her front teeth, sucking it into her mouth, as she tried to work out what she was going to say when she went inside. She made a conscious effort to stop the chewing, then started again a couple of seconds later as her mind turned to the task ahead of her.

There was no doubt in her mind the next few moments were going to be difficult. Bel knew that as soon as she opened the door and stepped into the building, she would have to start explaining herself, not just what she knew, but how. She wasn't sure that the how made any sense outside of her own head.

The alternative though, would be worse, both for herself and for the missing girl. One day at some unknown time in the future they would finally discover the body. From that moment on Bel knew she would carry the haunting guilt of knowing, unless she did something today, right now, to say something, to make someone understand.

Bel sucked in a deep breath, hoping to inhale a confidence she didn't feel, tightened her grip on the strap of her shoulder bag, and almost jumped out of her skin when her phone began to buzz in her pocket. Bel swiped the screen open and glanced at the message. Nigel. No surprise there. The first three words were please, please, please. Bel stabbed at the off button, stuffed the phone back into her bag. Too late for please, Nigel. Too late even for sorry.

Bel leaned on the brushed steel handle, then pushed open the heavy door and went inside. The reception area was empty. The soles of her sensible shoes squeaked with every step as she tried to make her unobtrusive way across the huge open space towards the counter. The floor seemed to be made of rubber, felt slightly soft underfoot, swept up in seamless curves where it met the bottom of each wall, so that Bel felt as if she was walking into the world's biggest wet room. She slowed her pace as she walked, trying to roll each foot over onto its side, but it didn't really help; if anything, walking more slowly only made the sounds worse, stretched out each squeak into an off-key lament. Not until she reached the counter and let it out with a cough did Bel realise that she had been holding her breath all the way across the floor. The inside of the building looked as careworn and shabby as the outside. The scuffed black counter had the same slightly rubbery feeling as the floor. There were deep scratches and gouges across its surface, and even a couple of places where it looked as if someone had tried to set fire to it with a cigarette lighter. There was a declaration of love from some guy named Jamie for some girl named Kirsty written at about knee height. Bel tilted her head to one as she tried make out a particularly boastful phallic cartoon on the front of the counter. The place was like a war zone. Bel shrugged, looked around while she waited, glancing at the jumbled collage of notices tacked to the walls, each of them offering advice or seeking information; a litany of lost dogs, stolen bikes, appeals for witnesses to various muggings and minor thefts. There was a heavy, cloying smell of disinfectant that didn't quite manage to hide the sharp nip of stale urine.

Bel went over again what she was planning to say, rehearsing key phrases that she hoped would help her explain what had happened, why she had come here. She talked herself through it under her breath, reminding herself to keep calm, to breathe slowly, explain everything that she knew, everything she though she knew, in a measured manner, not just blurt it all out in one hectic gasp that she was secretly worried might happen when she actually started to speak. The knot of anxiety that had replaced the bile in her stomach had already begun to tighten. Bel tried to recall some of the stuff from the two and a half lessons of Pilates she'd been to a couple of years ago, hoping that it might help her to relax a bit. Keeping the shoulders down came into it she recalled, and something about relaxing the diaphragm. Bel could feel her shoulders up around her ears somewhere, and her diaphragm felt like a block of concrete.

That was when she noticed the small sign placed discreetly on the counter next to the remains of what had once been some small shrub or plant but had finally given up the ghost, obviously choosing death and decay in preference to this gloomy environment. 'Press button for assistance'. Bel un-clenched her jaw, let out a small sigh, a headache already starting to gather in a hot bunch behind her eyes. She leaned across to push the button. A tired buzzer farted somewhere in the distance behind a closed door.

Bel went back to waiting, began to rub the palms of her hands down the sides of the dark blue trouser suit that she knew made her look frumpy beyond all hope, but was the only real choice she had for work, trying to keep the clamminess at bay.

Bel was here because of the dream. The first night she had brushed it aside, dismissed it as just a weird dream, but when the same dream woke her again the following night, and again last night at about four o'clock she made up her mind she had to do something, even if that meant making a fool of herself.

In her dream the girl was beautiful. Bel could only stare at her, captivated by the long tresses of auburn hair gathered together in a loose chignon with a silver buckle clip. The girl stood at the foot of her bed, playing the violin. There was a full orchestra playing somewhere too, but Bel couldn't see them. It sounded like they were in the wardrobe, so Bel got out of bed, in her dream, walked slowly across the deep pile of the bedroom carpet, opened the doors. The wardrobe was huge inside, cavernous. The music stopped the instant she looked inside. There were hundreds of musicians, seated in rows. They all paused mid-note and looked up, staring, scowling at her for being so rude. Bel took the hint, mumbled an apology, closed the door. The music started again, coming up to speed like one of those old wind-up gramophones. Bel turned to go back to bed. The girl still stood at the foot of Bel's bed, hadn't begun to play again, but held her violin at her side, the bow barely gripped in pale fingers. Bel could see the girl's lips moving but couldn't hear what she was saying. A metronome drip of tears fell from one eye, tracing a glycerine track on her cheek.

'Help me. Please. Help me.'

'What is it? What's wrong?'

The girl moved towards her, close enough for Bel to feel a warm sigh of breath on her cheek. She flinched back from the untouching contact, blinked.

As she opened her eyes Bel found herself in a tiny room. She was kneeling on the floor. The girl crouched a few feet in front of her, rocking backwards and forwards as she hugged her knees to her chest, a thin mattress under her heels. She was shivering, but Bel didn't think it was all because she could feel the cold. The ceiling was a low arch that pressed down just a few feet above Bel's head. There were no windows that she could see. The brick walls seem to be sweating salt. Everything smelled foisty, damp.

The girl stared at Bel, blinked a few times as if she wasn't quite sure what she was looking at, turned to slap her hands against the wall, began to pound and scratch at the bare bricks. Bel watched as the girl's beautiful nails dug into the mortar, snagging and splintering, the dull tearing sound making her cringe and shudder. A streak of blood ran from one torn fingernail, made a smear down the wall; a jarring note of colour in the stark place.

Dream dictionaries generally described music and musicians in positive terms; to the best of Bel's knowledge they didn't make any reference to small brick-walled prisons. Right up until that morning Bel had been trying to dismiss the dream as just that; a weird dream. It was a bit strange then, to see the same girl's face staring up at her from the local news feed on Facebook as she scanned the news pages, as if she had gone straight from her dream to her phone's screen. It read like a story that didn't quite add up; the girl had been reported missing from the college where she was studying the violin, and the police were investigating, but they couldn't seem to make up their minds whether the girl had just wandered off somewhere, perhaps decided to drop out of sight for a few days, or if something more sinister had happened. Bel knew though. Bel had dreamed the dream.

A clatter of noise; a door opening. Bel blinked herself back to the here and now, looked at the face of a woman in uniform scowling at her from behind the counter. 'Can I help you?' No smile here, no suggestion of customer service.

'I need to speak to someone about the missing girl, Emily Phillips. The one that's been in the papers.' Bel was quite pleased with herself that she had managed to keep her voice level despite the obviously aggressive vibes coming from the woman on the other side of the counter. The policewoman's eyes narrowed perceptibly. 'And your connection with the case is what exactly?' Her eyebrows, too wild, too bushy in Bel's opinion, and in desperate need of re-shaping, rose in interrogation. Bel was determined to hold her gaze though, so she stared right back at the other woman, braved it out, even though the little girl inside her was pleading that she should give up on this whole silly idea, come to her senses before it was too late, turn around and leave, run out of the door without a backward glance. The only thing that stopped Bel was that right at that moment she wasn't sure she could remember how to make her legs work.

'I have some information,' her voice sounded small now in the space. 'Something that might help.'

The policewoman looked back at her without blinking for long, long seconds before finally excusing herself with 'I'll just see if there's someone who can take your statement,' and Bel was left alone again with the scuffed plastic counter, the sluiceable floor and the disinfectant smell.

Detective Inspector Ian Fox sat at his desk; cold coffee ignored in a beige plastic cup. They'd stopped providing crockery at the station ages ago, too much of it kept going missing. He brooded as he stared at the large board mounted on the wall across from his chair. Things were not going well. It was a big board. Pinned right in the middle, looking small and alone, a photograph of Emily Phillips. She sat primly upright, with her violin resting on her lap, her dark hair a vast cable of a plait that draped over one shoulder almost down to her waist. Her broad face stared out at him, open, naive, not quite smiling. The girl's mother said the photo was taken a couple of years ago, that she didn't dress in pleated skirts and starched white blouses anymore, but that it was still a good likeness.

In any other case there would have been more than just the photo. The board would have been full of stuff; snippets, leads, contacts, but this time the photo was just about all Fox had. The case seemed to be going nowhere. This was supposed to be his big chance, his golden opportunity to "earn his bones", to shine for the D.C.I., and maybe even get noticed by the Superintendent. There was just the one tiny problem; Emily Phillips, seventeen years old and a rising star in the world of classical music, had disappeared without a trace.

Fox knew that was what you got in a missing persons case, but it had been five days now since she had disappeared from the college of music, five days since her handbag and other bits and pieces were found scattered in the corridor. Since then he had had the case almost completely to himself, and what did he have to show for it? Diddley-squat.

Fox had started looking into the girl's background, certain that he was going to quickly find that Emily had become smitten with some new boyfriend and had run away for a few days of secret sex in Scarborough, or that she had been kidnapped and killed by an evil step-father and hidden in the loft, or maybe even abducted by her besotted music tutor, but there was nothing. Emily had never had any sexual relationships that he could uncover. Her father had died ten years before, but her mother had never got re-married or shown even a passing interest in forming any new relationships. Her violin tutor for the last three years had been one of the leading teachers in the country but turned out to be a woman in her fifties. When he had spoken to her, the woman had talked only about how talented Emily was. Hardly the stuff of red-hot passion. There were no reports of stalking. Emily herself seemed to have only one relationship; with her violin. How could someone just disappear?

Fox scowled at the photo, willing it into revealing some information, then scooped up his tepid coffee, shuddering as the bitter liquid went down with a gulp. About his only chance now was that she would turn up dead. If she got herself murdered the case would obviously go up the line, but there would be a chance that he could claim a place close to the action because he'd already been putting in the basic legwork on the case.

WPC Barratt poked her head round the door, breaking his train of thought. 'Woman in reception says she's got some info on the Phillips girl.'

Fox had always felt a little intimidated by the permanent scowl on Barratt's middle-aged face, even though he out-ranked her. He scrunched the plastic cup, tossed it into the bin in the corner, scraped back the chair to stand. Maybe things were looking up, maybe this would be the break in the case he'd been waiting for. 'On my way.' As he made his way to reception, he intoned a muttered prayer that the woman waiting there would be carrying a blood-stained knife in one hand and a violin in the other.

Bel looked around some more while she waited, noticed the black bulb of a camera fixed in one corner of the ceiling. It didn't surprise her that she was probably being watched. They'd be cracking jokes at her expense right now, she thought, laughing at her, maybe even running a book on how long they could keep her waiting. That was the sort of thing they did, wasn't it? Bel began to count her heartbeats until a different door clicked open.

She couldn't help but stare at the man as he approached and held out his hand in greeting.

'Detective Inspector Ian Fox.' Bel had already built up an image of what the detective would look like, based mainly on watching detective stories on the telly, so she had been more or less expecting a gruff, scruffy old man in a greasy overcoat with a penchant for jazz music or real ale, but this guy looked to be only a handful of years older than her own twenty-six. He was tall, too, and decidedly handsome, in her opinion. No scruffy overcoat for DI Ian Fox; he had on a blue-grey suit that hung just right on his lean frame. Judging by his almost triangular shape, he worked out too. As he reached forward to take Bel's hand in his firm grip she wished she had pockets full of tissues to soak up the clamminess on her palms, but the man appeared not to notice, just shucked the cuffs of his shirt-sleeves where they poked out of his jacket, checking to make sure they were the perfect length after the handshake. Happy he was correctly dressed; Fox lifted his eyes to look at the woman in front of him properly for the first time. Bel wondered how she didn't faint as their eyes locked for a second. His eyes were the colour of the summer sky, with tiny flecks of sand and sea. Bel could feel the thick, hot flutter of her heart in her chest, and became embarrassingly aware of the crimson flush of heat as a blush began to rise on her throat. She was worried that it threatened to sweep across her face at any second. She made a conscious decision in there somewhere to close her mouth. He was so perfect that she felt lumpy and frumpy as she stood in front of him, shuffling from foot to foot in her blue polyester trouser-suit and flat shoes.

'Barker, Bel Barker. Isabel. My friends call me Bel,' she finally answered. She had been aiming for confident, casual, but her lips seemed to have lost all trace of moisture and for some reason her tongue had decided to stick itself to the roof of her mouth, so by the time she finished introducing herself she was barely able to form the words.

'And you say you have some information concerning Emily Phillips, Miss Barker?' His voice was a bit too loud. Bel felt a little bit scared, threatened even.

'Er, yes.' Bel could see eyebrow-woman out of the corner of her eye, loitering behind the counter, probably for the first time in history, ears set to maximum. Bel was determined that if she was going to make a fool of herself, she wasn't going to do it in front of an audience. 'Can we go somewhere a bit more private?'

No doubt Fox must have thought that this average-looking woman in front of him, rocking ever so slightly from foot to foot in her dark blue trouser-suit and flat, black shoes was a little weird to say the least, but what the hell. He shrugged, turned to go back through the door. He held it open for her to follow and Bel caught up in half a stride.

The door swung shut behind her with a mechanical gasp. The sharp, high-pitched smells of disinfectant and urine were replaced in her nostrils by the ripe, funky odours of leather polish and sweaty feet. Bel was more than a little relieved to find that her shoes no longer squeaked on the floor. As she followed Fox along the narrow corridor, she did what any sensible woman would do, craned her neck from side to side, trying to see into rooms as they hurried past, but there didn't seem to be anything of interest. Fox stopped at a plain maroon door, pushed it open, led the way into a tiny room. The cramped space made Bel's skin crawl; the walls were an insipid cream-of-seaweed green and they seemed to crowd in on every side. She felt herself growing smaller with every passing second. The only furniture was a small, square table, the surface scratched, the edges chipped, with a moulded plastic chair tucked under each side. Fox dragged one chair out and dropped onto it, dug a small notebook and a cheap biro with a badly chewed end out of his jacket pocket. He waved casually towards the other chair, inviting Bel to sit, the shadow of his hand thrown hard on the table by the single fluorescent light above.

'So, Miss Barker, you have some information you want to share with us. About Emily Phillips?'

'Yes, that's right.' Bel was nervous, sat perched on the edge of the chair. She could feel the plastic lip digging into the back of her thighs.

'Enlighten me.' Fox turned to a clean page and waited, pen poised.

'It's a bit complicated.'

'Complicated how?' He glanced up at her, a small frown on his face.

'Complicated's not the right word. Different might be better.'

'Okay, different.' His pen still didn't move.

This was it; Bel knew. This was where it would all start to get official, get strange, get awkward. She took a deep breath. In for a penny. 'I know you're going to think I'm crazy, but I need you to hear me out. I think Emily Phillips has been kidnapped. She's being held against her will, she's in a small room with brick walls and I think it's got an arched ceiling. She's trying to get out. She's cold and she's tired and she's scared.'

'Where did you get this information from?'

'Would you believe me if I told you it came to me in a dream?'

Fox looked at Bel for a few seconds, trying to size her up, trying to read some clue in her face to show if she was serious in what she was saying. The only thing he could see was a slight squint in her right eye. 'To be honest, yes, I think I would,' he finally said.

'That's such a relief,' Bel managed a thin smile, exhaled in relief. 'I wasn't sure how open you were going to be about this sort of thing. Anyway, it's not an ordinary dream as such, it's more like watching a movie while I'm asleep, but I was in the movie and so was Emily, and she showed me that she's locked away somewhere.'

'Does this happen often? These dreams?' Fox asked.

Bel was watching his face as he spoke but couldn't judge his expression. She carried on. 'No, hardly ever. I don't go looking for this sort of thing, it just happens. It's not usually dreams, either. Most times it's psychometry. You know, picking up information from inanimate objects. Anyway, Emily keeps playing the violin at me, in my dream, and then she starts crying and asks me to help her.' The words tumbled out in a stream, almost on top of each other. Until that moment Bel hadn't realised just how much she'd needed someone to listen to her, to believe in her. She paused, took another deep breath.

'That's why you're here? Because Emily Phillips asked you to help her in a dream?' Fox asked. Bel couldn't help but notice that he had put his pen down. The page of his little notepad remained unmarked.

'Well, like I said, it's a bit more than a dream, it's a kind of vision, I suppose.'

'And you've seen Emily in this, this vision?' His eyes seemed to frost over; all trace of summer gone.

It was about then that Bel knew that the interview was as good as over, that Fox had already closed his mind to anything she might try to tell him, that it had been a mistake to come to the police station, but she knew that she'd had no choice, she had to follow her heart on this. Snatching a gulp of air, she made one last try. 'You've got to believe me, please. It's like I said, she's been kidnapped. She's in pain. She's feeling scared and confused.'

Fox's chair creaked as he leaned back, stared at the ceiling, his hands clasped behind his head. The chair balanced on two legs. He stayed motionless for so long that Bel began to wonder what he had found to look at, glanced upwards herself. There was a long, thin crack in the plaster, and a few black spots of mould in one corner, nothing to get excited about. 'Can you describe her abductors?' Fox asked at last. 'How many there were, what they looked like, what they were wearing?' He didn't look at Bel as he spoke, continued to stare at the ceiling.

'No, er, one, there's one man, but I've not seen him in my vision, only Emily.'

'One assailant, but you've not seen him. What about the car? Assuming there was a vehicle of some sort. I don't suppose you got a registration number. Make? Model? Colour? No?'

'No, no, I didn't. Hang on. Look, you don't understand. It's not like that, I didn't see that bit, only Emily.' Bel could feel the conversation slipping away from her. It was so frustrating. This man wasn't even pretending to be interested in what she was trying to tell him. She began to feel uncomfortable, as if she was being mocked, played. 'It's not supposed to be like watching a documentary on the telly. It's more like a series of snapshots; feelings, emotions, impressions, that sort of thing.'

'Snapshots and feelings.' Fox's words dripped acid.

'I get better results from objects. If you like I could...'

Fox's chair slammed back down onto four legs, making Bel jump. 'I don't like,' he said. 'Was there anything else, only I'm a bit busy looking for a missing teenager.' The words came out as one long growl. He closed his notebook with a snap and rested the pen on top, taking care to line it up perfectly with the left edge of the little pad. He pinched the bridge of his nose, and Bel was suddenly struck by how weary he looked, the drawn lines of exhaustion on his face. After long seconds he exhaled a sigh, dropped his shoulders. 'Thank you, Miss Barker, we'll be in touch.'

'Hang on, I thought you'd want to know everything.'

'That's just it though, isn't it, Miss Barker?' He made the honorific a hiss. 'There isn't any everything, is there? It's all just bland, empty phrases. Snapshots and feelings? Music!' He didn't try to hide the sneer in his voice, scraped back his chair, got to his feet, opened the door. 'I'll show you out.' It took a second for Bel to realise that the interview really was over, that he was leaving the room. She scrambled to her feet, hurried to follow. Fox didn't once look back to check that she was behind him. She could feel her teeth clenching into a silent growl as she seethed at the sheer arrogance of the man. Fox pulled open a second door, walked through. Bel felt so frustrated. This wasn't how it was supposed to go at all. She tried to think of something else to say, something she could shout after him, something to get him to stop, to let her start again, try to explain the whole thing properly, but her tongue was a slab of stone in her mouth. She managed to stop the door before it swung shut in her face, walked through, found herself back in the foyer. Eyebrow woman was still there, loitering behind the counter, obviously waiting for any follow-up. 'If I had my way,' Fox turned, almost spat the words at Bel, his voice pure contempt, 'I'd prosecute your sort for wasting police time, but the Gaffer says we don't have the time or the resources, so I guess you can count yourself lucky,' there was a very significant pause, 'this time.'

'My sort?'

'You so-called bloody psychics. That's what your calling yourself, isn't it? Psychic? It's the same every time there's a big case. I can just about cope with the idiot phone calls, and a few crazy e-mails I can always delete after I've read them, but I'll never understand where someone like you gets the brass neck to just walk in off the street and spout all this crap as if it was real, as if it actually meant something.'

Bel felt a very different blush flash across her skin, gazed down at her shoes rather than meet his gaze. She risked a glance across at eyebrow woman, watched as one furry caterpillar rose in reproach. Enough was enough, Bel turned her back, hurried to the exit, pushed through the heavy door and out into the street.

The warm summer breeze brought a rash of cold prickles to her sweat-beaded brow.

~~~~~
~~~~~

Date and time unknown.
Sometime between Friday 14th June 2019 and Saturday 6th July 2019

Emily blinked, opened her eyes, tried to focus in the sallow light.

Her head felt too heavy, and seemed to be filled with a buzzing, electric fog.

She couldn't work out if this was the first time, or if she had slept and woke, slept and woke ten times, a hundred, a thousand. She let her eyes fall closed again, tried to dream of summer mornings, of a warm breeze caressing her arms as she snuggled back into the soft cotton sheets of her bed. A small smile played on her lips.

Emily's eyes fluttered open.

The cotton sheets evaporated in an instant.

She lifted her head from the crook of her shoulder where it lay, gulped back the wave of nausea that overwhelmed her as she moved, as if gravity had launched a personal vendetta against her. With a gasp of effort, she rolled onto her side to look around.

The room was tiny. A small lamp stood on the floor at one end. Its yellow light too feeble to dispel the shadows that lingered in the corners. The room looked to be about ten or twelve feet long, not much more than six or seven wide. She could almost stretch out her arms to touch both walls at the same time. Bare brick walls, oozing damp, leeching salt, rose on either side to meet in a narrow arch a few feet above her head. The mattress on the floor felt greasy, damp to the touch. A grubby white duvet, no cover, sat on it in a crumpled ball.

She closed her eyes, rubbed her temples with her fingertips, opened them again.

What the Hell was going on?

In the flat wall at one end of the room a rusty metal door, the only feature in the brickwork. She felt too dizzy, too sick, to even try to stand, so she crawled towards it on her hands and knees, trying not to let the claustrophobia that she could feel building in her chest boil up into outright panic. The door was less than four feet high. When she got right up to it, she could see it was a single sheet of thick metal, dull red brown with rust, large hinges welded to one edge. There was no handle. She couldn't see a keyhole. She forced her fingers under the lip of metal at the side, tried to pull it open. It moved about half an inch, stopped solid. No amount of pulling or rattling would make it budge. After a few seconds she felt exhausted, her muscles drained, her breathing laboured. She slumped down with her back to the door, resting her head against the cold metal as she listened to her heart pounding in her throat. She slowly scanned the room.

With a start she realised what was so obvious it was beneath notice. Light. There were no windows, but there was light. It was coming from the battery-powered camping lamp at the other end of the room. A chemical toilet sat next to it, with a couple of rolls of toilet paper, the soft kind, incongruously pink in the dim yellow light. Lined up like skittles on the floor were a dozen bottles of water. Plastic. Thirst hit like needles in her throat.

She crawled towards the bottles, ignoring her knees scraping on the concrete floor, scooped up a bottle with trembling fingers, spilling more than she drank as she gulped it down. She grabbed another. There was a supermarket carrier bag on the floor. She snatched it up and pulled it towards her as she drank.

Sandwiches. In plastic triangles. Pre-packed. Her hand dived in, grabbed one. She ripped it open with her teeth, wolfed it down, chomping and biting, gulping water between mouthfuls of bread. It was gone in seconds. She snatched up another, tore it open, taking a little more time over this one; chewing hurriedly but purposefully rather than the bite-swallow-bite of the first. She read the label. Super Sandwiches. Cheese and pickle. The morsels stayed in her mouth long enough to almost register their flavour. She glanced down at the first wrapper, now in tatters on the floor. Chicken. She hadn't even noticed. Emily took another swig of water, tipped the remaining contents of the bag onto the floor. She frowned as she looked at the strange collection. Along with four more sandwiches there was a box of tampons and a pack of toilet wipes. In a separate pack, five pairs of panties, bright orange with a lace frill. She stared at the strange collection, trying to work things out, picked up a toothbrush, still blister-packed, toothpaste, a bottle of anti-bacterial handwash.

She turned the toothbrush over in her hand, trying to put these bizarre pieces together into something that made sense. She could feel an acid-burn of reflux in her throat. The sandwiches wanting to come back. If only this fog in her head would clear, give her a chance to string a few strings of thought together. She couldn't remember anything after parking her car and hurrying into the College of Music this morning. Had it been this morning? She could feel another plug of panic rise into her throat and restrict her breathing. She told herself she remembered someone calling her name. She couldn't be sure.

And then here, this. This strange, bizarre, dingy, hateful prison of a place.

She screamed inside her head, rocking backwards and forwards on her haunches, desperate to not let the sound out into the real world where she worried that he would not be able to make it stop. She gulped down on her fear, her panic.

She felt so alone. 'Mum!' she whimpered in anguish. Overwhelmed, she fell into a heap on the mattress and finally let go the tears. Deep, heartfelt gulps of pain and anguish. She could feel an ache in her shoulder, hear her head begin to fill with a strange static hiss. Weariness overcame her.

Emily fell asleep.

~~~~~
~~~~~

Tuesday 18th June 2019
13:17
Day Five

Bel was spitting feathers as she came out of the police station, so she bought food. A chicken and bacon sub from the deli in the precinct, extra coleslaw, the bacon pieces crisp and crunchy, with a choc-chip muffin to follow.

She was still upset when she got back to the office. Who the Hell did he think he was, the arrogant prick? Detective Inspector bloody perfect. Did he think she'd gone to see him just for the fun of it, to draw attention to herself? Well, actually, now that she thought about it, that was probably exactly what he thought.

Shit. She started to squirm with remembered embarrassment. Then the anger at Fox kicked in again, and the anger at herself for being so bloody naive as to think she could just march in there and assume he would listen to what she was trying to tell him. Damn Fox, but he was right. She must have come across as a right nutter, talking about the dream like that.

The thing is, it wasn't the first time this sort of thing had happened.

There had never been a time when Bel couldn't remember having dreams, visions, 'visitors' for want of a better name, right back to her earliest memories. Lots of children had imaginary friends. Bel Barker's had been a girl called Sarah. Bel remembered her as being about her own age, give or take a year or two. Back then her exact age didn't matter, but now it fitted in a way that only made Bel feel sad looking back.

Sarah, the girl had told Bel her name was Sarah, would spring up and start talking to her, Bel remembered, at just about any time of day or night, mostly when they were alone in Bel's bedroom, but sometimes when she was downstairs too, butting into conversations between her and her parents, trying to put words in her mouth that if she wasn't careful would spill out; swear words and rude comments mostly, but later, as Bel grew older, vicious tirades against her parents, Mum mostly, that Bel was shocked to hear voiced even in the confines of her own head, and would never have dared to actually say. They used to play games too; hide and seek. Sarah always won, evaporating in front of Bel's eyes, hiding in impossible places, whispering encouragement as Bel got closer, then making her burst into fits of girlish giggles when she appeared, her head pushing out of the turned-off television screen, or best of all, sticking up out of the toilet bowl. They played another hiding game too sometimes, where Sarah would take an object that belonged to the grown-ups, a key or a pair of glasses maybe, or a single shoe perhaps, hide it away and not bring it back for days. When Bel asked her once where the missing things went Sarah became evasive, mumbling that it was difficult to explain. It wasn't always fun though. Sometimes the games Sarah played could be darker, more spiteful. One afternoon when Bel told her she wanted to play with her friends outside in the sunshine rather than sit in her room talking to her, Sarah slammed the bedroom door shut, not letting Bel out, despite all her protestations. It seemed longer at the time, but could only have been a couple of minutes, just long enough to let Bel know that Sarah could, if she wanted. The specifics of "could" were never explained, but Sarah underlined her actions by pushing Bel off-balance down the last two steps as she was finally allowed out of the room and ran outside to her friends. Sometimes Bel was scared of Sarah.

Bel's Mum didn't like Sarah either. Not because of the spiteful comments and hidden keys; Bel never did reveal the worst of what Sarah said, and tried to persuade her to return the missing items whenever she could, with mixed success. No, her Mum refused point blank to accept that Bel even had an imaginary friend. Bel learned that Sarah's should never be mentioned under any circumstances. The only times Mum ever physically chastised Bel had been when she mentioned Sarah. As far as Mum was concerned the subject of Bel's invisible friend was totally off-limits.

As time went by, and Bel's horizons began to broaden, she began to spend less and less time with Sarah or looking back it might have been that Sarah spent less time with Bel. After Bel reached puberty Sarah just seemed to fade into the background. Bel would still hear her occasionally, moving about in her bedroom, or shifting small items downstairs, but she seemed to have lost her strength, her power, as if in growing up Bel had grown away too, travelled to a country to which Sarah didn't have access. When Bel left home to get a place of her own, Sarah stayed behind. Whenever Bel went around to visit her parents in the years since she could sense that Sarah was there, lurking in the shadows somewhere, but she never came out to see her anymore. It was almost as if she was sulking.

Mum didn't like any of it; in fact, she refused to have any mention of Sarah at all and would come up to Bel's room to scold her if she heard her talking or playing with her invisible friend. It was wrong, she would explain, a sin, and Bel was not to do it. That was all very well but Sarah would be pulling faces as Mum spoke and sometimes, Bel would have trouble keeping a straight face.

So, although she knew she was going to get in a whole heap of trouble for it, something happened one day when Bel was nine that she just knew she had to ask Mum about.

It all started with someone knocking on the front door. Not just knocking, a hammering that rattled the stained-glass fanlight. There was the frightening sound of sobbing too, a high-pitched wailing that bit straight into the soul. A cry like that could only mean trouble, big trouble. Mum made a beeline down the hallway, drying her hands on the tea towel tucked into the waistband of her pinny as she went. The door burst open before she could get to it. A woman fell to her knees in the hallway sobbing and wailing. Her name was Angela. She was one of Mum's friends. Mum gathered Angela into her arms and took her through into the kitchen. Bel had been forgotten in all the commotion, so she did what any sensible nine-year old girl would do, she kept quiet, followed them through, settled herself into a corner out of direct sight to watch and listen as the drama unfolded.

After Mum's previous reactions to any mention of Sarah, Bel more or less already knew what the reaction was going to be, but after what I had seen she had to know, so the next day she asked Mum as casually as she could if the couple were friends again. Mum paused as she held the iron inches above one of Dad's work shirts and asked her daughter which couple she meant.

'Angela, of course,' Bel replied, trying to keep her tone light in the face of her mother's steely glare, 'and that man who followed her in.' Mum carefully placed the iron on its heat-proof pad, folded her arms, asked Bel to explain.

So, she told her. She explained how she had seen the man bustle into the kitchen a couple of seconds behind Angela and start pacing backwards and forwards near the back door, about the dirty overalls he was wearing as if he'd come straight from work, about how he had stood in one corner sobbing into his hands. Bel had assumed he must have done something really bad because he just kept saying 'I'm sorry, Angie, I'm sorry,' and saying how much he loved her, and asking her again and again to forgive him.

The silence that followed this little statement left a cold imprint on Bel's memory, even now, but worse was the look on Mum's face, the way every last drop of colour seemed to drain away until her skin was drip-white and her eyes shone like little beads of polished jet.

It turned out the crying man *had* done something bad, something really bad.

The man was Angela's husband. The reason the woman had been banging on the door was that she had just been told that he had been killed in the foundry where he worked. He'd been hurrying to finish early, so he'd been cutting corners. He was excited about something; Bel could still see on the screen of her memory how the man kept trying to show Angela the flowers he had bought her. No matter what he did he couldn't get her to see the big, bright pink bouquet as he held it out towards her and begged her to take it from him. The more he tried to talk to her and the more she couldn't see him the more he cried.

It turned out the gantry crane hadn't been rigged properly, something about the electro-magnet cutting out. Anyway, a couple of tonnes of steel off-cuts and scrap had dropped on him right where he stood. They reckoned he died instantly, but he'd still stopped off for flowers. It seems even the dead did displacement behaviour.

Later, Bel couldn't remember when exactly, it might have been weeks or months after, she found out that Angela had been to the doctor's just that morning to have it confirmed that she was pregnant. She'd phoned her husband on his mobile at work. He obviously couldn't wait to get home to her.

Angela had a boy. Bel sort of assumed Angela must have moved away, because she hadn't seen her around for years.

Anyway, after she'd finished explaining, Bel stood rigid with fear as Mum looked down at her for what seemed like a million years. She finally took hold of both of Bel's hands, pulling on them as she guided her to sit down with her at the kitchen table, then didn't let go but held them up close to her own chest.

If Bel had been hoping for comfort, some sort of support or reassurance perhaps, or maybe just a suggestion of understanding even, it turned out she was to be disappointed.

'Listen to me, Isabel.' The use of her full name told Bel this was serious. Mum only ever called her Isabel when she had done something wrong, or when she had important news to deliver. 'I want you to listen carefully,' she said. Bel nodded her compliance, shuffled in her seat, as much in fear as anything else.

'This thing you do,' Mum continued, 'this thing where you see people who aren't there, these dead people.' Bel nodded but couldn't hold Mum's gaze and the scowl that it showed.

'Isabel, the thing you did yesterday, and the thing do with your so-called imaginary friend, the girl that you pretend to talk to in your room,' Bel moved as if to open her mouth to speak, but Mum squeezed her hands tight to stop her before she got the chance. 'Don't think I can't hear you, laughing and singing and jumping around. You need to stop it, you need to stop it all, right now, do you understand?'

'But, Mum!'

'No. Don't "but, Mum" me. This thing that you keep doing is evil. It's the work of the Devil, and you need to stop it right now. If I hear one more word about what happened yesterday, or any more stories about this, this girl you keep talking to, I, well, I, she's not real, the girl isn't real, and you have to stop this childish pretence right now, do you understand?'

Mum squeezed her hands so tightly Bel began to worry her fingers might break. She couldn't say anything, so she simply nodded her assent, hoping that the pain would soon stop. Mum let go, pushing Bel's hands sharply away from herself as she stood up. 'No more, Isabel. Understand? No more!' Bel sat at the table as her Mum left the room. Silent tears fell from both their faces, though neither knew about the other.

The subject of visions and spirits was never been broached again, from that day to this. No-one ever explained to the ghosts that they were not allowed to appear, though.

Despite her Mum's protestations, Bel still saw dead people, and over the years had come to accept that it was just something that happened to her. The spirits never seemed to have much to say, they usually just wanted her to take messages to people she had never met, to tell them they still loved them, or in a very few cases something trivial about a brooch having fallen in the cat litter, or a warning about leaving the gas on. Mostly she didn't pass the messages on.

There was one disturbing thing that Bel had never been able to get used to though. She'd never been able to work out exactly what they were, but she didn't like them one bit. In fact, they gave her the creeps every time she saw them. She called them the cocoons.

They happened sometimes when someone was going to die. Not violently or in an accident, but from illness or old age. They didn't happen all the time, or Bel would have spent her whole life stumbling about blindly in an oily soup of other peoples' impending death. The best that she could work out, it seemed to begin a few weeks or months before a person died. They would start to leak a kind of greasy smoke that only apparently only Bel could see. The smoke would start pale, like cigarette smoke, getting thicker and darker as the days and weeks went by, until the person ended up wrapped in a heavy blanket like some terminal fog. Bel would still be able to see the person inside, and the smoke itself never seemed to affect them, or her, physically. One particularly thick one looked like the cocoon or chrysalis a maggot or caterpillar would make when it changed into a fly or a moth, so the name stuck in her head. She'd never mentioned the cocoons to anyone.

The first time she noticed one and realised what it was and what was happening she had watched, curious, as the smoke began to wrap its slow, rancid way around a neighbour, an old woman that Mum had known for years, when Bel had been about eleven or twelve years old. It went on for a couple of months. The poor woman had breast cancer; Bel later discovered. The vapour had been as insubstantial as a winter's breath when it first appeared, then began to grow thicker and curdle around the woman over the next few weeks, until Bel thought the poor woman was going to be choked to death by the surrounding vapours rather than succumb to her tumour. Then she died.

It was the knowing that upset Bel the most. The knowing in advance. The knowing and not being able to do anything to prevent or change any part of it. There seemed to be no rhyme or reason to it, no justice either. There had been one time when she spotted a young mother walking in the precinct, the one near the station with the little supermarket and the discount store. The woman was pushing her baby girl along in a pushchair, window-shopping as she went along. Her daughter was wearing a pink bobble hat and kept throwing a stuffed toy panda onto the floor every few yards. The young mother displayed endless patience, would stop to pick up the panda, leaning into the pushchair to giggle and talk to the girl, and all the while as Bel watched a liquid sliver of vapour wrapped itself around the woman's happy, smiling face.

Bel lost it. She decided, right there, in the middle of the little shopping precinct, that she couldn't just watch, couldn't just let this tragedy overtake this young woman that she had never seen before.

Bel made up her mind that she was going to change things, take control, make a difference. She walked up to the woman, tried to explain, not about the curl of greasy smoke that had begun to wrap pale fingers around her face, she knew even in her anger that the woman would never be able to take in any information of that kind, but rather that she should take care of herself, go see a doctor, get a check-up.

It didn't work. The woman's face crimped in fear and she put one protective hand down onto her child's head as she hurried away, more upset by the crazy witch ranting in front of her than at anything Bel had actually tried to tell her.

After that Bel didn't try any more. She could still see the vapour when it appeared, and it was still deeply disturbing for her every time she saw it, but she realised that there wasn't really anything she could do; people were too locked in their ordinary everyday problems to be able to open their minds to anything she might try to tell them, even if their lives were at stake. What was a girl to do in the face of the ordinary?

Then, while visiting her grandparents less than a year ago, Bel watched in cold fear as that first pale snake, thinner than a finger, less substantial than the palest mist, began to ooze out of her Granddad's nose as he sat watching telly and took with casual thanks the cup of tea that she had just made him. Bel couldn't look, turned away, tried to compose herself as she passed a cup to her Grandma, trying to tell herself it was all in her imagination. When she next looked over at Granddad the pale grey thread seemed to have gone, evaporated. She kept glancing across at him during the rest of the afternoon, but nothing more happened. She heaved a sigh of relief and made her way home. Five or six days later the greasy smoke was back, a little thicker this time, a little more substantial, wrapped around her Granddad's head like a macabre turban. After that it didn't go away.

Bel went into denial at first, refused to see it, put it all down to a trick of the light, or tired eyes, but the smoke-sign gradually got thicker, darker, heavier. Before the end her Granddad looked to Bel as if his whole body was wrapped in boiling tar.

The worst of it all was knowing that she couldn't say anything. Who could she tell? What could she say? "Granddad, you're going to die, and I reckon it's going to be in the next month or so."? Or tell her Grandma, or worse still her Mum, and spend the rest of her life being held responsible for bringing the bad news about Granddad? No, thanks; she knew that it would be the world's worst case of blaming the messenger, and Bel would end up in her Mum's head as being the person who had killed him. Bel did everything she could to make sure she was as shocked and surprised as everyone else when the heart attack took him in his sleep three weeks later.

There was one other thing about being psychic that had played on Bel's mind on and off over the years. A former friend had asked her straight out once; if she really was psychic, how come she wasn't stinking rich? How come she hadn't been able to pick the winning numbers on the lottery nine weeks on the bounce and buy her own private Caribbean island where she could lounge about in the sun all day, surrounded by a posse of muscle-bound hunks, all oiled-up in their budgie-smugglers, ready and waiting to peel grapes for her or pander to any other whim that might cross her mind. If only.

Apparently, it just didn't work like that. God knows, she had tried, more than once. Who wouldn't want money to come to them by "magic"? A couple of years previously, after a particularly lousy week at work, Bel had set her stall out to do exactly that. She'd decided that working for a living was a mug's game and she made up her mind that she was going to use whatever "extra" talents she could muster to get her hands on some serious money. So, she sat herself down one Saturday afternoon, pen and paper in hand, determined to make herself "see" the numbers that were going to be drawn out of the lottery machine that evening. After some serious concentration six numbers eventually pushed themselves forward for her to notice, so Bel wrote them down and trotted off to the shop to stake her claim to untold riches. After the draw that evening, she was surprised and more than a little upset to find she'd managed to get just two of the numbers. Her total prize? Nothing. Nada. Bel decided the fates were playing with her, making her wait a few days while they lined up the stars, so she tried again the next week, and the next. The harder Bel tried the worse it seemed to get. Eighty-six million quid the top prize had got up to by then, a King's ransom, and all Bel had managed to get was one number and two 'next-doors'. In the end she came to the conclusion that it just wasn't going to happen for her, that she wasn't destined to be rich; not in this lifetime. She would still buy a scratchcard every once in a while, trying to tell herself that this particular one was calling to her somehow, offering some sign that there was money to be won. The best she'd ever managed to win in one lump was two hundred pounds; nice enough, but hardly millionaire material. Mostly she didn't bother anymore.

So instead, Bel began to read up on her strange talents in a semi-serious way over the weeks and months, trying to work out if anyone anywhere had any real ideas about what these talents were and where they came from. The internet had a million pages full of it; all sorts of stuff about mediums, spirit guides, spooks and psychics, the whole caboodle. To be honest, most of it came across as just plain daft, obviously fake. The only bits that made any sort of sense to Bel were some of the serious physics stuff; paired particles, quantum time loops, and probability density fields. She also found there was a lot of mileage in the Jungian position of the superconscious, too, but even some of that seemed a bit close to the knuckle. The only thing she had been able to work out for sure was that she seemed to have access to some strange channels of communication that other people didn't.

All that would have been fine and dandy, and she could have carried on living a more or less ordinary life if it hadn't been for this strange dream. The problem was that the dream was different, and Bel knew it. Her previous visions when she had had them had all been of people she had met, either family or friends, or people she had worked with. Bel had never met Emily Phillips, never even heard of her, yet she knew that somehow, she had been given the responsibility of trying to find her, before it was too late.

Bel had pretty much calmed down by the time she got back to the office. She made coffee, sharing the chocolate muffin with Joan, the office administrator and general factotum, then tried to get on with her own work as best as she could. What Bel felt she really needed after her encounter with Detective Inspector Clever-Clogs was to go home and take a long, hot shower before slumping on the sofa with a glass of chilled white wine.

No such luck.

Her Mum had rung that morning while she was on her way to work, late again, asking Bel to do a turn as Little Red Riding Hood and pop in to check on her Gran. Her Gran hadn't been feeling too good this last couple of days. Mum explained that she would have called in herself, but she had already gone to Haworth with Dad for a couple of days on another of his World War Two memorabilia re-enactment group away day meeting thingies that he was always going to. None of this war stuff made any sense to Bel. For one thing, Bel's Dad hadn't even been born when the war ended, and the closest his own father ever came to active service was a stint in the 'Look, Duck and Vanish'. He had never got to fire a shot in anger, never went further on manoeuvres than Bridlington.

Bel quizzed her Mum about it once. How could she ever be so interested in anything to do with guns? She had just smiled and said it was Dad she was interested in and anyway it could have been a whole lot worse. When Bel asked how, her Mum just said 'Golf.'

Bel was hiding a little bit of a guilt thing about going to see Gran; she had promised she would call in that lunchtime, even though she had already made up her mind that she was going to go to the cop-shop. It was only a little white lie after all. No-one would be any the wiser if Bel called in on her Gran after work instead. What possible difference could it make? Gran for sure wouldn't notice. She 'wasn't feeling too good' more and more these days. For as long as Bel could remember Gran had been a pink-cheeked little old lady with a shock of white hair, always busy, always on hand to offer sugar-sweet sympathy or hard-as-nails advice as the circumstances required.

That all changed the day Granddad died. Gran had grown old overnight, lined, ill-looking in a general but undefined way. She had always been religious on an easy-come easy-go, righteous damnation sort of way, but now she dedicated herself like only a convert could. Most days lately she could be found polishing a pew with her backside at St. Michael and All Angels, where she would put all her energy into prayer and the rosary, working the mysteries relentlessly with arthritic hands. Bel's Mum reckoned she was checking God out, seeing if He was up to the job.

There was no answer when Bel rang the doorbell, but that wasn't unusual. Gran had been selectively deaf for most of her life. She would happily let the phone ring right next to her if she decided she didn't want to answer it, and anyway, if she really was as ill as Mum has said, she would be just as likely to be tucked up in bed. Bel let herself in with her own key. She only had to take a couple of steps into the house for it to wrap itself around her like a soft, comfortable blanket. This house, this home, had always been one of Bel's favourite places; full of warm, happy memories. She listened for the familiar sound of Granddad's clock, his retirement present, sitting on the mantelpiece, stomping too loudly through the seconds as she walked past the open door into the living-room, the fridge humming tunelessly to itself in the kitchen, smugly Bel sometimes thought, as she entered the room. She half-expected Gran to be sitting at the kitchen table nursing a cup of tea and ignoring the doorbell as she played with the crossword in today's paper. She wasn't there, though. She had probably decided to take herself off to bed for the rest of the day. Maybe she really was ill. There had been that new strain of 'flu doing the rounds. Bel opened her mouth to call upstairs, wake the old woman for a fresh brew, but if she was sleeping it wouldn't do any harm to let her sleep a few minutes longer. She made Gran a mug of tea, and a strong coffee for herself, slurping away at the hot liquid as she put away the bits and pieces she'd picked up at the supermarket on her way over as an apology for not calling at lunchtime.

Coffee finished, Bel rinsed the mug and tidied it away, before picking up her Gran's mug of industrial-strength tea and turning for the door. It was at that moment that Bel stopped, stood still. Something wasn't right. The human brain is a fantastic machine, quietly taking everything in, then, like some mystical Sherlock Holmes, picking out on the one thing that doesn't fit into the proper pattern. She scanned around the kitchen, checking things out systematically, until she spotted the bit that didn't fit. There on the kitchen table. High-fibre cereal in a bowl, milk out of the fridge but not poured, two slices of toast sticking up out of the toaster, cold.

Breakfast?

A silk glove of unease wrapped its fingers around Bel's spine and began to squeeze as she noticed that the cellar door was ajar.

Gran always kept it locked, for fear of burglars. Bel had nudged past it without noticing when she'd brought in the groceries.

Bel held her breath and took a small step towards the slightly open door.

'Gran?' Right at that moment Bel didn't know if it would be better if she heard an answer or not. She reached out and took hold of the edge of the door, pulled it fully open and looked down into the cellar. The silk glove dropped away to reveal a heavy leather gauntlet beneath, studded with spikes and clutching a knuckle-duster. It pulled on Bel's spine so hard she felt as if the top of her head was going to implode.

Gran lay slumped at the bottom of the steps like a bundle of rags, her left leg twisted under her at a strange angle, the knuckles of one hand white with effort as she pressed against the wall, almost as if she thought it was still not too late to stop her fall.

Bel felt her mouth open, but she couldn't remember how to scream. She leapt down the stairs, the teacup shattering on the floor somewhere behind her, as she jumped the last two steps and over Gran, to kneel at her side.

'Oh, Bel love,' Gran sobbed, her eyes fluttering and her breath coming in short gasps as she flitted up and down her own rickety steps of consciousness, 'I think I've hurt my leg.'

Bel looked at the old woman's lips, squeezed into a thin, bloodless line, at her sweat-beaded brow creased in pain, at her leg, sticking out at an impossible angle. 'Shit, shit, shit,' Bel muttered to herself as she tried to assess the damage, then forced a tight smile onto her face to hide her own anguish and took Gran's hand to try to reassure her. 'Stay there, Gran,' she found herself saying stupidly, 'don't try to move. I'll get help.' Her hand felt cold and painfully frail in Bel's own, and trembled as she held it.

Bel sucked in a sharp breath, swung herself upright in a single move and began to scramble up the steps, scattering the contents of her handbag across the kitchen floor until she found her mobile and dialled 999.

It seemed like about ninety-five hours before Bel finally heard the faint warbling of a siren growing louder, followed by the hectic bustle as the paramedics came in and took control. She grabbed a chance to phone her Mum as they strapped Gran onto the plastic stretcher and started grunting her up the narrow cellar steps. Bel explained as briefly as she dared, skipping over the part about Gran possibly lying on the cold cellar floor all day with a suspected broken hip because Bel hadn't turned up at the agreed time. Her Mum gasped in horror at the news, but didn't question her in any way, promising that she and Dad would be there as soon as they could.

So much for being psychic, Bel cursed herself as she stuffed her phone away and took hold of Gran's hand again.

'I'm scared, Bel,' Gran's croaky whisper stung her out of her guilt trip. They were in the back of the ambulance now as it jolted and bumped through traffic. 'It's okay, Gran, don't worry,' Bel patted her as gently as she could on the back of her hand, worried that the merest touch would cause her more pain, 'we'll soon have you to the hospital. They'll be able to look after you there.'

A few minutes later the siren cut out with a blip and the ambulance backed into a bay at the hospital. The rear doors were flung open. A tired-looking doctor and a harassed nurse leaned in, nodding as the paramedics spat a staccato stream of numbers and brittle, hard-edged words before passing the old woman into their care. Bel followed, ignored, as the gurney was pushed through a pair of heavy rubber doors and into a curtained cubicle.

The nurse took Gran's pulse. 'We're going to give you something for the pain, Mrs Briggs, and then we'll see about getting you up to x-ray.'

'Is there any chance of a cup of tea?' Gran assayed her best winning smile in spite of the pain etched across her face.

'X-ray first, Mrs Briggs, but I'll see what I can do.' She backed out through the curtain with a reassuring smile.

'Don't leave me, Bel,' Gran sobbed, as soon as the nurse was gone.

'I'm not going anywhere, Gran,' Bel answered and took her frail hand again, leaning over her to gently push a stray lock of white hair away from her eyes. 'I know you're worried, but they're going to look after you. You'll feel a lot better once they've sorted your leg out.'

'I'm not worried about my leg; I'm worried about afterwards.'

'Afterwards? What do you mean, 'afterwards'?' Bel frowned.

'I need you to help me, Bel, before it's too late.'

'I don't understand. Too late for what?'

'I was trying to sort it out when I fell. You'll have to help me now.' She looked small and frightened as Bel looked at her, and the lines of pain on her face seemed to crowd in around her eyes as if they were trying to squeeze the soul out of her. 'My handbag,' she pointed, fingers fluttering, to the bag wedged at the bottom of the gurney. She'd refused to let go of it as the paramedics had muscled her up the cellar steps. In the end Bel had scooped it up for her, plopping it down between her feet as they'd bundled her into the ambulance. She reached for it now, trying to not look at her Gran's foot, twisted at such a strange angle. The handbag was big and black and patent leather, just like you'd expect a little old lady's handbag to be. Gran fumbled open the clasp and dug about inside, finally producing two keys threaded together with a strip of sugar-pink ribbon. She thrust them into Bel's hand, almost stabbing her in her trembling haste. 'In the cellar. You'll know what to do,' she said. Her head dropped back on the pillow and she let out a sigh. Her face looked less tortured somehow, as if she had managed to rid herself of some heavy burden.

Before Bel had a chance to ask her Gran what she meant, the nurse bustled back in, holding a kidney dish in which rocked a loaded syringe, and Bel was gently moved to one side once again. The nurse smiled at Gran. 'Mrs Briggs, the doctor says you can't have a cup of tea until after your x-ray. I'm sorry. You,' she turned to look at Bel, 'will have to wait outside now. We'll let you know the extent of her injuries as soon as we can. We expect her to go up to theatre in the next couple of hours.' She started to usher Bel out of the cubicle with a gathering arm. 'Try not to worry too much. I'm sure she's going to be alright.'

'Bel,' Gran whispered, fixing her Granddaughter with a pale, watery gaze, 'I wasn't a bad woman you know, whatever they might say. Don't forget that, will you?'

~~~~~
~~~~~

Date and time unknown.
Sometime between Friday 14th June 2019 and Saturday 6th July 2019

Emily spun around at the sound, scrambled to her knees on the mattress, reached one arm out for support against the damp brick wall as a wave of nausea slapped into her face. She had heard a strange metal squeak. She gasped as the metal door swung open to reveal a man, faintly backlit, looking at her. She could smell grass carried in on the faint breeze from the outside world, and the cutting scent of pine needles. The man seemed to be weighing her up, appraising her, almost, waiting for her reaction. A sob escaped her lips as the realisation finally lighted in her mind; Rescue! He had come to rescue her, it had to be. She almost couldn't believe it.

'Please. Help me.' a hiccup of relief caught in her throat as she gasped out the words. A wave of exhaustion fell across her as she held one hand out towards her saviour, the other still clinging to the damp wall as she rocked uncertainly on her knees.

The man was wearing some sort of a uniform; Emily couldn't work out if he was a policeman or a fireman, but in the end none of that mattered, he was here, he had come to rescue her, and she was going home. Tears blurred her vision, tears of relief and joy, then started to silently fall. Emily's rescuer took a step towards her.

He seemed to change as he moved closer in the dim yellow light of the lantern. Emily squeezed the tears from her eyes, shook her head to try to shake off the fog inside. The man-mountain she had been looking at just a second before seemed to have shrunk and grown podgy, his face bloated and gross with a scruff of coarse black hair above a heavy monobrow. What Emily had thought was a rescue-services uniform turned out to be just a set of grubby brown overalls and a hi-viz vest. He looked almost like a parcel delivery man.

'Are you the Police?' Her forehead creased in a frown as she stuttered out the words.

'No, I'm not the Police,' he sneered as he took another step forward. A broad grin spread across his face as he leaned towards her. His voice sounded deep and hard, full of gravel, his breath coming in heavy, laboured gasps that grated in his throat.

Rather than the welcome arms of rescue she had been expecting just a few seconds ago, Emily felt the man's hand as it reached to touch her, the fingers running through her hair as he began to stroke it. She flinched back, brought up her hand to stop his podgy fingers touching her.

One hand snaked out so fast she had no time to react, grabbed her by the wrist. She felt the pain as he twisted her arm, forcing it down by her side, then behind her back. The twisting pressure made her crouch even lower where she knelt on the mattress. The man leaned his body in towards her, over her, pushing her down onto her back, overpowering her with his own weight. She whimpered in pain, in fear. The knowledge that he was far too strong for her to resist, that he had her completely under his control made her breath catch in her throat. 'Please. You're hurting me. What are you doing? Please. Stop.' The sweat of fear grew clammy on her brow and down her back.

'You want me to stop? You want me to stop?' the man growled. Emily stared up at him, morbidly fascinated by the flecks of spittle frothing on his wet lips. 'I'll stop soon enough, you bitch!' His free hand swung round in a fist and caught her on the side of the head. Stars swam in front of her eyes.

Emily couldn't work out what's happening. 'No. Please. Don't.' He hit her again. Her nose exploded in pain; tears boiled up in her eyes. His hand was round her throat in an instant, a band of cold, hard pain, squeezing, squeezing. She tried to fight him off, make him slacken his grip, but he was too strong. He put one knee on her chest, pressed down. She couldn't move, couldn't escape his weight pressing her into the mattress, fought for a breath that wouldn't come. The tears in her eyes were replaced by stars, at first bright silver, then growing darker; red, angry, blotchy.

And then, and then it just didn't seem to be worth the effort of trying to struggle any more. There was nothing she could do to stop him. She was going to die. She knew it, could hear her breath whistling in her throat as the world turned black around her. His powerful hands began to tug and pull at her clothes.

~~~~~
~~~~~

Wednesday 19th June 2019
07:42
Day Six

Bel could hear her phone chiming and cheeping, insisting it was time to get up, but she couldn't persuade her eyes to open; they just blinked a couple of times and fell shut again. The phone sounds were coming from the general direction of her jacket, the one she had so carefully tidied away when she got home yesterday by crumpling it into a ball and dropping on the floor at the side of her bed. She rolled onto her side under the duvet, reached out to grab the jacket, dug out the offending phone and started slapping at it until the noise stopped. With the sharp sound gone Bel dropped onto her back again, ran through a checklist in her head as she struggled to get her brain into gear. Her teeth felt furry and her head was full of throbbing red lumps. She hadn't even got out of bed yet, and already it was shaping up to be a bad day. She only had herself to blame. Wine o'clock had come too early and she hadn't gone to bed until it got to empty-bottle o'clock. Although she knew from personal experience that wine wasn't a good eraser, she had tried anyway, hoping to wipe away the cascade of images that had been ganging up on her, both from the incident with Gran yesterday, and these last few nights with the visits from Emily. She had slept, or at least it had been easy for her to fall asleep, but in the end, it was no good, the sleep she did manage to get had been little more than a jumble of crumpled sheets and lumpy pillows.

Bel swung her legs out and sat on the edge of the bed for a minute as she wiped the sleep from her eyes, then dragged herself to her feet, her heartbeat blurring into a throb inside her head. She scooped up her phone from the bed and checked for messages as she shuffled to the kitchen, munching down a couple of paracetamols as she waited for the kettle to boil for the first coffee of the day.

There were five missed calls, four of them from Nigel. Why was she not surprised? Each of the messages was a dis-jointed sob-story, a sorry-for-himself pleading for Bel to take him back, mixed with begging apologies. Bel deleted every single one of them without bothering to reply.

She slurped another mouthful of coffee and started to piece together flashes of memory from the previous evening. As she drank the first glass of wine, she'd decided to send a brief message to Nigel, just to let him know that she was going to stuff all his precious bits and pieces into bin liners, and that he should make arrangements to pick them up when he could be bothered. After a second glass the next message advised him that she was going to cut the arms off all his shirts, and his one jacket, leather, second-hand, old, scuffed and, Bel knew, his prized possession. In the end she didn't do either, just had another glass of wine.

Until a few days ago Bel had thought things were going okay with Nigel. To be fair, the two of them had still been a million miles away from swapping apartment keys, and she certainly wasn't going to pretend that she thought for a single minute that he was "the one", but she had more or less reckoned that they had a fairly good, open, honest relationship that was sort of going along okay. The sex was good too, which was always a bonus.

Bel could feel her teeth start to clench as she recalled the day just a week ago when she found that good, open, and honest appeared to be words that didn't necessarily apply both ways in her relationship with Nigel.

It was the day after Bel had had the first dream of Emily, so she was feeling weary and a bit grumpy after losing most of a night's sleep and still having to battle through a day's work, lots of legwork with no offers coming in that were anywhere near the asking prices. Bel decided to cut her losses, take an early afternoon break, an hour off, then go to it again, hopefully refreshed and re-energised. It was only a couple of miles to Nigel's; she could drive round for a coffee, put her feet up for half an hour or so, see if he'd made any progress in finding a new job. He'd been out of work more than a month, but seemed to be making all the right sounds, all the right moves. Bel found out that day that the sounds turned out to be just sounds, and as for the moves, well, Nigel seemed to have his own idea on what moves were the right moves.

Bel parked up, walked to the door and knocked. No answer. Maybe he'd nipped out to the shops, or maybe he was in the bathroom taking a shower, or reading on the loo, a man thing Bel had just never been able to understand. Rather than leave without a chance of a coffee, Bel went to the front window to have a quick look inside, just to check. Nigel liked his music; Green Day and Linkin Park, though she preferred Foo Fighters and Queens of the Stone Age herself. Nigel always had his MP3 clipped to the belt loop of his jeans, and if he was alone, he would have the volume turned up and the earbuds rammed home, impervious to any sound in the real world. So, it was with a half-smile on her face that she put her face close to the glass and shielded her eyes from the reflection of the bright sunlight behind her. She could see movement through the almost-closed curtains. Bel rubbed at the grimy glass, pressed her nose hard up against it. The living room was dark, but after a few seconds her eyes settled to the gloom and she could see exactly what was moving in there. It was Nigel. He was kneeling on the floor in front of the green fabric sofa with the dodgy spring that kept poking out at one corner, his pants round his ankles, skinny buttocks pale as they moved relentlessly backwards and forwards. The reason they were moving backwards and forwards was sprawled with her legs open on the sofa in front of him, naked from the waist down, some blonde girl that Bel had never seen before. The girl had a slack expression on her face, almost as if she didn't really care about what was being done to her. The anger spat out of Bel and she banged on the window with the side of her hand, hard, the glass wobbling with every thump. Nigel looked round, a frown disturbing his features. More than a second passed before he recognised Bel's face at the window. His hips frozen in mid-stroke, reversed as he withdrew, then he made to stand up, grabbing at the jeans around his ankles, the girl forgotten. By the time he opened the front door and hopped out onto the footpath to find her Bel was already in her car and heading down the street. She didn't look back.

The last message on Bel's phone was a voicemail from Mum, insisting that Bel call her straight back as soon as she heard this, but to be honest Bel felt too tired, too hung-over, too headachy, to cope with the undercurrent of guilt-bombing about what time she had actually arrived at Gran's the previous day that was bound to dominate the conversation, so much that Bel decided it would be a good idea to give it a miss. Her Mum hadn't mentioned Gran, so on the basis that no news was good news, Bel deleted the message. Mum would have to wait until later.

Bel made her way to the bathroom, started to get ready for work, brushed her teeth "minty-fresh" to take away some of the nasty fur and stale taste that clung to the inside of her mouth. Back in the bedroom Bel started hunting around for something to wear that wasn't too grubby looking. The floor had seemed the ideal storage solution last night, but in the cold light of day turned out not to have been such a wise choice. Finally unearthing a pale orange blouse that she managed to convince herself would lose its creases after a couple of hours body heat, Bel took a last gulp of coffee as she put on the trouser-suit that had become almost a uniform, shuffle-hopped into her shoes, scooped up keys, camera and briefcase, and headed for the door. Hung over or not, Bel had an appointment to measure up a house this morning.

As she opened her apartment door and stepped out onto the landing she almost fell over a huge bouquet of flowers and small box of chocolates lying on the mat.

The card, written by the girl in the shop no doubt, the script was far too neat to be Nigel's and had a total lack of spelling mistakes, begged forgiveness, proffered undying love.

Undying? They'd barely been going out four months, hardly an eternity, and besides she had no way of knowing if he's done this sort of thing before, or in previous relationships, for that matter. She had only been around to his place a handful of times. She didn't care for it much, to be honest, it was scruffy like only a bloke's place can be, and had a sour smell that Nigel didn't seem to notice but caught in her throat sometimes, so for all she knew he could have had a string of girls round every day of the week, getting up to, well, she'd seen through the living room window what he'd been getting up to. Bel kicked the flowers across the landing, then rammed them into the trash chute with an angry twist. The chocolates she pushed deep into her handbag. Joan could have them. Chocolate was chocolate, after all.

The house was in Crawshaw Crescent, Leaside. Bel could tell just from reading the address more or less exactly what she was going to find when she got there; a small semi, built in the twenties or thirties, a bay-windowed front room, reasonable-sized kitchen, two, maybe three bedrooms, a small lawn at the front, and if it was really nice, a twenty-foot garden at the back.

Leaside was Bel's stomping ground, such as it was. She'd been born and raised there, and in the four years she'd been doing this job she prided herself on the fact that she'd worked hard to learn, to turn that generalised feel for the area into a proper working knowledge.

Less than fifteen minutes later she pulled up outside the house at Crawshaw Crescent. Apart from the stuccoed walls and rampant skein of ivy, both of which Bel knew would probably detract from the selling price, it was exactly as she had imagined it would be. She'd more or less sorted out the blurb in her head on the drive over, so unless the vendors had decorated the living room in the style of the yellow morning room at the Palace of Versailles, as far as Bel was concerned, this one was in the bag; she just needed to measure up, take a few photos to go with the copy and it would all be written up and in the agency window before the end of the afternoon.

As she grabbed her phone and stood on the footpath to line up the shot, Bel had to squint against a ray of summer sun that shone straight into her eyes. At the instant she hit the button she realised there was probably going to be a problem with the photo.

Staring down at her from the bedroom window was a dead woman.

The woman came fizzing down the stairs as soon as Bel walked in, a summer sparkler too early for Bonfire Night. 'You've got to stop him,' she pleaded, almost shrieking. 'Tell him he can't sell the house!' If she'd been alive, she would have been hopping from foot to foot in obvious agitation; instead she flickered on and off like a faulty fluorescent light. Bel tried to ignore her as she shook hands with the actual, living, owner, the 'Him' the ghost had obviously been referring to. Bel wasn't particularly worried about the ghost; she'd come across a few over the years that she'd been measuring up properties. Spirits like this usually turned out to be the little old man or woman who had lived there alone and died in their bed. They usually faded to random creaks and taps after a few days or weeks, unless they had a continuing mission, some grievance or unresolved problem. Bel figured this one must be the dead wife, the reason behind the sale. The woman had been dead about three months, they had told her when she had picked up the house details in the office the previous day, and now Mr Curtis was ready to down-size to an apartment in the newly-built "mature residents' complex" that was in fact a renovated textile mill close to the river. To be honest, the dead wife looked more alive to Bel than the living husband did right now. His face looked tired, hollowed out, as if he had come to the terminus but not got off the bus yet. His hands trembled as they hung at his sides. Bel could smell the distinct juniper scent of gin on his breath even at this hour.

'I'll leave you to it then, shall I?' the man stated flatly, and before she could open her mouth to answer he had turned on his heels and shuffled off into the front room. Bel could hear some daytime television presenter as the door opened briefly, trying to stir up a controversy about breast-feeding in public. Both the presenter and the public needed to get a life, in Bel's opinion.

'He can't sell the house, he mustn't!' The dead woman screamed, about an inch from Bel's face, before launching herself to ricochet off the walls like an electric porcupine. 'Jessica won't know where to go if he sells the house. You've got to stop him!'

Bel turned her back on the dead woman, moved into the kitchen, determined to ignore her. It wasn't as if she didn't have enough on her plate already.

The kitchen turned out to be a decent size; Bel measured it up at twelve feet by twenty. She took a bit of a scan around, that was her job after all, searching for anything to make a note of, any potential selling feature, but to be honest there wasn't much to brag about. The walls were half-tiled in a flat cafe-au-lait colour that only made the room feel tired and grubby. There was an old, off-white net at the window, and the cold tap dripped relentlessly into a stainless-steel sink that in spite of the name had an ugly patina encrusted on its surface. The smell of rotting fruit led Bel by the nose to a cut-glass bowl on the small pine dining table, where a pear and three bananas were slowly working their way back to the soil.

Whoever bought this place would want to rip it all out and start again, but the potential of the place was plain to see. Bel gazed out of the window, into the back garden. It was big, probably a thirty-footer she reckoned, lawn spreading and overgrown, flowerbeds choked with weeds, a solitary apple tree at the far end, and, close to the house, a lop-sided trampoline with netting, one of the circular ones that looked almost like a tiny mixed martial arts arena, the metal frame flaking rust like dandruff, ready for the next challenger, or maybe just waiting for the return of Jessica.

As if on cue, Mrs Curtis came stomping through the closed kitchen door, snapping Bel back in an instant from her idle daydreams into the here and now. The fact that the here and now contained a woman from the nowhere and no-when didn't jar in Bel's mind.

'He...' a teaspoon leapt out of a cup on the draining board and skittered across the worktop, 'can't...' the cold tap splashed a gush of water into the sink, 'leave!' Yesterday's paper swept off the table onto the floor as the dead woman's anger rushed around the room in a ball of blue sparks.

Maybe this made things a little different. The late Mrs Curtis wasn't giving the impression of a spirit that was going to slowly fade to a whisper. Bel began to wonder with a chuckle what a poltergeist would do for the selling price of the house. Maybe, she decided, if she just listened to the dead woman's story, heard what she had to say, it might help calm her down, let her dissipate her energy, allow her to finally fade away.

Bel took a deep breath and turned to face the spirit of Mrs Curtis. 'Tell me about Jessica. Is she your daughter?'

'I've looked everywhere for her, but she's not here.' The dead woman stopped bouncing around, her fizzing incandescence settling to a thrumming pulse. 'I thought she'd be waiting for me, but I can't find her anywhere. She's still alive, I know she is. She must be. If she comes home and Gerald's moved away, she won't know where to go.'

Bel hesitated. She knew she might end up regretting this but asked anyway. 'Can you show me what happened?'

The woman took a single step forwards, paused about a foot in front of Bel, stared up into her face, her eyes black mirrors. She dropped her chin to her chest, then lunged at Bel as if she was going to headbutt her in the ribcage. Bel staggered back, taken completely by surprise. It felt as if the old woman was standing in exactly the same space as she was. Bel fought to stay calm as a tingling sensation began to build up behind her eyes, almost as if the old woman was trying to look out at the world through them. The tingling feeling spread along every nerve until Bel could feel a buzzing numbness running through her whole body. A big pink bubble burst in her mind and Bel became instantly aware.

Jessica was eleven.

It was her first week at high school. She played the flute, had done for a couple of years. She was never going to be brilliant, but she enjoyed herself so much they found the money to pay for private lessons, even after the lessons in junior school ended. They dropped her off as usual that Saturday morning, kissed her goodbye, watched her skip up the path to the tutor's door. They never saw her again.

They always went for breakfast in a little market cafe a couple of miles away after they dropped her off. Mr Curtis liked his Full English breakfast. When they came back out of the café one of the tyres was flat. Mr Curtis muttered a bit as he got the spare out, grunted and cursed as he changed the wheel. When they got back to the tutor's house, they were more than twenty minutes late. That was what broke him in the end, that breakfast in the Olympic cafe, that flat tyre. The delay, the interruption, the change in routine that had happened on that Saturday morning became his all-consuming "what if", became his wife's soul-eating blame.

The image blossomed in Bel's mind; a beautiful September morning, warm, bright, the first bite of autumn in the breeze; perfect. Jessica had already left.

She'd rejected her tutor's offer to wait inside, explained how she was all grown up now and quite capable of walking the three or four miles home, especially as it was such a nice day. So, she smiled, waved goodbye, skipped down the path - and disappeared off the face of the Earth.

Mr and Mrs Curtis were a little surprised at their daughter's sudden rush to independence, but they laughed it off, got back in the car and followed the route she would have walked. They didn't spot her on the drive home, but they were still smiling as they walked up the garden path to the front door. They knew she would already be inside, waiting for them.

The door was locked. They went in anyway, called her name, but she wasn't there. It was then that the first icy shadow of fear crept into their hearts.

They pushed the fear away, reassured each other as they got back in the car, telling themselves they must have just missed her on a corner or something. This time they drove slowly, checking carefully, scanning all around as they made their way all the way back to the tutor's house to check again, and back home for a second time; this time in a slow, silent frenzy of foreboding. Only when they let themselves into their locked house for the second time did the fragile facade of sanity collapse and crumble around them.

They descended into a hysterical, wailing flat spin, panic making them irrational. They ran up and down the street calling Jessica's name. They knocked on neighbour's doors. They visited or phoned every one of her friends they could think of. No-one had seen her; no-one had heard from her.

Jessica had simply vanished.

The shadow became an abyss two hours later when they phoned the Police. They fell headlong into that dark pit, never to climb out.

The Police arrived in record time, a procession of blue uniforms marching into their home to investigate. They looked around. They kept on looking. They searched the house from floorboards to rafters. Suspicion fell on the music tutor for a while, but there were witnesses who definitely saw her coming out of his house. They searched his house anyway; nothing.

They took Mr Curtis to the Police station, just to ask a few questions they said, check over a few facts, you understand. They kept him there for almost three days and nights, grilling him endlessly, making the same sick suggestions over and over again; about what he must have done, how they knew that he loved his daughter but perhaps things had got out of control, he had let his physical urges get the better of him, how he must have panicked when she had screamed, or maybe she had threatened to tell her mother, so he had struck out, hurt her, then struck he again to stop her crying, and how he must now be filled with remorse, and how he would feel better if he would only admit to himself, and to them, what he had done. Mr Curtis could only cry, which made them more certain of his guilt. Eventually they stopped asking questions, let him go home.

The search had by then moved on to gardens and streets and fields. The police poked about in hedgerows, put frogmen in the river, canvassed door to door, and the days staggered past in a haze of anguish, and then the weeks, and then, well, it just didn't seem so urgent anymore. It was almost as if the whole thing had never happened, as if their little Jessica was somehow no longer real; worse, had never been real, was just some story they had made up, just a picture they'd given to the Police, just a name, a figment of their imaginations.

Saturday, September tenth, two thousand and five.

There was another pink twang somewhere inside Bel's head, as if the universe had suddenly let out its breath, and she dropped into the chair at the kitchen table, a bit heavier than she'd meant to. She felt a weariness sitting heavy in her bones from having shared her body, her mind, with the dead woman. She'd never tried anything like that before, and to be honest she wasn't in a rush to try it again. It had left her feeling worse than the hangover she'd woken up with that morning, her head thumping, her stomach pinched and nauseous. Coffee probably wasn't a good idea, but right now she felt as if she needed one, and a couple of ibuprofen. Bel could see the slight tremble in her hand as she filled the kettle and dug a cup out of the cupboard where everyone always kept them; close to the sink, head height, lowest shelf. She knew it would be frowned upon, not quite polite, if they found out back at the office that she was helping herself to the clients' stuff, but they weren't here, and in all honesty, she doubted if Mr Curtis would either notice or care. Blowing on the hot liquid and ferreting two tablets out of her handbag, she chugged them down, scalding her throat in the process.

Bel stared at the clock on the wall. The battery was running down and the second hand kept trying to climb towards the ten but dropped back after every tick. Bel stood watching as the same single second played out in front of her again and again, couldn't shake the image in her head of the Curtises wandering the streets, day-in, day-out, year after year, like a couple of well-heeled hobos, peering into faces instead of bins, searching endlessly for their little girl, their beloved Jessica, never able to rest, their souls stretched thin in torment. No wonder the dead woman didn't want her husband to leave.

Bel stood up, tried to compose herself, looked out of the kitchen window at the neglected trampoline, the rubber sagging and cracked, picturing the joy Jessica had brought into their lives, and the final sorrow. 'Mrs Curtis,' Bel spoke aloud, though she knew she didn't actually need to when she was talking to a spirit, it just made it easier for her to articulate her thoughts, 'I'm sorry about what happened to Jessica, but I can't help you, no-one can help you anymore. You're dead, Mrs Curtis. You need to go to the door, the bright door. I know you can see it. You need to go to the place where the door is and open it and go into the light.'

Bel could tell her words hadn't got through because Mrs Curtis turned, gave a plaintive wail and pushed through the wall into the living room.

Although Bel knew she would have to go in there to measure up sooner or later, she didn't think she could bear to look Mr Curtis in the face right at that moment after what she had just discovered, so she took the chicken's way out and made her way upstairs.

The bathroom had an avocado suite with black and white chequerboard tiles, a hideous design combination from more than thirty years ago. Bel scribbled notes, measured, moved to the next room. The master bedroom. Nothing worth noting apart from a truly gopping wallpaper in shades of orange and yellow. She took the measurements and moved on.

It wasn't until the next door swung open that she realised this was Jessica's room. She stood dithering on the threshold, moving her weight from foot to foot as she looked into the bedroom. Somewhere at the back of her mind she was half-expecting something to happen, which was a bit silly because if Jessica really had been haunting the place, her mother would have found her after she herself had passed over and wouldn't have pounced on Bel like she did. She chided herself for being so timid, but still didn't step inside, just leaned forward a little to look into the room some more.

It was an ordinary little girl's bedroom, bed neatly made, clothes folded away in wardrobe and drawers, a bookcase filled with 'Tracey Beaker' and 'The Worst Witch', but only the first four 'Harry Potter' novels, Bel noticed. Jessica must have disappeared before the rest of the books were published. That thought more than anything filled Bel with a deep sorrow; the realisation that Jessica must have been more or less exactly the same age as herself. She tried to shrug away from the emotion, turned her attention back to the room. Westlife and Gareth Gates pearly-white-smiled down from the walls, alongside pictures of fluffy kittens and prancing ponies. It was obvious that the room hadn't altered a jot since the day Jessica vanished, no dust had been allowed to settle, no clutter allowed to contaminate the shrine.

It didn't take a massive leap of the imagination to picture Mrs Curtis coming in every day while she was still alive, and maybe still visiting even now, trying to find things to tidy, desperation etched on her soul as she longed for her daughter to reappear and take up her life where it had left off, despite the fact that the girl hadn't set foot in the room, alive or dead, for more than twenty years. This was silly; Bel knew she had nothing to fear here, the place was empty. She took a deep breath and stepped into the room.

Nothing happened. No boggarts rattled in the wardrobe; no bogeymen clambered out from under the bed. She realised that she was holding her breath. She let it out with a gasp, allowed herself a self-conscious little grin as she realised that a tiny part of her must have been expecting something dramatic to happen, like in a ghost story when the hero enters the haunted chamber. That was just plain silly. The place was empty; Jessica simply wasn't here, hadn't been since the day she disappeared. Bel plopped down on the bed, let her gaze drift around the room, coming to rest in turn on the now meaningless milestone items in Jessica's life; the swimming badges, the music books. A line of dolls and teddies sat propped up against the freshly plumped pillow. Bel scooped one up, more for the feel of the baby-soft fur than anything and sat stroking it against her cheek.

Faint traces blossomed in her nose as she held the teddy close, old scents trapped in the fur and carried down the years; talcum powder, and the unwashed smell of a child, bruised grass, and an animal smell, dog maybe. Bel could feel a cramp growing somewhere in the back of her shoulders, her head felt hot and for some strange reason she found she couldn't quite focus her eyes as she looked around; everything seemed to be shimmering, like those images of heat rising in the desert. Nothing was straight or still. For a second Bel felt almost as if she was falling forward, and then saw with a gasp that she was. She barely had time to put her hands out before the carpet came up to hit her in the face.

The deafening roar of an engine rolled past like a physical force and the acrid stench of diesel fumes bit at her nose. A gasp rose in her throat as Bel tried to work out what was happening around her. She was standing in a dirt lay-by at the side of a narrow road, blinking against bright sunshine. An articulated lorry juddered into life, the roar of its engine rising and falling like a giant beast panting as the cab dipped and thrashed with effort. The lorry stuttered, paused, hunched as the next gear bit and dragged it forward out of the lay-by and onto the blacktop. After a few seconds the curve of the road carried it out of sight behind the trees and the loud sound faded.

Bel turned, not quite trusting her own legs, trying to take in her new surroundings. The road was crowded in on both sides by trees, tall and straight, thickly planted right up to the tarmac's edge. Darkness filled the spaces in between. Bel hunched her shoulders, hugging herself as a shiver began to reverberate through her body and threatened to shake all her teeth out.

A dog barked once, somewhere off to her left. She turned towards the sound. A black Labrador came lolloping down the lane, heading straight towards her. It stopped, as if it was checking that it had Bel's full attention, then, once it was sure, turned and cut into the trees. As soon as she saw it jink to the side, she knew she had to follow. She set off after it, her movements stilted and brittle as she pushed her way between the closely planted trees. It only took a few steps, barely enough for Bel to make it through the first twist of undergrowth before she was wrapped in a desolate quiet, a not quite silence; the only sound a soft soughing of the breeze in countless branches. Bel hesitated, turned to look back the way she'd just come. The trees were more densely packed than she'd realised at first, cutting off most of the bright summer sunlight that shone down on the outside world, giving the place a gloomy, monochrome feel. Bel realised that already she could no longer see the road.

The dog barked again as if chiding her, reminding her to keep up, to concentrate. Bel took another step, all the while trying to not think too closely about what she was doing; following a dog into the woods in a dream in a teddy-bear in a dead girl's bedroom. Another bark. Bel squinted, concentrating on keeping her gaze locked on the dark smudge moving ahead of her in the gloom of trees.

After a many minutes of stumbling about Bel started to get the impression the undergrowth had begun to thin out a bit, and in a few more steps she found herself standing in a small clearing.

The dog paced backwards and forwards just inside the treeline, stopped, sat down, tail thumping on the dry earth. After a few seconds it leapt to its feet, ran to a spot at one side of the clearing and started scrabbling at the ground, kicking up a spout of soil as it clawed away at the soft detritus of countless autumns on the forest floor.

Bel began to inch her way forward to where it was working, her breath blossoming in front of her face, a fog of condensation in the air that seemed to have grown cold and damp in the last few seconds. The dog's paws moved like pistons as she watched, scraping, scraping. When she was almost close enough to touch, the dog backed off, watching, head down as she crept closer to the shallow scrape it had made in the crumbling soil. With one last glance to the dog, almost seeking permission, Bel leaned forward, peered in.

A breath of air stirred a tiny will 'o' the wisp of dust in the newly made earthen bowl.

Something shone, spectral white in the dark, dark earth.

Puzzled, Bel knelt down to take a closer look.

The dog was circling now, head low, eyes intensely following her every move.

Bel reached out to move a clump of soil to one side. It crumbled to powder at the first touch of her fingers, soft and dry to the touch.

Bel scraped some more, the soft soil compacting under her nails. The thing in the ground seemed to float up towards her, a pale curve, incongruous in this dark, desolate place.

A few more scoops.

Every nerve in Bel's body jangled as she recoiled in horror.

A face.

A girl's face.

White skin. A curl of auburn hair moving across her forehead, tugged in a greeting wave by a stray wisp of wind. The girl's mouth, open in silent scream, was packed with black soil. Her eyes stared up at Bel, unblinking. Bel watched with bated breath as a single tear bloomed, glistened, rolled down the girl's soil-dusted cheek. The cold earth drank it up in an instant.

Bel realised she was falling over, scrambling backwards as she tried to find her feet, desperate to put some distance between herself and the strange scene in front of herself. She didn't even realise she was screaming until she heard the trees echoing her own scream back at her, mocking.

Bel let out a gasp and her head jerked up. She found herself surrounded again by the reality of Jessica's room. She was kneeling on the floor now, one hand digging deep into the soft, rich pile of the carpet, the other fastened in a death-grip on the teddy's throat. She stayed like that for a couple of minutes, until her head stopped spinning, counting the thud of the hammer in her chest as her heart slowed, then pulled herself to her feet, which was a bit tricky, because her legs felt about as strong as drinking straws. Bel made her careful way to the bathroom, splashed cold water onto her face, stared into the mirror, willing the image of the buried face to fade from her mind. There was no point trying to convince herself otherwise, the vision she had just seen could only be of Jessica.

Shit.

She really didn't need this, on top of everything else.

Jessica was dead. It sounded callous, but it was true. Bel knew there was nothing she could do to help her. Yes, she had just seen a vision of her buried in some random woods somewhere, but random was the important bit. Jessica could be buried anywhere; Bel didn't recognise the place in her vision, and even if she had known to the inch exactly where it was, based on the way DI Fox reacted the other day, there was no way she was going to go within a million miles of the police about this. The best thing she could do right now was to finish measuring up for the sale and get out of this sad, mildewed little house, sharpish. If the ghost-mother couldn't be persuaded to move into the light there wasn't a great deal Bel could do about it, and besides, most people were about as psychic as a tonsillectomy. Whoever bought this place probably wouldn't even notice Mrs Curtis' ghost if it bit them on the bum.

Bel stood in the hallway, in front of the closed living room door, took one long, slow, deep breath, released, forced a smile onto her face, pushed open the door. 'I just need to do in here, then,' she said, poking her head into the small room, trying to sound cheery, holding her clipboard in front of her chest like a shield as she walked in, trying to affect an air of casual professionalism. She needn't have bothered. The room turned out not to be a copy of the yellow morning room at the Palace of Versailles after all, just a cluttered little space about twelve foot by fifteen, the sofa against one wall covered with old newspapers and dirty clothes, a single armchair pulled square-on a few feet in front of the television, a half-empty bottle of gin on the rickety coffee-table next to it, alongside a half-full glass. A cup of coffee stood on the mantelpiece, a deep rug of mould congealing to jelly on the surface.

Mr Curtis' lifted his head. He dragged one knot-gnarled hand across a chin that hadn't seen a razor in at least a week. The sound made Bel think of old horror films, the scrape of ancient parchment and mummies' tombs. 'Right then, I'll go for a pee and leave you to it.' He stood and shuffled out of the room without looking back.

Bel zipped out a tape and made her way to the window, mentally rolling up her sleeves, goading herself to get her act into gear. It had got to the stage now where all she really wanted was to just get done as quickly as possible and get the hell out of this place. She turned and faced into the room, taking in all the clutter and disorder that only seemed to bring the walls in closer. The old man was obviously starting to turn into a hoarder; there were piles of newspapers, and, for some unknown reason, plastic food containers, stacked one inside another, the lids forming a separate tower at their side. Bel wondered if the obvious decline had started after Mrs Curtis died, or if the seeds of the problem stretched all the way back to the day Jessica disappeared.

Bel's gaze was drawn to an old credenza, made of cherry wood, with lion's claw feet, leaded glass doors, tucked into the corner of the room. It looked so out of place, inherited perhaps or just bought "because it looked nice" at the time, and then left wherever it would squeeze in. She moved a step closer to take a proper look. On various shelves stood the tiny treasures of a small life; a cheap cut-glass decanter with two matching glasses, a single willow-pattern plate on a plastic stand. Pride of place, top shelf, front and centre, a silver-framed photo, six by four.

The girl in the photo was sitting with her knees to the left, her gaze turned square-on to the camera, her buck-toothed smile dominating her face. A shock of auburn ringlets cascaded down either side of her face, framing her freckled features perfectly. She looked as proud as anything in what was obviously her brand-new high school uniform. She could never be described as beautiful, but the life shone so brightly from her eyes that they seemed to twinkle out of the frame.

Bel recognised her in an instant, sucked in a gasp of surprise.

'That's my Jessica,' Mrs Curtis appeared at Bel's shoulder, pale now and drained of energy, flickering slightly. Bel could feel the softest of sorrows pulsing out of her in waves. The flush of the toilet and a heavy tread on the stairs announced that Mr Curtis had started his return journey.

'She's dead, Mrs Curtis,' Bel explained to the ghost again, speaking in a hectic whisper, her eyes focussed on the photo on the shelf in front of her face. 'She showed me just now in her bedroom. You've got to go to the light. She'll be waiting for you there.'

A look of weary resignation fell across the dead woman's face. 'Find her for me. Bring her home. Please.'

'I will,' Bel replied, not meaning a word of it.

'Promise me,' and she faded into the dull air.

Bel had thought afterwards about what happened next, and for the life of her she would never be able to conjure up a plausible excuse to justify what she did. She could hear the door handle turning behind her. In a few seconds Mr Curtis would be back in the room. Bel's hand moved without conscious bidding, turned the tiny brass key, opened the cabinet door and snatched up the silver-framed photo. Placing it on her clipboard, she hugged the board tight, clutching Jessica's image to her chest. Smiling and nodding her way through the next few minutes almost as if she was in a trance, Bel concluded the formalities as quickly as she could, shook the old man's hand, headed for the door.

It wasn't until she was sitting in the car a few minutes later that it finally sank in what she had just done.

~~~~~
~~~~~

Wednesday 25th September 2002
14:22
A beginning

David Mason stood next to the girl, as nervous as any teenage boy had a right to be. She smelled of flowers, some sweet perfume that he never would discover the name of. The only thing he knew for sure was that he loved her, and from that instant forward always would.

Her name, he discovered, was Mandy Armitage. She was in the year below him, year ten. The first time he saw her in the corridor that day after the bell sounded and the whole school moved from room to room in readiness for the next lesson, he took in everything about her, almost in a single visual breath, creating a gestalt stamped on his consciousness, etched on his soul; her smile, her hair, the way she walked, talked, giggled. He knew he had to find a way to speak to her, explain how beautiful she was, how he loved her and wanted to be with her forever. He learned that she played the violin, so he searched out the music teacher even though he didn't know the first thing about music, ingratiated himself, persuaded the teacher to sign him up in spite of the fact that he had already missed the first three lessons of term. The school even lent him a violin.

Mandy had a talent that shone like a beacon. Next to her he looked, sounded, felt, ham-fisted, gauche. He gazed in slack-jawed rapture as she drew an effortless motif from the strings, then felt his face flush with embarrassment as she caught him staring. She by turns tolerated him, smiled sympathetically when he dropped his bow from nervous fingers, laughed behind her hand at his caterwauling attempts to coax sound from the instrument, sniggered as he reddened in his stuttering attempts to make small talk.

If he could only find a way to talk to her properly, without getting flustered and tongue-tied, explain his feelings for her, tell her of the love he carried for her, the burning passion that swelled in his heart. He already knew that he wanted to spend the rest of his life loving her. He had to find a way to show her just how much she meant to him. He didn't know music, so he tried the best he could with words.

It took him weeks of devoted attention to bring everything together. He drew pictures, intricate images of their two hearts entwined, copied poems of love and longing from library books, pressed pretty flowers between pure white, embossed cards. When he had finished, when he had filled a large pink box with everything his heart contained, all his hopes and desires for the future, he left it for her in the year office, a hostage to fortune with her name written on top.

She sat with giggling friends as she opened his discovered offering. He listened at the door, his heart alight with joyous anticipation, ready to march into the room, sweep her off her feet at her first gasp of recognised love, carry her away to an eternity of romantic bliss.

'What is it? What have you got?' one friend asked, eager to know.

'Mandy's got a secret admirer,' another friend snorted.

'Does it say who it's from?'

'No. I don't know. Shush, let me take this ribbon off.'

'What's inside? Let's see.'

'What's this? "Shall I compare thee to a summer's day?"'

'Wow. Shakespeare.'

'Somebody loves Mandy. Is there a note or anything? A name?'

'I'm looking, I'm looking. What's this? A pressed flower. I wonder who could have sent it.'

'A picture. Drawings of hearts. He really must love you.'

'It is romantic, isn't it?'

'See who it's from. See who it's from.'

Mandy snatched up the envelope, tore it open to read the card inside. 'All my love, David Mason.' She snorted her contempt.

'Oh, my God. David Mason!'

'Not him.'

'He looks like an ape.'

'He's so short.'

'A Neanderthal.'

David's mind reeled as he listened. Tears welled into his eyes and hot breath caught in his throat. He felt his heart torn into thin painful strips, couldn't suffer this any longer, turned to hurry away down the corridor, stomped into his next class and sat in a purple sulk at the back of the class as the history of Europe from 1870 to 1945 was introduced to disinterested minds.

The conversation in the year room continued.

'Hngh. Imagine those stubby fingers touching you, all sweaty, like fat little sausages.'

'No wonder he can't play the violin.'

'What's with the monobrow?'

'He breathes with his mouth open.'

'And he sprays when he speaks.'

'What are you going to do?'

'You're not going to go out with him, are you?'

'Not in a million years.'

'Imagine him kissing you.'

'Yeuch.'

'I couldn't bear him to touch me.'

'I think I'm going to be sick.'

'Maybe we should teach him a lesson.'

'How do you mean?'

'Why don't we play some sort of prank on him?'

'Like what?'

'I dunno.'

'I've got it. This is what we're going to do. Listen.'

~~~~~
~~~~~

Friday 11th October 2002
14:54

School finished, lessons over, the usual rush for the doors, for freedom, for the weekend, began.

'You're David Mason, aren't you?' The two girls stood together, arms linked, blocking his path. The one who hadn't spoken stared at him as she worked the gum in her mouth backwards and forwards, side to side.

'Who wants to know?'

'Mandy Armitage, that's who.'

David felt his pulse quicken; a flush come to his face. 'What about her? What did she say?' It had been almost a week since he left the present for her in the year room, since he heard the cruel taunts begin, since he fled, his hopes for love dashed on the rocks of scorn. He skipped school, missed lessons, didn't dare go to violin class, scared to face his lost love, his Mandy. And now; these two girls stood between him and the door.

'She wants to see you. Now. In the senior girls' cloakroom on the first floor.' The girl smiled as she spoke, her companion looking him up and down, pulling a string of gum from her mouth then chewing it back until it disappeared between bright white teeth.

David pushed past almost before she finished speaking, fighting against the tide of bodies pressing in the other direction, hurried up the stone staircase and along the corridor, fewer people here, he was almost running now, paused at the door, glanced both ways, entered.

The room smelt pink.

She was sitting on the long-slatted bench that ran down the centre of the room, one leg to each side, her dark green pleated school skirt hitched up to her thighs. Her hands rested between her legs, but he caught a glimpse of her panties, a flash of orange, didn't know if he should look, couldn't tear his eyes away.

'Hello, David.' She looked up at him through long lashes, a coy smile on her face.

He opened his mouth to speak, but the only sound he could muster was a lustful grunt. He licked his lips, tried again. 'Hello, Mandy.'

'Hello, David. Pleased to see me?'

He nodded, glancing around, the long row of closed stall doors, no urinals, the walls painted pink to match the smell.

'I haven't seen you around for a while. I liked your present.'

Another nod in response. 'Did you?'

'Do you want to go out with me?'

'Oh, Mandy, yes! I've wanted to go out with you since forever.'

'So, can you think of anything you'd like to do?' She parted her hands. He stared at her crotch, deep orange panties with a lacy frill. His mouth fell open. 'Do you like what you see?' She smiled up at him.

'You mean, do it? You and me? Here? Now?'

'Why not? School's finished, no-one's going to come in. Besides, it'll make it more exciting, don't you think?' He stood staring at her, crippled with confusion, hesitated. He thought he heard a sound, but it might have just been his breath catching in his throat.

'Come on,' she encouraged him, her voice soft now and deep, 'don't be scared, Come closer.' He took a step towards her. 'Wait.' She put up a hand - stop. 'If we're going to do this, we need to take our clothes off. Come on, hurry.' She leaned towards him, her hand now tugging at the front of his shirt, popping buttons. Encouraged, he stepped forward, stood over her. He reached down to touch one breast, but she brushed his hand casually aside. He saw the grimace of repulsion in her face but mistook it for a lustful smile. She stroked the front of his trousers, intrigued in spite of herself as she felt his hardening penis through the coarse fabric, fumbled to loosen his belt. He quickly took over, letting his trousers fall around his ankles.

A flicker of acid in her eye as she spoke, staring straight at him. 'Okay, girls, you can come out now.'

There was a sound like an animal attacking. There must have been twenty of them, pouring out of the toilet stalls, a stream of laughing, cackling, gasping girls, and the light, the hard blue-white flash of cartridges as cheap cardboard cameras were pointed towards him, as he stood there, shirt open, trousers around his ankles, penis erect. He stood for eternal seconds as they surrounded him, some laughing, some screaming, some covering their mouths in shock. He couldn't work out what was happening, looked towards Mandy for guidance. She was speaking, but he couldn't hear the words above the riot of noise, could only see the cold sneer across her face. He fumbled his trousers up to cover his groin, his penis losing strength by the second, turned towards the door, pushing through the cackling, jeering phalanx of teenaged girls. He didn't stop, hurried along the corridor, down the stairs, out into the courtyard, ignored the curious stares as he ran, ran, ran away.

After a few weeks the school sent a letter to his home pointing out that he no longer appeared to be attending music lessons and asking him to return the violin.

~~~~~
~~~~~

Date and time unknown.
Sometime between Friday 14th June 2019 and Saturday 6th July 2019

Emily was laying on the damp mattress when she came round. She'd wrapped the duvet around herself as she slept, trying vainly to keep out the cold that struck up through the concrete floor. She stared at the brick ceiling, trying to work out why it was there and what it might mean, then let her eyes fall closed again. Fractured images, glimpses of memory, fluttered across the shutters of her mind. Her whole body ached, and a chill gripped her heart. She tried to swallow, but the act caught against a steel bar of pain in her throat. Clenching her teeth, grunting with effort, she rolled over to sit up.

She couldn't seem to stop the trembling that ran in cold electric lines along her arms and legs. Every inch of her body was sore, beaten, bruised. She looked down at her arms, puzzling at the deep red scratch marks had been gouged into her skin. Each one throbbed raw. More scratches covered the length of her legs, all the way from her ankles to the top of her thighs. She felt exposed, vulnerable, tried to tug down the hem of her skirt.

The man.

She thought he had come to help her, to set her free. She shuddered as the images of what happened next tumbled across her mind. She pulled the duvet tight around herself, hugging herself, trying to hold in the sobs that threatened to crawl up inside her chest, tried to halt the shivering that wouldn't stop. Her right breast felt sore. She looked down, frowning as she pulled open her top, saw the strange raised, red patch on her skin. It throbbed and pulsed as if it has it a heart of its own. Teeth marks.

OhmyGodOhmyGodOhmyGod! She'd been bitten.

Another splinter of memory. The man looming over her. She remembered his weight as he forced her backwards onto the mattress, laid on top of her, covered her, the rancid, sour stench of him in her nose making her breath catch in her throat. She could still see his sneering face in front of her, feel the grip of his hands around her throat as the dark walls had swallowed her. The man hadn't come to rescue her. He had raped her.

She could feel the anger building in her stomach.

She should have fought him off, hit him, scratched him, something, anything, but it had all seemed to happen so fast. He had been too strong, overwhelmed her.

Emily sat on the mattress, rocked backwards and forwards, hugging her knees.

She had been kidnapped. She could barely hold the thought in her mind as it screamed and ran to hide in a dark corner. She wondered how he had chosen her. Why? Had he done this before? For all she knew there were other rooms just like this one, all lined up next to each other, inside each one a young woman held captive in squalor, waiting for him to let himself into their cell.

Emily needed to know, to find out. Now. Right now. She took a deep breath, called out. 'Hello.' Her voice cracked, came out as little more than a croak. She took a gulp of water, tried to clear her throat. 'Hello.' Better, stronger, the word rang out like a bell against the closed-in walls. Emily held her breath, listened for a reply. Nothing. She crawled to the door, tried again, shouting at the top of her voice, banging with the flat of her hand on the cold metal. The sound died away with barely an echo. She waited a moment. Nothing. She took a deep breath, poked a finger into each ear, then screamed until her lungs were crumpled bags in her chest. She freed her ears, listened carefully against the rusty door. If there was anyone else here, anyone anywhere, they must surely be able to hear her. Long, quiet seconds passed. Nothing. No sound at all, just the beat of her heart in her chest and the rasp of her breath in her throat.

A thought hit hard, jarred inside her head. He hadn't covered his face. She had seen her share of TV detective shows, read her share of books, she reckoned she knew the score. If he hadn't bother to conceal his identity from her that could only mean one thing. He wasn't worried about her being able to identify him, because he knew that she never would. She was never going to get out of there alive. The thought jangled through her whole body in a cold electric jolt of adrenalin, a shudder of absolute fear. She wondered if he would kill her soon, in some frenzy of lust and anger, or if he planned keep her there for months, years, until he got bored with his captive plaything, before he cast her aside like a piece of rubbish or a discarded toy. Maybe there were others, but instead of different rooms the scene had been played out again and again at different times. Maybe there was only this one room, occupied by one woman at a time.

She sobbed in despair as she lifted a bottle of water to her lips, took a long drink, letting the cold water wash a soothing course down her throat.

Emily lowered the bottle from her lips.

Something wasn't right.

On top of everything else that had happened to her, she could feel something nagging at the back of her mind, a tiny voice, a whispered warning.

She took another swig of the water, rested the bottle in her lap, tried in her trembling fear to look carefully around the small confines of her prison, trying to work out what was so important that it was able to sit inside her mind and nag away at her.

Long seconds passed as she tried to take in every detail of her tiny cell. She gave a mental shrug. Everything seemed to be perfectly normal, for a given value of normal. She laughed at the absurdity of the thought. How could any of this be normal? She raised the bottle to her lips, took another swig of water.

She snatched the bottle away from her lips, the bolt of water in her mouth slowly warming as she tried to allow the thought to develop in her head.

Did she break the seal, or was it already cracked? She tried to recall opening the bottle, twisting the top, breaking the seal, removing the lid. Had she? Hadn't she?

She put the bottle down on the concrete floor, picked up another. The lid was screwed shut, yes, but the seal was already broken. She dropped the bottle to the floor, picked up the next. The same, closed tight, but the seal broken, the bottle already opened. And the next, and the next. Why? A tightening panic rose in her throat.

He must be putting something in the water, doctoring it before he gave it to her, so that every time she took a drink she was being drugged, drinking in another dose of some sick potion; some drug or concoction to keep her quiet, keep her docile. That must be at least part of the reason she felt so weary. If only she could get her act together, concentrate, even for a few minutes, just long enough to make some kind of plan, work out if there really was any way she could try to escape. She looked at the cold brick walls. No hope there. Maybe she could break open the door or dig a tunnel. Something, anything, if she could only think clearly.

Emily took a slurp of water, then recoiled in horror as she realised what she had done.

After a while she began to feel a warm weariness creep over her. She curled up on the mattress and fell into sleep.

~~~~~
~~~~~

Monday 1st July 2019
11:55
Day Eighteen

It never crossed Bel's mind that Gran could have known so many people. For as long as she had been able to remember Gran had been nothing more or less than a slightly cranky but loveable little old lady. Now it turned out that she had had a full and varied life for the last thousand years, and knew about seven million people, most of whom were now crammed into her front room. There had been so many people at the funeral service that dozens had been left to stand at the rear.

Bel stood just inside the living room door, trying to take in the room. The snug little lounge was simply full. The closed in feeling was accentuated by the fact that everyone was dressed in black. People stood or sat in small groups, making muted conversation. The hot weather didn't help; men pulled at collars and loosened ties, women took to fanning themselves with whatever they could lay their hands on.

For every face that she could recognise there were half a dozen more that Bel had never seen before, all of them old, most of them female. A coven of crones was sitting on the sofa under the window, critically observing everything and everyone, their heads coming together every few seconds to exchange hoarse whispers that only they could hear. For all Bel knew they'd known Gran all her life; probably worked with her in the mill, gone to the same school even. Now they were here to say a final goodbye relishing that it was not their turn today.

Bel glanced across as the kitchen door swung open, watched as her Mum came out backwards, balancing trays of open sandwiches, pork pies, sausage rolls. She looked tired, brittle, emotionally exhausted, as she moved crablike from group to group. Bel hadn't had the courage to call her Mum, let alone go round to talk things through, since the day of Gran's fall. She knew that a difficult conversation was waiting for her somewhere in the future, a dark, heavy conversation about blame and responsibility, full of sorrow, resentment and recrimination, but Bel wasn't ready to face that day just yet. She risked a glance as Mum went past, caught her eye for the briefest instant. There was only a cold distance that reflected her own feelings of guilt.

The worst part was that Mum had tried to phone Bel the night Gran actually died, but Bel had missed her call. Gran's injury had put a strain on everybody, and Bel had got to the stage where she felt as if she needed a break, just one single evening where she didn't have to think about Gran or Emily Phillips or her bastard ex Nigel. Gran had been in hospital three days by then, and the old girl looked like she was making a good recovery after the operation to re-set her hip. The surgeon was happy, the nurses all said she was doing well.

So that evening Bel decided to take the night off from all the pressure. She made a few calls, arranged to meet up with a couple of girlfriends from her schooldays, had a few drinks, let her hair down, tried to blot out all the crap, if only for a few hours. So, just to be bloody-minded, that was the night Gran took it into her head to up and die. And of course, Bel didn't find out until she picked up her messages the next day.

Bel had always hated formal stuff like this, but then who in their right mind actually enjoys funerals? Paying your respects is one thing but sitting bunched up together in fidgety silence in a small room with mostly strangers after a boring service in church was enough to make Bel lose the will to live, no pun intended. Apart from the whispering crones the loudest sound was coming from one old man who had brought a sniffly cold with him and seemed to want to share it with as many people as possible. Behind everything Bel could still hear Granddad's clock marking off the seconds to eternity on the mantelpiece. She wracked her brains, trying to think of something, anything, that she could use as an excuse to make her escape, but she knew that there was nothing she would be able to come up with that would be good enough to get past Mum's radar.

Dad came barrelling out of the kitchen with a clatter, brandishing a bottle of whiskey in each hand. He made his way round the room, taking no prisoners as he poured a generous measure into each cup of weak tea. By the time he'd completed his circuit a few random conversations had broken out; there was even a snort of laughter as one man leaned close to the woman at his side and muttered something in her ear. As Dad began to go around for a second time smiles and open grins began to light up faces, and cups were proffered freely. Even Father Jenkinson, the priest who carried out the service and had wangled himself an invite to the wake on the back of it, joined in, holding out his empty teacup with the best of them. Bel moved away as she heard the Holy Father begin to tell the old joke about the nun and the blind man. The room was getting too warm. She could feel the walls pressing in. She headed for the kitchen. As she passed the sofa, she could see that Dad had been sucked into the clutches of the coven. They had him cornered, smiles in their eyes, their teacups pushed close to his face.

The kitchen was empty. Mum was still circulating, dishing out sandwiches. Everyone had an appetite now. That would be the booze. Bel didn't feel like drinking. She flicked on the kettle for a coffee, dug in her bag for a stick of gum as she waited for it to boil. Her fingers brushed against Gran's keys, forgotten since that desperate day she had given them to her, now a whole lifetime ago. Bel weighed them in her hand as she looked across the room to the closed cellar door. Gran had set off down there for a reason, that much was obvious, and the reason had been important enough for her to make that strange request of Bel in the back of the ambulance, the promise that she would make it right for her, though she never said what or how, and Bel didn't have the foggiest what Gran might have been talking about. Bel flirted with the idea that there might be a wad of money hidden away, or a piece of jewellery perhaps; some special ring or brooch maybe that Granddad had given her when they were younger. Bel knew that she was deluding herself about either probability; Gran had lived an ordinary life and money had always been tight. Besides, Gran's words had carried an edge of guilt and fear far stronger than mere money. Bel knew there was only for her to find out; she had to go down into the cellar and take a look. She knew that Gran's funeral wasn't the right time, but she doubted when that right time might ever be, so she gripped the keys anyway, crossed the kitchen, turned the old Bakelite handle and swung open the cellar door.

Bel froze, her foot hovering over the first step. As she looked down at that cold stone waterfall the memory of Gran's fall slammed into her mind, confronted her again just as it had just two short weeks ago; the sight of Gran's frail, twisted body at the bottom of the steps, the pain on her face, the tears in her eyes, the tremble barely contained on her lips. Bel squeezed her eyes shut, trying to make the image go away, took a deep breath, hoping it would help. When she opened them again the image had gone. She let the breath out and made her way down the cellar steps.

The cellar was smaller than she remembered, just two small rooms. The door on her left was open. Bel leaned in to see the cramped room lined with shelves, each shelf stacked with tins of soup, veg, stewed meat. On one shelf alone there were more than a dozen tins of peas; next to them pickles, porridge, pulses. Gran must have been stocking these shelves for years, hoarding provisions, not against some future shortage, realisation dawned in Bel's mind and a tear came to her eye, but against the haunted memory of a childhood in wartime.

Bel stood, halfway into the room, tried to quieten her mind, tried to look through Gran's eyes, find a way to tap into a feeling, a memory, anything to help her understand what had made the old woman need so desperately to come down here. What was it she had been trying to sort out? Bel looked down at the keys in her hand, held them tight against her chest, close to her heart, a talisman, a touchstone, as she turned slowly on the spot, waiting for the thing, whatever it was, to leap out and offer itself. Nothing.

Bel stood and looked at the paint-flaky door into the second room, took the two steps to stand in front of it, tried the handle. Locked. She hefted the keys in her hand. The larger of the two keys looked like a good bet. She offered it to the lock, slid her tongue across parched lips as it turned. That could only mean that Gran's secret treasure was in here, somewhere. She had to give the door a shove to open it fully, pushing it over a little lip of stone that scraped against the wood at the bottom. She leaned forward to look into the small room. A clean smell. Bleach? Reaching in to flick on the light, Bel winced as the tiny room was swamped in the hard, white glare from a powerful overhead fluorescent light. Strange. Why would anyone want to have such a bright light in such a small room? Stranger still, most of the room was taken up by a massive old rustic pine table. It took up so much space Bel wondered how they had managed to get it in there in the first place. And why? What possible use could Gran and Granddad have had for a big old table like this in their poky little cellar? There were no clues to any hiding place, or the hidden treasure, unless a big table and a bright light were the clues, but what they pointed to, Bel couldn't imagine. A Belfast sink was fixed to the wall in one corner, a huge brass tap above it. An ancient water heater squatted above the tap like a calcified flamingo. The room looked and felt cold, clinical. To top off the effect, all four walls were clad in wooden tongue-and groove cladding, painted gloss white.

Standing in the doorway, the sound of the scraping door fresh in her mind, Bel grinned at an unbidden recollection. The last time she could remember being in this room she had been twelve years old. She had persuaded Martin Johnson from her class in school to come exploring with her one rainy day, she couldn't remember when exactly, it might have been during the summer holidays or just an ordinary weekend. After a few minutes in the cellar they had run out of things to explore, so they'd sat next to each other on the table and their little interlude gradually turned into something altogether more intimate, more adventurous.

The two of them had been so engrossed in the educational possibilities offered by comparative anatomy that neither of them had been aware of the soft scuff of shoes on the steps, hadn't heard the gentle scrape from the bottom of the door that Bel had heard again just now. They were brought back to reality in a heart-thumping instant when Gran announced her presence with a loud "And what do you two think you are up to?"

Martin had been sent packing, sobbing from a resounding slap around the ear. Bel had been treated to a lecture on the sins of the flesh, threatened with eternal damnation, being struck blind, and having all her fingers fall off for the sins of the flesh that she had just committed. Bel had begged Gran to forgive her, and she finally, begrudgingly relented on her threat to tell Mum. Bel earned her reprieve in the shape of months' worth of chores and errands.

Bel flexed her fingers as the memory ran its course. They never did fall off, not even half a decade later when she met up with Martin Johnson again and brought that interrupted anatomy lesson to an altogether more satisfying conclusion in the back bedroom of his council house.

Bel stood in the cellar doorway completely flummoxed. Gran had been so insistent, so upset in the hospital. She had wanted to 'make everything right' and 'everything' pointed to this room, but as Bel looked around again, she couldn't see anything to make right. The room was empty, the only furniture that big old table. No treasure chest, no secret panel, nothing.

Secret panel. That had to be it. Bel began to work her way round the walls, tap-tapping every few inches, not really knowing what she was doing or what she might be looking for, but desperately hoping she'd recognise it when she found it.

She found it halfway down the third wall. If this had been in the movies it would had been because she had spotted some secret sigils, made visible only through the subtle play of light on Coptic runes, glanced out of the corner of her eye as she brushed past, kind of like in "The Da Vinci Code", only this wasn't the movies.

There was a drawer in one end of the table. It opened with a wooden squeak. Inside was a small box, about six inches square, metal, patinaed and scratched on the top, a dent in one side. It looked like an old cash box. Just for a second as she took it out of the drawer Bel entertained the wild hope again of finding gold and diamonds.

Instead, when she used the second, smaller key to open it, she found she was looking at a small black leather-bound notebook, that fitted snugly into the little tin box.

She took the book out. Is this what Gran had been worrying about, an old notebook? Actually, now that Bel thought about it, this was all starting to make sense. The notebook had to be Gran's secret diary, probably from the time when she had been courting Granddad. The chances were that it would be filled with the slightly smutty secret thoughts of a teen-aged girl from the nineteen-fifties. Some things were just not talked about back then, especially anything of a sexual nature. Gran would have been mortified to think that anyone would read it. She'd only trusted Bel to take care of it because in the end she'd had no choice.

It was wrong to look, Bel knew, a little bit seedy. What gave her the right to pry into Gran's most intimate thoughts and feelings from a lifetime ago? What she should do, she knew, what any sensible person would do, was stuff the book deep in her pocket, take it away so that nobody else could ever see it, destroy it the first chance she got, shred it, burn it, kill it. It was only right. So, very carefully, Bel flicked open the first page with a fingernail.

Gran's unmistakeable copperplate script sat neatly upright on the page looking up at her. To see Gran's familiar handwriting laid out in front of her brought tears to her eyes. She lifted her chin, blinked them back, began to read. Instead of the heartfelt adolescent longings she had been expecting, the book was laid out almost like a ledger, a bare statement of facts.

At the top of the first page was a name, Anne Hardaker. Below that a set of dates, 9th May 1940, 2nd March 1960, 27th September 1959, a string of letters and words under that, S., P.G., 15/40, F.H.H., Q(n), and some other stuff, none of which she could understand. She turned to the next page. It was laid out just the same, a similar list of dates and letters, a different name at the top. At the bottom, the words five guineas written in a different hand. Bel stared at the words, trying to find some clue, some pattern, to help her understand what she was looking at. Whatever code Gran had used was obviously good enough to stall little old Bel. Maybe she should use a less direct method to understand what the letters and numbers meant. She closed the book, rested it on one hand, pressed the other flat on top, tried to relax, tried to let suggestions, glimpses, hints, come into her mind. Sometimes it worked, sometimes it didn't, sometimes the signals were so subtle that she dismissed them out of hand.

Bel gasped in surprise as a tiny, incandescent white star that outshone even the overhead fluorescent light seemed to pop out of through the cover of the closed book, hover for a second, then sprang upwards and began to silently orbit her head. A second light popped out of the book, then a third. Within a few seconds more than a score of sparkling lights brighter than anything she had ever seen, awake or in her dreams, were circling her head, dancing, pirouetting, teaming into pairs and triplets, then separating to spin off and join again with others as they moved silently around her. For that brief moment Bel felt herself enfolded in a joy she had never known before, a feeling so sweet and simple.

The lights dived back into the book, the string of bright pearls blinking out of existence, and the sweet feeling faded from her heart, to be replaced a few seconds later by a new brew of emotions, a raw mix of loss, grief, sorrow, that seemed to grow deeper and darker with each passing second, churned and rolled in her stomach, that made her feel as if she was going to throw up across the table. And then it was gone. Bel looked down at the book in her hand. What the hell did all that mean?

Bel knew that for her, about eighty percent of being psychic was psychometry, the feelings and emotions attached to an object. Some psychics did tea leaves, for others it was Tarot. Whatever they did, however they did it, it was all about picking up energy. Most of what Bel got came from holding an object, tuning into the energy implanted by the person who had held it last, or who owned it. She had never been able to explain it properly, not even to herself. Truth be told, even when she was reading up on the subject and all the conflicting theories, she spent most of the time looking for clues as to why her of all people; what made her so different? The best she could work out, some objects seemed to take on some form of embedded resonance, or object tape-recordings, and for some reason that nobody could explain Bel was somehow able to pick up the frequencies these recordings were transmitted on. It made sense to anyone who wanted it to, but equally came across as a load of mumbo-jumbo if you didn't want to understand. For Bel the psychic thing worked, it was as simple as that. Ninety-nine per cent of the time being psychic didn't matter. In real life, the only thing a teapot had to tell you was 'milk, two sugars', and a library book would sometimes show you the emotions of the last person to read it, which made choosing a good thriller a touch easier, but the thing was, it was all normal, humdrum, day to day stuff. Just from that brief contact of a few seconds though, she could tell that this little book was an altogether different kettle of fish. Whatever the book's secret was, whatever Gran's, she had been so emotionally charged that she had been off the scale.

Bel took a deep breath and opened the book again. At least this time she was mentally prepared. Although she could still feel some of the joy and the sorrow that had held her a moment ago, the main force of the connection seemed to have dissipated. She tried to compose herself, took what she hoped was a cleansing breath, then flicked to a page at random, about halfway through the book. It was empty. She furled back with a thumb until she found the last written page.

The name at the top read Margaret Barker. Mum's name, or if not, the notebook included the biggest coincidence of all time. There was nothing else, no clues, apart from a date: 12th September 1990. Bel frowned. That was just a couple of years before she had been born. Like a lot of people, it was difficult for Bel to realise that her own mother had had a life before she herself was born. What was even more difficult for her to get her head around was the idea that her Mum was somehow tied in with this strange little book of Gran's. Bel turned back a page, just to make sure there was no mistake, read the name Susan Pearson. Whoever she was, her name was followed by another list of letters, numbers and abbreviations, just like the ones Bel had seen on the other pages, none of which made any sense. She began to feel again the same murky brew of emotions running as an emotional current through her body; the dragging ache of loss in her stomach, a cold fear that skidded through her heart, freezing it as it passed. All of this was carried on an overwhelming sense of personal loss and bitterness.

Enough was enough. This creepy old place was starting to get to Bel. Whatever the little book was about, whatever she was supposed to be doing to make it right was going to have to wait for another day. She flicked off the fluorescent light, turned her back on the sudden dark, began to climb the steps. She stumbled as she opened the door at the top and almost fell into the kitchen. She made her way to the sink, splashed cold water on her face, took one more slow, deep breath. The nausea in her guts was starting to ease, and she felt as if she was mostly back under control. Right now, more than anything, Bel needed a drink. She pushed open the door into the front room, grabbed a vol-au-vent so that she wouldn't be drinking on an empty stomach, then poured herself a large vodka and very small tonic.

~~~~~
~~~~~

Thursday 20th May 2004
07:12

Mason never did go back to school, but he heard the stories, about his humiliation in the girls' restroom, about the hundreds of photographs pinned up on the walls across the whole school building, about Mandy Armitage's vehement outburst against him.

He had little to recommend him to potential employers; he had never been very good at formal lessons, his grades never rising above average, but by Christmas he had managed to find a job about twenty miles from home, at Manorgrove, the stately home of Lord Standale, sixth Earl of Buttershaw. Manorgrove wasn't palatial like Highclere or Castle Howard, and death duties had taken their toll with every passing generation, but Lord Standale tried to keep the place going. A small retinue of staff were responsible for a wide range of tasks across the estate. Mason settled in to his new life. As season followed season, he mowed and weeded lawns, planted shrubs, made repairs, painted sheds and fences. He was given a cottage on the grounds to live in, tiny, with one bedroom, stone built, tucked away out of site at the back of the main house. Although more than a year passed, the seething bitterness inside him didn't go away, just became burnished, hardened.

In his spare time he wandered, exploring the grounds and woods beyond. One particular track took him past a teeming warren. He liked to go there just after dawn, the morning mist still hanging in pockets between the trees, to watch as a handful of does kept guard, ever alert, over their playful kits while they foraged.

Mason made his way along the narrow track created by countless generations of rabbits until he found what he was looking for. A rabbit caught in a snare, the wire digging into its back leg. It lay on its side, panting, its eyes wide with exhaustion.

He smiled to himself, remembering the shock of surprise he had felt the first time he had seen a trapped rabbit. Now, thanks to an old book on woodcraft he discovered in the library back at Manorgrove, he was able to make his own wire traps, set them, checking regularly for trip-kills. His smile broadened as he saw the animal lying on the cold ground this morning. There was a mat of half-dried blood on the rabbit's leg. He reached down, resting his hand on the soft fur of the rabbit's warm flank. The feel of its hectic pulse set his own heart racing.

Mason lifted the rabbit a few inches off the ground. It hung loose in his grip; all fight gone. He dug his knife into the ground, freed the wooden stake that held the snare in place. The rabbit's other leg jolted in a spasm of pain.

Sheathing his knife, he carried the frail animal to a small clearing a few yards away, not much more than a circle of bare earth and tufts of scruffy grass.

He placed the rabbit on the ground. It lay still, panting, its eyes a black glaze of fear.

Mason looked around the little clearing. This had become one of his special places over the years; a place where he would bring small animals like this rabbit, uncaring of their fragile lives.

There was no struggle left in it, no fight, no flight. He dispatched it in an instant with a single stab of the blade.

A fly landed, began to search the newly discovered landscape. He watched it crawl to the edge of a blood-splash before wafting it away.

Jagging the blade into the ground he began to dig a shallow scrape, then flopped the body in, scuffing dry earth over it with his boot.

~~~~~
~~~~~

Date and time unknown.
Sometime between Friday 14th June 2019 and Saturday 6th July 2019

'Wake up!' The toe of the brown leather boot jabbed into her ribs. She came to with a gasp, rolled over, struggled quickly to her knees. Her whole body felt brittle with the cold that struck up through the thin mattress from the concrete floor.

The man was standing over her again, his heavy frame blocking the light from the lamp.

'It's time to play.'

She shrank back, sucking air in fear. Last time, he had played by choking her until she passed out.

The man grabbed her by the arm, shaking her as he dragged her up from the mattress to her feet. She wailed at the pain he inflicted and sobbed inside at how easily he picked her up, how strong he was, how weak and unable to resist she felt.

'I said it's time to play!'

He pointed, and she followed his finger, confused and still sleepy. There was a music stand, a sheaf of manuscript pinned in place, next to her mattress. Propped against the wall was a violin case.

She recognised her case instantly, the smileys and a Day-Glo "yolo" sticker she had put on at the start of term. It felt like a million years ago now. She fell to her knees, sobbing with raw emotion at this glimmer of normality in this mad maelstrom, reached out to take the violin, hesitated in case this was some new sick kind of trick. 'Open it.' His voice sounded almost normal, almost friendly.

She reached forward with trembling fingers to touch it, felt the worn texture of the rigid black case.

As she lifted the lid and saw her violin it felt like greeting an old friend. She gently stroked her finger along the front, tracing one of the f-holes with the tip of her finger.

'Take it out. I want you to play it.'

She frowned at his words. 'I don't understand. What do you want me to play?'

'The music's on the stand.'

Emily stood up, looked at the score. Mendelssohn's E minor violin concerto.

How did he know? This was the piece she had been practising for the last few months, in preparation for the recital. The recital. It belonged to a different world, a world she wondered if she would ever see again. Tears welled in her eyes. She brushed them away with trembling fingers as his voice dropped to an urgent hiss. 'I said play.'

She took the violin from its case, trying to keep her breathing under control. She no longer felt the cold. A deep well of emotion began to swell inside her. Not for a second had she thought she would ever hold her precious violin again. It sat in her hand like an old companion. Her fingers caressed the almost-soft feel of the maple wood neck, stroked the ebony fingerboard, plucked gently at the strings. They were still in tune. She clutched the bow, thinking for an instant it might serve as a weapon, but she didn't dare risk it. She could still feel the weakness in her muscles from the beating he had given her the day before.

She lifted her violin, and with an ease born of a lifetime's intimacy cupped it under her chin in a single fluid movement. It balanced there feeling weightless. The calming breath came automatically, the bow bit into a string, and the first notes filled the tiny room. The cold, the bruises, the aches and pains, all fell away. For one ecstatic moment she was able to escape into the music, swoop and rise with the passion, carried on the raw emotion of the piece. She felt herself lifted to a place she knew in her heart of hearts she would never visit again, could hold now only as a memory. Tears gathered in her eyes, but she refused to cry in the face of this gift.

'Bitch!' The man lashed out without warning, struck her across the face with the back of his hand.

She gasped, her head reeling.

'Fucking bitch! You think you're so special, don't you?' He grabbed her elbow, his fingers digging into her soft flesh. Emily whimpered, scared that her arm might snap.

'I'll show you just how special you are.' He thumped her in the meat of her bicep. All the strength fell out of her arm in an instant. She watched as the violin fell to the floor, a slow arc that ended with a clatter. He locked eyes with her, then stamped down his foot with a grunt. The instrument splintered into a thousand shards. He kicked the bits to one side, a sick smile on his face, slowly brought up his fist, held it in front of her face. Emily couldn't control the tremble on her bottom lip, the tears that welled in her eyes. The blow when it came slammed into her stomach. She buckled under the impact. She had never known a pain so deep, so hard. Her lungs couldn't move to suck in air, and she wondered if this was how she was going to die. The man forced her backwards against the wall, pressed his forearm across her throat, the sharpest brittle pain bit into her windpipe. He began to fumble at her crotch, tugging at her panties under her dress. She felt the fabric creak and tear in the grip of his fingers. All the while the pressure continued on her throat, crushing, closing. He was saying something; she could see his lips moving but couldn't hear any sound, just the roar of blood in her ears and the wheeze and rattle of her own breath as she fought to draw vital air into her lungs. Black walls began to close in around her.

The man knelt across her chest, ripping at her dress, pulling her panties down across her thighs. His erection stiffened as he glimpsed a flash of orange. He forced her thighs apart, using one knee as a crowbar.

'You're not so precious now, are you, Mandy?' His words were a harsh hiss of evil as he pushed into her, his jerking thrusts matching the pace of his words. As she fell from consciousness the tears she had held back in joy began to fall down her cheeks in sorrow, unseen.

~~~~~
~~~~~

Tuesday, 2nd July 2019
09:50
Day Nineteen

Waking up was hard work. There was a pulsing throb inside Bel's head that got worse when she tried to sit up, and because she had neglected to undress properly the night before, the make-up that hadn't transferred onto her pillow had smeared into her eyes, making for a gritty feeling every time she blinked. She had no choice, the bathroom beckoned, so she braced herself, swung her legs out from under the duvet, felt for the floor. Even her toes hurt.

The first drink had been as a reward to herself for having found Gran's notebook, whatever it might mean, in that table drawer in the cellar. Bel had made it on the strong side, no pub measures at a wake, so it had been easy to persuade herself that the second drink was also a good idea. By the time she'd topped up her glass for the third time, she was able to assure herself that this was all just a plan to get a night's dream-free sleep. No such luck; Emily had spent most of the night practising the same short phrase of music a few inches from Bel's left ear.

Much as she hated to admit it, Detective Inspector Fox had been right. He had wanted hard facts and rational leads; all Bel had been able to offer were bits and pieces, random feelings, impressions, pain. What, when it came to it, did she actually know? She felt sure in her own mind that Emily was still alive, but she had nothing she could call proof. As for her feeling that the poor girl was being held somewhere underground in a remote location, if you were going to kidnap somebody, isn't that exactly where you would hide them? Fox was right, Bel had nothing the police could use and that had made her come across as naive at best, a time-wasting idiot at worst. There had to be some way she could get hold of some solid facts that Fox would be able to understand and use. Bel padded into the bathroom, feeling fragile as she headed for the toilet and the shower. Hot needles scoured her skin when she stepped under the jet of hot water. More punishment. Bel stood there for a long time, and the aches in her bones began to wash away. When she finally turned the water off, she wrapped a big soft towel around herself and shuffled to the kitchen, flicked on the kettle. Coffee wasn't a cure for a hangover, she knew, but she needed something to wash down the ibuprofen. The tablets went down in a single slurp. By the time she had made her way to my bedroom and begun to dry herself off, she was beginning to feel almost normal again.

What she needed now, Bel told herself as she dug out jeans and trainers, was something to eat. It felt like days since she had eaten properly, snatching bits and pieces when she got the chance. There had been food at the funeral, but she been a bit busy. Her boss Mr Murdoch had told her to take a few days off after the funeral, give herself time to get her head together after Gran's death, so today she had no time pressures. There was a greasy spoon a couple of streets from her apartment. A bacon butty felt like the answer to at least some of her problems so Bel scooped up her phone and purse and headed out in search of food.

The breakfast rush was over, but the place was still busy, so Bel ordered herself a bacon butty, got a flat white with an extra shot to start on while she waited, and sat at a tiny table by the door.

People-watching has always been one of her favourite pastimes, so she glanced round as she took a sip. A young mother at the next table grinned and cooed as her infant son sucked on a slice of buttered toast. Her eye caught Bel's, and they shared a brief smile. Bel turned to look out of the window, watched a man sitting on a bench, juggling a sausage roll and takeaway coffee as he tried to turn the pages of his newspaper, all under the watchful eye of a corpulent pigeon that strutted about close to his feet, anticipating the blizzard of pastry flakes that was sure to fall. An old couple, still cherishing each other after all these years, held hands as they walked by. They were so different from the Curtises that Bel could think of nothing but them for a few seconds. The old couple turned a corner and were gone.

Bel turned back to the man and his pigeon audience, caught sight of the front-page headline as he held it up in front of him. Some corrupt local politician had been arrested on suspicion of embezzlement, apparently. So, Emily Phillips had slipped down the rankings of what counted as newsworthy. No news just isn't news. That would change the instant she turned up, Bel knew, especially if she turned up dead.

She was still alive though. Bel knew it in her bones, could taste it almost. If you were to ask her straight out how she knew, why she felt that way, the closest she would probably be able to come up with by way of an explanation would be that there was something about the dreams. It was as if they were too vivid, too fresh for Emily to be dead, but how do you explain that to yourself, never mind some stick-in-the-mud copper? Bel felt herself weighed down by a mixture of frustration and guilt, wondered if the reason she hadn't been able to uncover any specific information about where Emily was and what had happened to her was that the girl was still alive. Maybe if she were dead, she would be able to show up in a dream and lead Bel straight to her body. Bel couldn't wish the girl dead though, that would be ridiculous. What she really needed was some sort of a map to follow, a route to trace with her mental finger.

Who was she kidding? It wasn't as if she could just do a 'Google' search, was it, type a URL into the search-bar for a missing girl?

The young waitress, chewing gum, a bored look on her face, clattered the plate down on the table in front of her, but Bel was already standing up. She put the sip-lid on her coffee, snatched up the bacon butty and was out of the door before the plate had stopped rattling.

Bel couldn't get her legs to carry her fast enough. It was only a couple of streets, but she was out of breath by the time she got back to the flat, cursing the extra pain her hangover was causing. She stood panting at the door, squeezing her coffee and sandwich a bit too hard in one hand as she fumbled for the key with the other. A piece of bacon dropped onto the floor as she pushed at the door, but eating was no longer any part of her thoughts. She hurried into the living room, muttering a prayer to herself, begging for the co-operation of un-named gods as she carelessly perched the remains of the bacon roll on a chair arm, working with fumbling fingers to clip the keyboard onto her tablet and stand it on the coffee table.

Firing it up, Bel stabbed at the keys, scrolled across to 'Google', and typed in, 'Emily Phillips - Yorkshire'.

As it does, Google gave her seven hundred thousand answers in less than half a second. How stupid could she be?

Bel hunkered down to look at the screen. The first few lines were a link to Emily's Facebook page, news articles from the local feeds about her going missing, some stuff about her background in music, a Wikipedia profile, of all things. There was also an Emily Street in Hull, and another in Huddersfield, a Phillips Crescent and Close in Selby, but as for some bright, flashing arrow pointing to where Emily Phillips was being held prisoner, forget it. That sort of thing didn't happen in real life, and deep down Bel knew just how much of an idiot she had been to think otherwise.

Bel sat glaring at the open 'Google' page. Sitting in the cafe she had been so certain she was on to something. She slammed her hand down on the coffee table in frustration. 'Come on Emily, tell me where you are, damn it!'

But Emily didn't actually know where she was, did she, not to give her a street name or a house number. That was the problem Bel was trying to solve. Maybe if she could find a way, Emily might be able to show her the route she'd been taken after she was kidnapped. Bel had read about this sort of thing over the years. Map-dowsing they called it. There was this guy in America who used some sort of crystal on a string dangled over a road atlas to find oil. Made a fortune, so they reckoned. Just for a second Bel wondered if she'd missed her calling.

Well, she didn't have a crystal and she didn't have an atlas, but she did have her tablet and she did have 'Google'. She clicked onto 'itv.com/calendar', one of the local newsfeeds for Yorkshire, typed in Emily's name. She was looking for a home address for the missing girl, a place to start from. Bel scrolled down the page until she found what she was looking for; Buttercroft Holt at Chapel Allerton, Emily's home address, number seventeen.

Hang on, though; think, Bel, think.

Emily wasn't snatched from home, was she? She'd been at the College of Music, practising for that recital thing. Changing tack, Bel searched for the address, found it in a couple of seconds. The Northern College of Music, Clarendon Road, Leeds 2. A quick cut and paste and the postcode was in 'Google' maps, and there it was. This was the place Emily had been seen last, on the front steps of the College.

Bel stared at the image on the screen until she could feel her eyes started to bulge and feel itchy, but nothing happened, no stunning psychic insights leapt out at her. There was one thing she had learned when she had used her powers to try to win the lottery, and that was that forcing the issue just made it less likely that she would be able to get any useful information. Bel felt so frustrated. Emily had been missing more than a week now. Bel needed to make something happen. Simple logic told her that one of these nights Emily was going to come to Bel in a dream and tell her to stop looking, that it was too late, she was dead.

The cursor blinked at her, offering no advice, no comment.

She rubbed her finger backwards and forwards across the touchpad, making the image on the screen slosh from side to side, watching as the city streets came and went. She swiped at the touchpad, making the cursor move to the right, watched as it tracked across Leeds city centre until she found herself on the York road, followed it out of town. She was hoping for some spark of enlightenment, but nothing came, no bright flashes. She slid her way back to the College of Music, decided on a hunch to move south this time.

It began to dawn on Bel just how big a task this was turning out to be, even with the power of the internet. The M1 motorway started right in the middle of Leeds, heading south all the way to London. The M62 ran just ten miles south of the city centre and straddled England from coast to coast. Whoever snatched Emily Phillips could have been fifty miles away from the College of Music in less than an hour. Bel scrolled further and further south, past Sheffield, but she had no luck, no insights, no inspiration. She started to wonder how many screen-pages it took to cover Yorkshire. Even that might not be enough, though, she realised. Cars didn't just suddenly stop at map edges or county boundaries, did they? They're not marked on the road, painted on like white lines, you just kept on driving.

Bel knew she needed to change tack; alter the way she had been thinking about this search. That was what was wrong, she realised; she was thinking too much. Her mind was bouncing about all over the place instead of staying calm, settling onto some point of focus. Emily, Emily. She needed to be thinking about Emily, needed some way to keep her mind focussed on the girl, to stop all these random, negative thoughts from clogging up her mind.

The 'Calendar' news pages soon gave up a photo of Emily, but sadly, as with the newspaper she had seen in the cafe, it wasn't near the top of the feed anymore, not anywhere close. The image showed Emily standing with her violin in one hand, her hair up in a bun, grinning broadly as she was presented with a silver cup for winning some music competition. Bel hit print. Her old printer clattered into life on the sideboard. The photo came out a bit grainy and it looked like the inkjets needed cleaning, but it was good enough for what she had in mind.

Bel put the flimsy print down on the coffee table next to the tablet. The silver-framed photo of Jessica Curtis she'd "borrowed" was there too. How stupid had she been to pick that up? It amounted to theft, a simple way to lose her job in an instant if she was looking for one. She'd only taken it in the first place because of the empathy she had felt for the girl's dead mother. Bel promised herself that she would take it back the first chance she got, even if it meant just knocking on the door and apologising to the drunken old man as she handed it back to him. With any luck he would be too pissed to understand what was going on.

She stared at the photo for a few seconds, figuring that if she could get her conscious mind to switch off, let go, Emily might get a chance to get close enough for Bel to hear her. So, trying to separate herself from her own conscious thoughts, Bel began to move the cursor over the map at random, letting her fingers do the thinking. All the while she focussed her gaze on the photo of Emily, ignoring the screen and whatever it might be showing for the moment. 'Come on, Emily, come on,' she whispered as she flicked seven times in quick succession in one corner of the screen, then five in another. She was determined to not allow any rational thoughts she might have influence this in any way. If her gift really could find the missing girl, she reasoned, it wasn't going to get any help from her conscious mind.

After another random minute of swishing backwards and forwards Bel risked a look at the screen, just out of curiosity, wondering where she had ended up. Not that far, actually. The main Harrogate to Skipton road wandered across the page from the top left-hand corner. A smudge of blue on the right denoted Swinsty reservoir, surrounded on all sides by green blocks of trees. The cursor was blinking away near the middle of the screen, over a small, red blob.

She couldn't make out what it was, so she leaned forward, zoomed in a couple of clicks.

The strange red smudge didn't seem to be pointing to anything more interesting than a clump of trees, but it was getting slowly bigger on the page for some reason, even though Bel had stopped working the cursor. It began to spread, almost as if it was breathing, moving over the roads and the hills, flowing like a living thing, in an increasing circle of red. In a few short seconds, half the page had disappeared under the red stain. The smudge was growing darker now, obliterating words and lines alike. It must be a virus, some computer bug that was going to destroy the hard drive, leave her with a blank screen and computer dementia. Bel quickly hit ctrl Z, trying to reverse her actions, get away from this strange screen. Nothing. She clicked Escape. Escape. Escape. Still the virus moved across the screen. Bel stared helpless as the crimson stain oozed over the landscape like a viscous liquid, filling the screen from edge to edge. It seemed to pause for a second or so, then, with a cough, a sticky red bubble burst out of the screen and splashed across the keyboard. She desperately wanted to move her hands out of the way, but they were frozen, glued to the keys. She could only watch transfixed as the sluggish ooze pumped out like a torpid heartbeat, oozed across her hands, washed over them in a sticky, warm slime. A metallic stench rose in swirls, filled her nostrils. The cancerous crimson flower bloomed and spread, covering the coffee table, dripping onto the floor, a sludge of rancid bile and mucus. Make it stop! Make it stop! she screamed inside her head; her breath stoppered in her throat.

With a grunt of effort, Bel wrenched her hands free from the keyboard, tried to close the lid with greasy-sticky fingers. It wouldn't go down. Please let the lid go down, please let the blood stop. The pressure of the hidden crimson heartbeat was too strong. There was nothing she could do to make it stop; she was going to drown in blood in her own apartment! With a strength born of panic, Bel pushed herself backwards, away from the machine, rolled off the sofa, began to scramble across the floor, anything to get away. At last her tongue freed in her throat. Eyes closed against the horror in front of her, Bel sucked air into her lungs and screamed at the top of her voice.

She didn't stop screaming until she ran out of breath, then opened her eyes, gasping.

The tablet sat smugly on the coffee table, the cursor blinking like a slow pulse in the middle of the screen. All trace of the blood was gone. The stench had evaporated. There was just the cursor. Bel looked at it blinking innocently on the screen. Trapped between fear and curiosity, she edged closer, trying to make out the image on the screen.

The place the cursor had stopped wasn't much more than a handful of houses, a crossroads and a couple of farms. Bel leaned in nervously to read the name of the little village, ready to jump back if the cursor so much as twitched, too scared to touch the machine.

The cursor blinked sedately on Thatcher's Hamlet.

~~~~~
~~~~~

Date and time unknown.
Sometime between Friday 14th June 2019 and Saturday 6th July 2019

Emily told herself she would be ready for him the next time he came to visit. She went over the plan again, whispering to herself as she ran through her flimsy plan. Hit him hard, hit him fast, put him out of action as quickly as possible, use surprise to her advantage. She just had to grab his key, he must have a key, she reasoned, get past him, lock him in and get the hell out of there. She would throw the duvet over him as he crawled in through the low doorway, then punch him in the head, kick him if she could, hit him again and again until he lost consciousness and she could make good her escape. She just hoped her strength would hold out long enough for her to put her plan into action.

A sound at the door, the key rattling in the lock. He was here, he was already coming in. She'd been so busy psyching herself up, she almost missed her chance.

She snatched up the damp and heavy duvet, ran as hard as she could at the crouching figure as he struggled to get through the low entrance on hands and knees. Before she got there, she already knew that she was too late. She was still a couple of steps away when he began to stand up. She started screaming at the top of her voice as she threw herself at him, the blanket spread in an arc like a gladiator's net, lashed out with her feet and fingernails.

She only had time to get in one good kick before everything started to go bad.

Her foot connected with the man's face, a solid blow below his left eye, but he just seemed to shrug it off. A hand whipped out, grabbed her foot before she had chance to put it down again. The hand clamped round her ankle like a vice. He twisted, yanked. Hard. Emily squealed in pain, struggled to break free, but he was too strong. She lost her balance, fell to the floor. She tried to kick out at him with her other foot, but the blow was weak and ineffectual. He smiled a long, slow smile, pulled her towards him. He raised a fist and hit her with a single blow to her stomach. All the breath coughed out of Emily in an instant. She sagged into a crumpled ball around her pain, gasping for breath, crying out more in sorrow than in pain. She knew she had already lost.

'I suppose I'm surprised you haven't tried that before,' he smirked as he knelt beside her on the floor. He dug his fingers into her hair, yanked her head a few inches up from the floor. Emily tried to focus on his face. More than anything she wanted to spit in his eye, to show him that she wouldn't allow him to win, but he had hit her harder than she had ever been hit in her life. She could feel her stomach buckle as she tried to pant breath after hectic breath, tryed to not throw up. She struggled to escape his grip, but she had nothing left to fight with. She started to sob, her body heaving with effort.

'I have something special for girls who don't behave themselves.' He pulled a metal object out of his pocket and held it out for her to see. It reminded Emily more than anything of an electric razor. 'Do you know what this is?' The smile on his face was broad, lazy, sardonic. She tried to speak but didn't have the breath to form any words. 'No? I'll show you, shall I?' He flicked a switch on the side and a blue, flickering light danced between two metal spikes at one end. Emily watched the buzzing spark as he moved it towards her, then stopped a couple of inches away from her arm, a twinkle in his eye as he paused. He waited until she was looking at him, until he was certain they had made eye contact, then let go of her hair, and in the same instant touched the device to her bare skin.

Emily's world turned inside out with pain.

Every muscle in her body shuddered as the electric pulse hit her. Her jaw locked, clamping her teeth so tight in her mouth she thought they might crunch and shatter. Her back arched as the sparking current drove through her. She couldn't even try to breathe, her ribs were locked tight around her lungs, her heart hammered in her chest, a heavy painful throb. She could feel her eyes bulging in their sockets as a steel clamp wrapped itself around her skull.

After a million years the current ceased.

Emily lay on her back, panting up at the ceiling, feeling as if she'd been thrown against the wall. Her eyes refused to focus.

He rolled her over onto her stomach, as limp as a ragdoll, powerless to resist, pushed up her thin summer dress, pulls at her knickers, the bright orange ones with the frill, tearing holes in the flimsy fabric as he dragged them down across her thighs.

Her breath caught in her throat as he pushed into her. Salt tears streaked her grimy face. Broken; she lay motionless, unresisting under his assault.

~~~~~
~~~~~

Friday, 15th October 2004
16:06

This little trip had become something of a ritual over the last few months. He couldn't remember exactly when it all started, but he found himself coming back now every few weeks, whenever he got the chance. The van was his to use as and when he wanted, provided he didn't abuse the privilege, but there was a tank of diesel on the estate, and to the best of his knowledge no-one ever checked on his mileage. He made his way through the streets that had once been so familiar to him, but now felt as if they had somehow strange, shrunken somehow. Every time he set off to come here he told himself he was going to visit his mother, who still lived in the old house, but every time as he drew nearer, he turned left instead of right at one particular corner and drove towards a different address.

Mason parked the van on the other side of the street, a few doors down. He wondered sometimes how he she didn't notice him, didn't recognise him, but the evil bitch probably didn't even remember him.

He sat, watched, waited. This was all supposed to be in the past, long forgotten, except it wouldn't go away. He wasn't aware of the passage of time, didn't know how long he sat there, waiting, watching, until the evening began to draw in. She wasn't usually this late. That was the problem with public transport; unreliable. He already knew she didn't have a car.

Then he spotted her, walking on the opposite footpath, head down, bundled against the autumn chill. She didn't give the van a glance, turned up the garden path, fumbling in her handbag to find her key, unlocked the front door. He watched lights go on and off as she moved about the house, upstairs and down. He imagined he could see her ritual through the walls after observing the scene so many times; kettle on, cup of tea, something out of the fridge for the evening meal, thermostat cranked up. The mother would be home soon.

The house door opened. A dog bounded out at the first crack, clattering the door back on its hinges, dragging Mandy Armitage behind, tugging at its lead. 'Slow down, Shadow. Wait.' The heavy dog dragged her along the street to a narrow snicket between two houses that led to the fields behind. Mason remembered the day she brought the dog home, a fluffy bundle of wriggling legs and tail, cuddled close to her chest. He wondered how old it was now, how long he had been doing this, how many years he had been coming here to pine over a love that had long since shrivelled to nothing more than a bitter taste in his mouth. Why did he keep tormenting himself like this?

He turned the key and drove away, a broth of hatred souring to bile in his stomach.

~~~~~
~~~~~

Wednesday, 3rd July 2019
10:20
Day Twenty

Bel leapt about six feet in the air when she heard the dog bark. By the time her feet landed back on the ground every single nerve-ending in her body was jangling and she could hear the piston-clatter of her heart rattling in her throat and ears. She spun round on the spot, not knowing if she was going to scream, attack or run away, only to find some bloke trying to persuade a reluctant Border Collie to climb into the back of his rusty old red hatchback. Her lungs emptied with a gasp, making her realise how badly spooked she really was by all this. She forced herself to calm down, to gather her thoughts, sort out what she was going to do next.

If there was a better way to focus the mind than phantom blood and bile pumping out of a laptop, Bel hadn't been able to think what it was. It had chosen a weird way to go about it, but it looked like her strange talent had found a way to get the information out of her after all. Emily Phillips was being held prisoner somewhere in the village of Thatcher's Hamlet. That was what the blood and the cursor had been about; a trick played on herself by her deep subconscious to show her exactly where Emily was being kept prisoner. All she had to do was drive over there, find out exactly where Emily was being held, and then, well she wasn't sure that she had thought it all through properly after that, maybe she could break in to the place where she found her and rescue her or phone the police and have DI Fox come hurrying over with his tail between his legs to apologise before freeing Emily. Fox. Tail between his legs. It all sounded good to Bel.

When the thing with her laptop had happened, it had taken Bel long, long minutes to get her nerve together and risk touching the keyboard. When she had finally plucked up courage, shielding her face with one hand, and tapped the space key with a stretched-out finger nothing had happened except a thin metallic bleep. She had uncovered her eyes, tried again. Nothing. She stared at the cursor, blinking away on Thatcher's Hamlet. When she eventually realised nothing bad was going to actually happen, she'd printed out a route map to the village, then spent the rest of yesterday putting together what she was starting to call her rescue kit. If she was going to do this, she decided, she was going to do it right.

Bel dug out an old rucksack, legacy of a former boyfriend who had been into mountaineering more than he had been into her, started to pack it with the bits and pieces she reckoned she might need for rescuing a missing girl. She started with water, a couple of large bottles of the stuff, and a first-aid kit obviously, a torch and a small trowel in case there was any light digging to do. She put in a packet of high-energy biscuits in case Emily had been starved, and some painkillers. Bel packed away a change of clothes for herself, along with two spare pairs of socks. Next, she decided to cram in some jogging pants and a sweat-top, big and baggy, for Emily if she needed them. Bel could only guess at her size, a bit smaller than herself, but too big was always going to be better than too small.

The man in the hardware store had given her a look of pure, old-fashioned misogyny when she'd walked in with her list, stating without speaking that he was going to criticise everything she said and did. He added to the effect with a telling glance when Bel put a pair of bolt-cutters on the counter that she had barely been able to pick up, never mind open and close. She stood her ground though, adding a compass with a fluorescent needle that she just knew she had to have the second she saw it, regardless. For the first time in her life Bel actually knew which way was north. When she got home, she tucked it into the rucksack with the rest of the stuff. The bolt-cutters she left in the boot of the car because they were far too heavy to carry up to the flat. At the back of her mind Bel already suspected they were a mistake, but she had bought them anyway rather than lose face in front of the man in the shop.

Bel had woken early that morning, too fired up to sleep through to the alarm, her mind alive with preparations for her forthcoming expedition. At last she was beginning to feel as if she was doing something useful, putting her psychic powers to good use. Instead of the visions happening *to* her, she was taking control, making them work for her, and, she hoped, work for the missing girl. She'd laid off the booze last night, even got herself an early night, so she felt surprisingly good as she got out of bed for a change, and actually enjoyed the two croissants she'd had with her coffee. Cup rinsed and dried, Bel dragged the rucksack down to the car and stowed it in the boot. It felt as if it weighed about a ton. She was seriously starting to think she might have over-prepared. Still, this was her big chance to find Emily and put Fox in his place, so there was no way she was going to abandon her plans now. Bel punched the co-ordinates for Thatcher's Hamlet into the satnav, checked she had her sunglasses and hit the road.

There was no particular rush, so she took it easy on the drive out of town. After twenty minutes or so the city of Leeds had fallen behind, and she was cruising through the rolling curves on the back roads towards Swinsty reservoir. There was no doubt the view was majestic, this was God's country after all, but Bel had always found the act of driving a tedious chore no matter how pretty the surroundings, so she leaned across to turn on the radio, twiddle with the tuner. It was a bit weird, she knew, but since the visions of Emily began, she'd started to develop an interest in classical music. She even told herself she was beginning to recognise one or two of the pieces on the radio when she heard them. She'd kept telling herself she was going to programme in a couple of stations, maybe even find some stuff to Bluetooth, but hadn't got around to it yet. So, as she took a long, sweeping corner, trying to work the radio, Bel glanced up, gasped, tugged at the wheel, and spun off the blacktop. The car did a tight little pirouette before slowly sliding sideways into one of the million trees that seemed to have been planted everywhere. When the car came to a halt with a loud bang, Bel swore every bad word she knew, and there were many, then clambered out of the car to inspect the damage.

It turned out not to be as bad as she'd at first feared. There was a lot of paint missing from the passenger side, and a big dent in the door, but it looked like the car was still driveable. Once she'd finished checking out the car Bel was able to take a proper look at her surroundings for the first time. The hairs on the back of her neck prickled up in an instant.

She was standing in a lay-by just like the one she had seen in her vision, the vision she'd had of finding Jessica Curtis.

Shit! This was not part of her plans.

This didn't make sense. How could she have ended up here, of all places?

All of her plans, all of her focus, had been to go to Thatcher's Hamlet, take a bit of a prowl around, see if her gift could find Emily Phillips. That was why she had printed out the picture of Emily, put it on the coffee table, and, she now realised, placed it right next to the framed photo of Jessica Curtis. Never mind focussing in on Emily, her mind must have jumped the rails, given her a connection to the wrong girl. Looking round, Bel realised she wasn't supposed to be making her way to Thatcher's Hamlet after all. The whole thing must have been manipulated somehow by her sub-conscious to bring her to this lay-by, to follow the vision she had had, to find Jessica Curtis. Damn. What should she do? She really wanted to carry on, get back in the car and go to Thatcher's Hamlet, find Emily, bring her home to her family if she could, but there was another bit inside Bel, maybe the bit with an awareness of synchronicity, that was trying to explain that she had obviously been sent to this little stretch of dusty country lane for a reason, and that she should accept that and go with the flow rather than try to follow her own agenda. Again, shit!

Bel took another look around while she argued with herself about the right thing to do. A cloud of midges had already drifted in to hang in the air over the bonnet of the car. It hadn't rained for a couple of weeks, and the summer sun seemed to have baked a grey dust onto everything; the trees that had been bright and green and vibrant in her vision were sombre dark pines in real life, their needle fronds sharp, hurtful looking. The whole place looked eerie, closed in. In her vision she remembered she'd been standing somewhere just about here when the black dog had come lolloping down the lane towards her.

And that was when the Collie had barked.

After she'd managed to settle her heart back into her chest and calm herself down a bit, she tried to look and act normal, though the man in the red car kept looking at her with a puzzled frown as he coaxed his dog into the space behind the seats and dropped the lid. After a couple of minutes and a ridiculous pantomime over his seatbelt he drove off up the lane, giving Bel one last quizzical stare as he left. After that everything fell silent. Bel had never been comfortable in the countryside; it gave her the creeps, somehow. When you'd been brought up in the city a certain amount of background noise came with the territory, the rumble that comes from traffic, the low thud of distant sound systems, the ceaseless hum of a million people living cheek by jowl, so to hear nothing louder than the pip-pip of some tiny green and yellow bird as it flitted about in the branches of a nearby tree left Bel feeling a bit unnerved. Right at that moment she felt almost as if she was the last person in the whole world, the only survivor in some post-apocalyptic nightmare. She shook the thought away; she had watched too many zombie movies.

Bel knew that at some stage in the next few minutes she was supposed to go marching off into the woods, but to be honest she was in no rush. It looked dark in there, oppressive, even on a bright day like today. Being psychic didn't mean you don't get scared, and besides, which way should she go? The dog in the vision might only have been a thing from an imaginary world, but without it, Bel didn't have a clue which way to go, which way to turn. A tree was a tree was a tree as far as she was concerned, and these trees looked far too dark and gloomy for her liking.

She could always leave, she reasoned, get in the car and just drive away, set off again for Thatcher's Hamlet, or just give up and go home, take it easy on herself. Knowing her luck though, she would probably somehow drive herself round in a massive circle and end up right back here in this lay-by, probably crash the car into the same bloody tree. Resigned to her fate Bel reached into the car and sprung the boot-catch. The rucksack sat there looking smug, and, in the cold light of day, far too big for her to realistically think about carrying. Cursing herself for a being a naive fool, Bel un-buckled one of the pockets and dug out a bottle of water, and, remembering the graphic vision in Jessica's room, the trowel and a small torch. She knew she had put it off as long as she could, so she took a deep breath, stood up, slammed the boot shut and turned to face the trees.

There was a black dog staring at her. It looked just like the dog from her vision in Jessica's bedroom. A hard chill jangled up her spine. The dog looked so solid, so "there" that for a moment Bel wondered if it might be real, but deep down she knew it was another creation of her psychic imagination.

The dog sat there, about fifty feet away, on the grass verge just on the edge of the tree line, tongue out, tail thumping, looking straight at her. Damn. Now she knew that it was too late for her to change her mind, that there was no way she could back out of this. Another shudder shook down her spine, and she had to rub her hands over the skin on her forearms, trying to scrub away the goose bumps. It looked so gloomy among those dark pines. As she started walking forwards towards it, the dog jolted to its feet and started to run in a tight, giddy circle in front of her, yipping with excitement, before turning and plunging into the undergrowth.

As if to confirm that she was never going to be a wilderness explorer, the very first branch whipped across her face with a stinging slap. The little yellow-green bird started pip-pipping its patch of turf for all the world to hear, hopping backwards and forwards between two branches, an incongruous stab of colour among the dark, dusty foliage.

The going was a lot harder than she remembered from her dream, too. The ground all around her was littered with a dense carpet of fallen needles and small shrubs struggling to grow in the half-light. Long streamers of ivy seemed to cover everything, and big, waxy-leaved plants that the smart-arse at the back of her mind whispered were probably rhododendrons, crowded in on every side. She noticed that the carpet of pine needles was shot through with green shoots; life forcing its hand even in this bleak place.

Bel kept going, not fast but she liked to think relentless, unstoppable. Mainly she knew she was trying to keep up with the dog, which she realised was a bit silly because the dog was all in her imagination so it shouldn't matter how fast she went, but she knew that somehow it did. The dog seemed to be taking great delight in staying almost out of sight. He, Bel had started to think of the dog as a he because it looked more stupid than any dog she had ever seen, moved forward a couple of yards, then stopped and waited for the slow, stupid human to catch up. This was a first: she couldn't recall ever being made to feel inadequate by her own psychic vision before. She stopped to look around at one point, just to check her bearings back to the lay-by, but the whole world now seemed to be made of tall straight pine trees. She had imagined they would have allowed in a sort of dappled play of light, but in reality, she felt herself encircled by gloom. And, of course, the compass that she should have been using to navigate her way through all this undergrowth was still tucked away somewhere in the backpack in the boot of the car, so on top of everything else she was now officially lost. Bel knew she didn't really have much of a choice after that, so she tramped after her imaginary companion some more, cursing herself every few steps for being so stupid. If this had been about anything less than finding Jessica Bel knew she would have given up and gone home by now.

She managed to duck under the next branch just as it flicked back and tried to take her eye out. The sky seemed to suddenly lighten, the trees appeared to fall back from each other, and Bel found herself standing on the edge of a little clearing. The ghost-dog moved to the far side, circled around, turned to stare at her, watching as Bel took in the scene.

The trees had left empty an almost perfect circle about thirty or forty feet across. Pale pink flowers that were not daisies and were not roses grew in small clumps to one side among tussocks of coarse, dark-green grass. The place was like a hidden jewel in the surrounding gloom. A slim shaft of bright, yellow sunlight had somehow found a channel through the canopy of branches. It stood in the still air like a glass totem. Seemingly captured in its translucent walls a single butterfly tumbled and spiralled, its wings beating tiny, metallic reflections back up to the sky. Bel stood transfixed by its shimmering beauty. It was tiny moments like this that made her wonder if there really might be a god after all.

The dog was having none of this metaphysical introspection. It bounced to its feet and leapt forward, snapping and barking, scraping at a patch of dry soil at the far side of the clearing, shattering the crystal column of light. A plume of soil kicked up between its back legs. Bel's whole body felt numb. She took a greedy drink of water, tried to gather her thoughts. The ghost-dog continued to scrape at that little patch of soil, yapping in admonishment every few seconds at the human's apparent refusal to comprehend. The last traces of doubt in her mind evaporated. She hefted the trowel, it looked far too small now that she knew she was about to use it for real, moved towards the dog inch by careful inch. As she finally came to the little patch of ground, Bel struggled to sort out the double image in front of her, the undisturbed patch of ground in the real world, overlaid in her mind with the dog's scraping efforts.

The black Labrador backed off, began pacing backwards and forwards a couple of yards away. Bel hunkered down on her knees and started to dig.

The soil was dark and dry, crumbly almost like sand. As fast as she scooped it out small cascades ran down the sides of the hole, filling it back up.

Something didn't look right. Shuffling forward on her knees a few inches, she peered down into the hole. Another tiny landslide of soil scattered down one wall. There was a strange yellow-brown crescent bulging out of the powdery ground like a giant lizard's egg. Frowning as she looked at the puzzling shape, Bel brushed more soil aside with a finger, then gasped in horror as her brain finally worked out what she was looking at.

This giant egg had an eye-socket.

~~~~~
~~~~~

Thursday 21st October 2004
09:39

Mason sat in the van, waiting. The morning rush hour over, the street quiet now, no passing traffic. He could take his time; he wasn't expected back at work for the rest of the day. Now that he was here, he didn't really have a plan, just a few general ideas. After a while he walked to the corner where the ginnel ran behind the houses, high wooden fences on either side. He counted houses as he walked along, until he was standing at the back of Mandy's. Cautious about the dog, he tried the gate. The catch lifted. The dog started barking, a sharp sound in the quiet morning. He leaned on the gate and pushed. It hadn't been opened for a long time. He tried to not add to the noise as he moved it inch by inch, forcing a gap. He squeezed through, stopped just inside, waited for long seconds, ready to turn and flee at the approaching growl of the dog, or a sudden shout of challenge from some nosy neighbour. None came. Now that he was here, he began to doubt himself, but reckoned he had nothing to lose so took a cautious step forward. The dog started to bark again. Where was it? Why hadn't it attacked?

He called the dog's name, moved forward in inches, cautious, cautious, until he could see round the side of the house. The reason the dog hadn't attacked was clear; it was tethered to a downspout, a thick chain tied to its collar. It lowered its head the instant it spotted him, a low growl rolling in its throat. A plan arrived in Mason's head in an instant, fully formed. He knew now what he was going to do.

Back to the van. He searched in the back for his bolt-cutters, picked up the sandwiches he had made for his lunch, ham and cheese, stuffed them in his pocket. A long, slow look around the street as he closed the van door, then back to the snicket. He moved fast; this was not a time for caution. He called the dog's name, trying to sooth it with gentle words. The dog stood on point, alert, cautious, but at least it had stopped growling. Digging in his pocket he tore off a lump of ham from a sandwich, threw it towards the dog. It lunged forward, snapped the piece out of the air, swallowed it down with a gulp. Mason inched forward, careful to stay out of reach of the snapping jaws. He dropped a couple more pieces on the ground. The dog sniffed, moved forward, lapped up the sweet meat. It was gone in seconds. The dog watched Mason, tail beating, waiting for more, any threat gone. Mason waved another piece of meat in front of its face. A promise offered.

He waved the morsel from side to side, making sure the dog was following with its eyes, threw it to the ground between the dog's legs. The dog tried to turn itself inside out, fold in half in its efforts to locate the scrap of ham. As the dog dropped its head to scoff up the piece of meat, Mason moved quickly; he leaned forward, cut the chain with the bolt-cutters. It snaked to the ground with a metallic hiss. He slipped a screwdriver under the dog's collar, twisted it half a turn. Breath rasped in the dog's throat. He had it under his control now. 'Come on, Shadow. Let's go walkies.' He tightened his grip, waved another piece of ham under its nose to keep it interested, led it to the gate and down the ginnel.

The dog kept its eyes on the food, thick black tail beating fast, as Mason opened the back of the van. He tossed the piece of meat in, the dog scrambled after it without hesitation.

The van started first time. So far, he had acted on impulse. Now he needed a plan. He drove until he spotted a corner shop, bought two tins of dog food. He peeled one tin open like a soft drink and dropped jellied chunks onto the metal floor in the back of the van. The dog licked up pieces from the dusty floor, its tongue finding morsels between the spades and secateurs. Mason drove to the main road, turned towards Manorgrove.

Mason kept talking all the way; the dog seemed to be listening to him, its tail swinging a rapid beat in anticipation of more food. When they arrived at Manorgrove, he drove straight round to the back near his cottage, out of sight of prying eyes. He cracked open the rear door of the van, let the dog take a scrap of cooked ham off his open hand. It licked and snuffled, searching for more. He reached in, grabbing the collar, pulled the big dog towards him. Now that he was able to look at it closely, he could see that it was fat rather than powerful. He slipped a length of rope under the collar, tied a quick knot, pulling it fast with a jerk, drew the dog out of the back of the van. He reached back inside, picked up a claw hammer, paused for a second, then dragged out a narrow-bladed spade. The dog jumped down, sniffing the new air, tail thumping wildly. Mason waved a fresh tin of opened dog food under its nose, tugged on the rope. Shadow didn't hesitate, fell into step at his side.

This was Mason's territory. He knew he was safe here, knew he wouldn't be spotted, wouldn't be challenged. He left the van where he had parked it, tucked away a long way behind the big house, led the dog up a narrow track, into the woods.

Shadow snuffled at the undergrowth, exploring this new place; rotting leaves, pine sap in the trees, the whole rich smorgasbord of life in the forest. Smells he didn't recognise stood out like spikes in his nose; rabbits, a male fox deep and pungent, squirrels and rats, their scent-trails like threads woven into the ground; a deer; fear and pheromones in equal measure. He was happy to follow the man deeper among the trees.

They arrived at the clearing, this one larger, further from the beaten track. Mason stopped. The dog sat in front of him, looking up in eager anticipation. Mason dropped the spade to one side, hefted the hammer in his hand, then raised it above his head. It caught the sunlight, dropped a spark of reflected light onto the pine-carpeted floor. He called the dog's name. Shadow cocked his head to one side, tail sweeping pine needles backwards and forwards in a wide arc.

Mason brought the hammer down on the dog's skull, killing it with a single blow. He knelt beside the cooling body, unbuckled the collar before picking up the spade and digging deep into the pine strewn ground.

When he had finished Mason fell to his knees and started to cry, fatigue and frustration finally overwhelming him.

~~~~~
~~~~~

Wednesday, 3rd July 2019
12:46
Day Twenty

Bel could see who was driving even before the car stopped. She could feel her insides doing a cramped little flick-flack as she stood in the cloud of dust thrown up as the wheels locked washed over her and the tall figure of DI Ian Fox unfolded himself from behind the wheel. Just for a second as the car rocked to a halt on the handbrake Bel hoped that he hadn't twigged it was her, but the sneer on his face as he let the door of the dark blue coupe fall shut and he began to walk towards her told her that she had obviously made as big an impression on him as he had on herself.

"Well, well, well. If it isn't Miss Psychic Barker. Why am I not surprised?" He looked as handsome as Bel remembered, which she didn't think was fair, to be honest. This time his lithe frame was adorned in coffee-au-lait trousers and a pink shirt, the sleeves folded neatly to the elbows rather than rolled. A pair of designer sunglasses protruded an inch from the breast pocket. Bel did a quick compare and contrast with her own current appearance; dirty, scruffy, sweaty, feeling as if she'd been dragged through a hedge backwards, her hair all over the place, sweat itches running in lines all over her body; arms and hands covered in hundreds of tiny red scratches from pushing through the undergrowth. On top of that, she had been followed every step of the way back to her car by a cloud of about a million flying, biting insects, which had now settled on and around her face and neck and had started tucking in for a feast of her blood. It seemed to just about perfect that once again she had arranged to meet DI Fox in order to have the maximum impact possible. It was just a pity the impact was all negative.

Bel took a sip of water from a fresh bottle out of the car boot and stood upright from where she had been leaning on the tailgate.

'This had better be good,' Fox growled as he stood in front of her, a few inches too close to be comfortable to be honest, she thought, 'because in spite of what the gaffer says, this time I *will* prosecute you for wasting police time.'

'I promise you; I did not plan this.' Bel clenched her jaw, determined to not break eye contact. It wasn't easy; she felt as if he was almost standing on top of her, as if he was deliberately trying to bully her. 'I was just out for a drive.' Bel had already made up her mind that she wasn't going to admit to anything more than was absolutely necessary to this sour-hearted man.

'So, I can see.' He nodded towards the damage visible on the side of Bel's little red Fiesta. 'The report said you'd found a body.' His words came out in a flat sigh. As far as Fox was concerned this was already a complete waste of time, and he was determined to not be here a second longer than necessary, but he knew he was more or less obliged to check out the report, even if it turned out to be from a woman who he considered to be about 90% fruit-loops. Fox reckoned Bel was just the sort of flaky pastry who would get herself all excited at finding a mannequin or a blow-up doll. 'Right, so where is it?'

'It's in the woods, but, well, it's not a body as such.'

'Ah, here we go again,' he snorted, 'the story starts out full of itself, and the closer we get, the smaller and flakier it gets.'

'You're not going to believe it until you see it for yourself, so why don't I just show you?' She had intended to be calm, rational, focussed, but there was something about Ian bloody Fox that just made her lose her focus. Once or twice during the few quiet moments she had been able to snatch during the last couple of days she'd run through various scenarios in which her scathing wit had put him firmly in his place, but now that he was here in front of her she once again felt herself turning into an imbecile. How come every time she saw him, she felt almost as if she should be wiping her chin to check that she wasn't dribbling. 'It's this way,' she mumbled, timidly waving one hand towards the small gap in the trees. She started walking. Fox tutted his contempt as he fell into step behind her. Not a single word of conversation passed between the two of them as they walked back along the twisting little path that would take them to the clearing; Bel definitely wasn't in the mood for small talk. She did allow herself a small smile as she heard him stumble and curse on the uneven ground behind her. She didn't bother to ask if he was okay.

The trek back through the undergrowth seemed to take on an almost surreal aspect, and Bel was beginning to doubt herself, to wonder if she had somehow managed to get herself actually lost when she finally spotted the sweat-top she had left draped over a high branch drooping in the stagnant air like the surrender of a defeated army. 'It's just over here,' she pointed, pushing through the final overhang into the clearing.

The shaft of sunlight, the play of light in the canopy, the dancing butterfly, all were gone now; the colour and magic seemed to have drained out of the little clearing, leaving only flat greens and dirty greys. Bel could still hear the little yellow bird though, somewhere off among the creaks of branches that moved under an unfelt breeze. The whole place sounded sharp now and brittle, and her mouth felt so dry and full of dust. Bel tried to mentally hug herself as she led Fox to the little patch of scuffed earth where she had just been digging. She felt so cold all of a sudden that she thought she might start shivering. 'This is what I found.' Bel wanted to be able to speak clearly, confidently, but she seemed to have lost her good voice somewhere deep inside her chest, and the only part that made it to the outside world was a little squeak.

'So, you've found a hole in the ground?'

'I did the hole. You need to see what's inside.'

Fox aimed another glare at Bel as he took a pair of disposable latex gloves from his trouser pocket, snapped them on. Even that sound seemed to Bel to be full of contempt. She watched as he took what looked like a silver pen out of his pocket, telescoped it open like an old-fashioned car aerial. He hunkered down on his haunches and started to poke about with it in the dirt at the bottom of the hole.

He scraped around for about four or five seconds before a jolt of recognition flashed across his face. His whole frame was struck rigid in an instant.

'Shit, shite, and double-fuck!' He scrambled backwards on his heels, almost falling over his own feet as he leapt up, licking at his dry lips, looking down into the hole. He moved from foot to foot, as if he needed to start pacing but wanted to stand still at the same time and had settled on this poor compromise. 'When did you find this?' he asked, looking at Bel properly for the first time.

'About an hour ago or so, I guess.'

'And have you touched anything?'

'Well, obviously I touched the skull, while I was uncovering it,' Bel said, almost apologetically, 'but as soon as I saw what it was I stopped digging. That's my top stuck on the branch over there, so I could find this place again, and the trowel lying on the ground's mine, but apart from that, no, I haven't touched anything.'

'Right, er, good. Well done.' He uttered the words almost as if they were a foreign language, then turned his back on Bel and dug out his mobile phone, stabbing at the numbers before holding it to his ear. 'This is DI Fox. Get me a SOCO team, right now!' he said, his breath rasping in his throat. Bel stood sipping at a bottle of water as she looked at his back, didn't offer him a drink when he turned back towards her. As far as she was concerned, he could bloody well fend for himself.

Whenever you see a forensic pathologist portrayed in one of those television dramas, or a best-selling detective novel, they're always some eccentric old duffer with a tweed jacket and leather patches, or a bow-tie and monocle, making condescending jokes about the deceased in a plummy voice, before sauntering off to finish a rubber of bridge, or returning to their research into verrucas in sixteenth century Spain that has been so rudely interrupted by some thoughtless person dying in another set of bizarre circumstances.

The man who eventually turned up in the clearing about an hour later looked to Bel as if he was barely old enough to be out of short trousers, but that didn't matter because whatever clothes he was wearing had been engulfed under the disposable white paper boiler suit he was wearing that was at least two sizes too big for him. For all the world he looked like a mischievous little schoolboy as he marched into the clearing, right down to the rosy-red apples in his cheeks and the spike of dark hair poking out at the front of the paper hood. His feet sloshed backwards and forwards in a pair of white rubber wellies as he walked, and he had a massive plastic cool box slung over one shoulder. He looked as if he'd been on his way to a picnic at a nuclear power plant when he got the call.

By now quite a gang had turned up. They all seemed to know what they were supposed to be doing. One rolled out an endless streamer of blue and white striped tape, while four others began to erect a bizarre inflatable plastic hut that Bel supposed would eventually go over the hole where she had found the skull. Bel had been moved to one side in stages, bumped a few yards, then another few, until she ended up having to watch from the other side of the clearing, forgotten in the buzz of activity the forensics people had brought with them. Her water bottle was empty by this stage, and she debated if she should go back to the car and get the last bottle out of the boot, or maybe just get in the driver's seat and go home. No-one seemed to have any pressing desire to speak to her, and to be honest she was starting to feel like a spare part. More than anything right now she longed for a long, hot, soapy shower and a long, cold bottle of Chardonnay.

The schoolboy-forensics guy assumed centre stage, and after a whispered conversation with Fox, shuffled forwards on his hands and knees to poke about in the hole. A tall, thin woman, more white paper boiler suit styling, stood to one side, a large camera in one hand. Every couple of seconds she took a photograph as the forensics guy pointed out various items of interest. The piercing blue-white light of the flash made Bel flinch every time it pulsed back from the encircling trees, which seemed to leap forward in the false light, their branches reaching out towards her like claws. After a few minutes and dozens of flashes forensics guy reached into the hole and picked up the yellowed skull. Bel was almost expecting him to hold it up as if he was auditioning for a part in that Shakespeare play, which was what you would get if this had all been happening on the telly, but this was real life and he just stuffed it unceremoniously into a large brown paper bag on the ground beside him.

As another flash jarred against Bel's senses something caught her eye, a shimmer of movement just on the edge of sight, from in among the trees a few yards to her left. She blinked a couple of times, shaking her head as she tried to focus in the strange light.

And then Bel saw.

Standing in the dappled light, seeming to hover a few inches above a little patch of pale blue flowers, auburn ringlets turned orange as they caught a stray sunbeam, her face a cappuccino-dusting of chocolate-drop freckles, stood Jessica Curtis.

Bel gasped in shock and turned away for a second, trying to compose herself as her heart ricocheted around in her ribcage, before looking across again to confirm that she really was looking at the dead girl from the silver-framed photo. Jessica was sobbing the sort of long, breath-stretching sobs a small child makes in the depths of exhaustion, the kind that you think might go on forever. Bel took a hesitant step towards her, unsure of what she was supposed to do, stopped about ten feet away.

'Help me,' Jessica wailed, lifting her face towards Bel, her cheeks wet with tears. She held out her clenched fists towards Bel as if she was holding something that she wanted to show her. When she opened them the only things she could see were the girl's own twisted, broken fingers.

'Help me. Please. He hurt me.' Her voice disintegrated into sobs again.

Bel glanced across the clearing for a second to check on Fox. The last thing she needed right now was for him to see her talking to a girl who wasn't really there. It would be like watching someone have a conversation with a vacant patch of air, and Bel knew that he'd already made his mind up that she was as crazy as a box of frogs. She needn't have worried; Fox was too busy pacing around dishing out orders to worry about her. He seemed to be relishing his role. For a single sardonic second Bel wondered if he viewed this grim discovery as a career opportunity, his chance to impress.

When she turned back to look at Jessica, there was a second girl standing with her, one arm around Jessica's shoulder as if to console her. Jessica was still crying though, in spite of her companion's attention.

'Have you come to take us home?' the second girl asked almost matter-of-factly as she patted Jessica mechanically on the arm. Bel found herself looking into old, old eyes that stared out from such a young face and calmly held her gaze.

'My name's Suzanne Foster,' she said, 'Can you tell my Mum I love her?'

'Are you both here? Are you...?' Bel wanted to say dead but couldn't make the word come out of her mouth.

'There are five of us here,' she responded. 'I think there might be some others too, somewhere else. I saw another girl once, a different girl. I think he took her to another place.'

The blood in Bel's veins ran cold, topped off by an icy cap of sweat that spread across her forehead. 'Shit! I mean, sorry, that's awful. Who? Five? Can you talk about it? Can you tell me what happened?'

'I can't remember all of it. Sometimes it hurt too much.'

Bel turned to check on Fox again. He was hunkered down on his haunches now, pointing to something in the hole. The hole where Jessica lay. Bel looked back to Suzanne. 'Wait here. I'll be back in a minute. I just need to talk to that man over there.'

'What man?'

She couldn't see Fox. Bel frowned. She must only be able to see Bel because of her psychic empathy. A dark sorrow enfolded her as she realised just how alone these girls must have been for all this time in this tiny bleak clearing among the cold, unfeeling trees.

Bel scrambled sideways the dozen or so steps to where Fox knelt glaring into the hole, looking back as she walked to make sure the girls were still there. The forensics team had been busy. They seemed to be moving down the length of the body, exposing more and more bones as they went.

'Quick,' she said, standing over Fox, 'I need a notebook. And a pen. Suzanne's got names.'

'Suzanne?' his eyes tracked across to the brown paper bag containing the skull, lying on the ground next to a stack of forensics equipment a couple of feet away.

'No. That's Jessica. Jessica Curtis. She's standing over there at the other side of the clearing. Suzanne's with her. Another girl. She says there are more bodies. At least three more.' Bel watched his lips moving as he tried to take in what she was saying. She had to admit it must have been difficult for him at first, but even after a few minutes to think about it, he still looked like he had trouble coming up to speed.

'Let me get this right. You're talking to a dead girl?'

'That's right. She says there might be five girls buried here altogether. And some more in another place, but she's not sure where. She's going to help us find the bodies, if she can.'

'Five? Five bodies? Here, in this little clearing?' He craned his neck to look past Bel to the place she had just been standing, as if he was going to insist on checking for himself that what she had just told him was correct.

'Can we just agree that what I'm saying is right, you give me a notebook, and we sort out the details later?' Bel held out her hand.

'Hang on, hang on. You're really serious about this, aren't you? You're telling me there's another girl,' he slipped on slick pine needles as he struggled to stand up, 'different to the one whose body we're digging up, and she's telling you about even more bodies buried here?'

'That's what I'm saying. Notebook?'

'And you really do believe what you're saying, don't you?'

'What do you mean?'

'All this "talking to dead people". Okay, so you got lucky with the skull, I'll give you that, but don't you think you're getting just a bit carried away with yourself?'

'I'm not asking for your approval or permission. Are you going to give me a notebook or not?'

Fox scowled at her for a long second, then took out the small notebook Bel had last seen in the interview room, slapped it begrudgingly into her hand. She snatched the proffered pen from his fingers and turned on her heels to walk back to where Jessica and Suzanne were standing, stopped in front of them. 'Do you know where you are, where you're buried?' Bel asked Suzanne as gently as she could.

'You're standing on me,' she said, pointing matter-of-factly down to Bel's feet.

Bel jumped about three feet in the air, then hurriedly shuffled a few feet to one side.

'Do you know how stupid you look, talking to yourself like that?'

Suzanne blinked out of sight at the sound of Fox's voice. Bel spun around to find him standing right behind her.

'Stupid or not, Suzanne has just explained where she is buried.'

'This is the other girl you've been talking about? Okay, where?'

'Right here, right where we're standing.' Bel kicked a little cut in the powdery earth with the toe of her trainer to emphasis her point, scraping up a little spray of dust.

'Fuck! Are you serious?' He looked at the ground, then back up at Bel.

'I've never been more serious in my life,' She looked him in the eye, not blinking. He looked confused, started moving his jaw as if he was about to say something. When he did speak, he sounded weary, exasperated. 'Okay, I won't pretend I believe you, but you obviously do, so I'll just say that anything you give me, any information no matter how far-fetched, I promise I will at least try to look at in a sensible, rational way. I'll get somebody to start digging in this spot just as soon as possible, but until then, I'm a bit busy.' He didn't wait for Bel's response, turned to hurry away, digging out his phone as it started buzzing in his pocket.

Bel had been so surprised that Fox had agreed to support her that she had to take a minute to bring her focus back to the girls.

'Suzanne?' she whispered. 'Can you show me where the other girls are?' The girls shimmered back into sight.

'I'll see if they want to talk.' The spectre of the girl turned away, blinked out of existence like a light. For a second it was as if Bel had moved into a different place while she waited for Suzanne to return, found herself encircled by a strange little eddy of calm, the muted atmosphere in this small space accentuated by the distant soughing of the wind in the trees. In a breath she was brought back from her reverie as Suzanne appeared again right in front of her, as if she had been hiding just a whisper away, and Bel should have been able to see her if only she had concentrated.

A squeeze of pain so intense that Bel thought she was going to pass out clamped itself around her hands. Bel pulled them close to her chest, closer to her heart, hugging them to try to ease the pain. 'What's going on, Suzanne?' As she looked up again, Bel saw two new girls standing with Suzanne, huddling together in fear.

Suzanne shrugged as she spoke. 'I asked Kathy to come see you, but she won't come. She doesn't want to talk. She doesn't do much anymore, just stays where she is in the ground.' She nodded towards the newcomers. 'This is Kimberley and Chelsea.'

One of the new girls spoke. Her voice sounded as if it was coming from a place right on the edge of hysteria. 'Kimberley's not well.' She held the other girl tight, hugging her to her side. Her own mouth and chin were streaked with blood.

'What's wrong with her?' Bel asked, looking across at Kimberley, wondering what could be worse than a face full of blood. The girl seemed barely able to stand, her legs splayed at the knees, trembling so bad they seemed to be almost vibrating. Like Jessica, she was cradling her hands to her chest, as if to comfort herself. Her face was frozen in a grimace, a silent, eternal open-mouthed scream of pain and fear and dread. Bel looked down at the poor girl's hands. The thumbs had been hacked off about halfway down. The wounds showed red and angry, full of blood and bits of flesh.

The pain in Bel's own hands flared again, a pulsing fire spiking up each arm, as if her very bones were filled with splintered glass. 'What happened?'

'Have you come to take us to Heaven?' asked Chelsea.

'Is that what you want to happen?'

'If it will stop Kimberley's pain, yes.'

'And what about you? Are you hurt too?'

She tilted her head back in answer and opened her mouth wide. The blood on her chin was more than matched by the mess inside.

At least four of her top teeth were missing, and more than one from the bottom too, by the look of it. Bel couldn't understand why this girl wasn't screaming in agony alongside Kimberley.

'What happened? Who did this to you?'

'The man,' she spoke calmly. 'He pulled them out with pliers,' she shrugged.

Bel could feel the hot wash of tears fill her eyes. It was all she could do to not burst into tears and fall to her knees sobbing. 'You poor thing.' Bel could only guess from the hot pulse of pain in her own hands what the girl was going through. In an instant the pain evaporated, to be replaced by a soft, pink, caress like woolly mittens.

'Is that better?' The girl smiled at Bel.

She couldn't help but smile back. 'Did you do that?'

'It doesn't have to hurt when you're dead. I tried to explain it to Kimberley, but she doesn't want to understand. She thinks it's all her fault, so the pain never goes away. The only way she's going to get any peace is when she goes back to her family.' She shrugged her shoulders in resignation.

The tears that had welled in Bel's eyes spilled out now, cutting wet lines down her dust-shabby cheeks as they fell. She rubbed the back of one hand across her face, wiping the streaks away with swift strokes. This was no time for emotion, she needed to get her shit together, write this stuff down. 'Her name is Kimberley?' she asked, fumbling open Fox's notebook, turning to a fresh page. Suzanne and Kimberley, she repeated as her hand began to scratch a jerky scrawl across the page.

'She's from Rochdale, I think,' the girl stated in a matter of voice, 'but she can't tell you anything. She's all locked in behind the pain.' Bel looked across at the other girl's face. It was still fixed in that same rictus of agony.

'How long has she been here? Do you know?'

'She just turned up one day in the ground next to me. It's difficult to keep track of the time when you're dead.'

'If you tell me your name, we can try to take you home too, back to your family.'

'My name's Chelsea Ambrose. I lived in Harrogate. Six Raynville Drive. I was born on New Year's Day, nineteen eighty-six, and I died on May the twenty ninth, two thousand and two.'

Bel tried to scribble more notes, hoping that she would be able to read her own spider tracks later. She found herself staring at Chelsea, where a single drop of bright red blood gathered at the corner of the girl's mouth, made its slow way down her chin. She could only imagine the strength of mind the poor girl must have to lock away all that pain, to cap it off like a burst water main.

'Do you know how you died?'

'He killed me, the man.'

'Can you remember what happened?'

'I think he must have drugged me or knocked me out or something. I just remember I was in a tiny, damp, smelly little room. He used to rape me and beat me. I screamed and cried the first few times. That made him laugh. He told me that I could scream as loud as I liked, but no-one would hear me.'

'And no-one did,' Bel offered as response.

'No,' Chelsea opened her mouth. It was supposed to be a smile, but the bloody, gap-toothed mess made Bel's mind reel. 'He raped me, and he beat me, and he pulled my teeth out. He was right. No-one heard me scream. In the end I think I just got too tired and died. The next time I opened my eyes I was here.'

Bel sobbed quiet tears for the girls lying there in that small clearing for all that time, and for all the others, wherever they were.

She could see the confusion on Fox's face as he came over a few minutes later. From his point of view all he could see was Bel staring at a gap in the trees, talking to nobody, a snot of tears running down her face. Fox stopped a couple of feet away, opened his mouth to speak, closed it, passed Bel a bottle of water. She took it from him, drank heavily, then took a deep breath and started to outline what Chelsea had told her. She held out the pad with the scribbled notes. 'It's all in there, as best as I could get it written down.'

'So, this is all things that these dead girls have told you?'

'If they didn't tell me, how would I know? How did I know to come here, to this god-forsaken, middle of nowhere place, to go scratching around in the woods, looking for the bodies of girls that you lot,' her anger flared as she spat out the words, 'didn't even know were dead?'

'Give us a chance. We've not even begun to dig at the places you said they were buried, never mind started to check out this information. We do know, because I asked some questions, that Jessica Curtis has only ever been officially listed as a missing person. Her parents never petitioned for her to be declared dead.'

'That would be her mother's doing. She still hasn't accepted that she's gone.'

'Hang on, are you saying you've met the mother? This is starting to sound like a set-up to me. What's going on?'

'The mother's dead. It was her ghost I met. She wants me to find Jessica, to bring her home. I guess that's why I've come to this place; to find Jessica.'

Fox looked at the notebook in his hand, then back at Bel. 'But what about Emily? I thought you said you were looking for Emily Phillips.' He looked perplexed.

'I was, I am, not that you care. You basically told me to fuck off when I tried to tell you at the police station.' A wall of exhaustion had dropped across Bel's mind. She felt so weary after everything that had happened, and the last thing she wanted right now was to get into an argument with Fox. She shrugged her shoulders in resignation, decided she may as well head back to the lay-by and her car. She just wanted to go home, take a shower and crawl into bed. 'Where are you going? What about these notes you just gave me?' Fox called to Bel's receding back. 'What am I supposed to do now?'

'That's up to you. I'm only one girl, I can only do what I can do. Whether you believe me or not, I know that Emily's still alive. I'm going to keep looking and I'm not going to stop until either I find her, or you show me her body.'

~~~~~
~~~~~

Thursday, 21st October 2004
15:51

Mason took the collar off the body, stuffed it in his pocket, buried the dog where it lay, just yards from the rabbit. He had hoped the hot red thickness inside his head would fade, but it wouldn't leave him. Losing the dog would hurt Mandy, he knew, but she wouldn't actually know it was dead, and she wouldn't know it was him that had killed it. Or why.

He cried into his hands, feeling the well of frustration in his heart, his bones, his fists. There had to be some way he could make her feel the pain, the humiliation he still felt at her scornful words, her rejection. He wanted to stand in front of her and look into her eyes as she shared the pain he felt in his heart.

He screamed his frustration at the trees. Rabbits scattered, bolting for safety underground. He followed the white flash of a tail with his eyes as it disappeared into the undergrowth. Killing the dog wasn't enough. There were rabbits in here somewhere. He needed to find them, hurt them, stab, kill. He tore at clumps of grass and skeins of ivy with his bare hands, grunting with effort until he had uncovered a bolthole that ran at a sharp angle down into the cool earth. He stabbed the spade into the ground like an axe, tearing at the soil, uprooting foliage, slashing scoops of earth into the air. The spade grated against a rock. He pulled at the plant matter until he could see a house brick, bright red against the black soil. He tried to dig it out, scraped some more. There was another brick next to it, mortared into place. Curiosity took over. He slowed down, dug further, working the blade of his spade with purpose, scooping away clods of earth. After a few minutes he had uncovered a small curve of bricks poking up out of the earth. He leaned forward, renewed his efforts. An hour later, his frustration long forgotten, he stood back and looked at the arch about four feet high and three feet across that his efforts had uncovered. It seemed to run straight into the side of the hill like some man-made cave. The entrance was still blocked with fallen earth. Maybe it was some kind of ventilation shaft for a mine, or an old kiln maybe. He knelt down, started scooping at the loose soil in the entrance. It came away old and dry as he drove in the spade deep and hard. A few scoops more and the spade jarred in his grip with a metal clang. He scraped dry soil aside in a spray until he could stand looking at a metal door, unused for years, thick with rust. Dark green paint showed through the rust in places. A corroded lump of metal to one side must be the remains of the padlock. A single slicing blow from the spade and the tired metal fell to the ground in pieces.

Mason stabbed the spade into the gap at the door's edge, levering it backwards and forwards until his fingers found a place to grip, then grunting his anger at the stubborn metal, tugged the door open by stuttering inches, until he was able to shoulder the door to one side and twist his way inside.

The summer sun had fallen behind the trees now, the tunnel ahead thrown into stark contrast. He sat for a minute as he caught his breath, trying to gain some night-sight. He really needed a torch, but the nearest one was back at the workshop at Manorgrove. He scraped more earth aside, shouldered the door from the inside, forcing it back until it would open no more, hoping to let in more light. If anything, it made things worse. He moved forward, stooping under the low-arched ceiling. His fingers scraped against another brick wall in front of him after about ten feet. Moving his hands to each side his fingers found more metal. There was a door to either side, solid, padlocks, these not so weathered. A quick shake told him these are not going to fall to a single blow from a spade. He turned and made his way back out into daylight.

It took almost an hour to make his way down to Manorgrove, collect the tools he needed and make his way back to stand at the tunnel entrance again, armed now with a large torch in one hand, meaty bolt-cutters in the other. The outer door opened easier this time. He stooped and shuffled in. The padlock on the first door carved apart like liquorice. Mason pulled the door open. It swung slowly on hinges frozen with rust. A two-second scan with the torch revealed a small room, empty, not much wider than the entrance tunnel, about ten or twelve feet long, brick-walled, concrete floored, the ceiling curving in a tiny cathedral arch just above his head. The room smelled dry and musty. He turned to the other door, the cutters making light work of the brass padlock. A sweep of the torch revealed that this room was furnished with an old upright wooden chair and tiny white-painted card table, the felt top holed and threadbare. He pulled the chair up to the table and sat down. There was the stub of a candle in a brass sconce, and an age-old box of matches on the table. More out of curiosity than anything else, Mason pulled a match out of the box, struck it against the sandpaper side. It flared in the torch-lit gloom. Mason chuckled to himself, put the match to the candle. A spit of wax and the flame caught. He killed the torch, smiled as he looked around at the dancing shadows thrown by the flame onto the close, salt-bleached red-brick walls.

Now he knew how he would make Amanda understand. He would bring her here, explain to her how she had hurt him, let her see the pain he had suffered. Then he would make her understand his pain the only way he knew how. The thin candle flame ran like liquid along the blade of his knife as he turned it in his hand.

~~~~~
~~~~~

Thursday 4th July 2019
10:55
Day Twenty-One

She was so tired by the time she got home that Bel was already trying to walk out of her clothes as she turned the key in the lock to let herself in. By the time she reached her bed it was all she could do to fall into it without hitting the floor first. She didn't surface until her bladder forced her out from under the duvet next morning at a little after eleven. Shower next. Bel stood there for ages, letting the hot water spit at her tired bones, and didn't turn it off until she was satisfied that she had scrubbed away every last dusty trace of that little clearing in the woods off her skin. After a brisk rub dry, she threw on some scruffs and checked her phone. Only two messages from Nigel today. Maybe he was starting to get the hint. The first was the usual mix of grovelling apology and perplexed indignation that she had actually finished with him. He seemed to be aggrieved that she had actually caught him in the act.

The latest message asked if they could arrange a time for him to come around to collect his stuff. Bel hoped that abrupt and dismissive would come across in her response as she replied to say his stuff would be on the doorstep in a bin-liner if he wanted it and thought no more of it. With a smile Bel promised herself to remember to put in the stinky pair of socks he had left in the laundry hamper. Maybe he would be able to persuade his new paramour to wash them for him, though Bel seriously doubted it. From the little bit of her that Bel had seen, she didn't look the washing type.

The events of the previous day had left Bel feeling lost, soft, listless, in spite of her lie-in and the hot shower, so she made herself a large mug of deep dark coffee, grabbed a packet of choc-chip cookies and parked herself on the sofa. Yesterday had seriously taken it out of her, not just the physical side, although she could feel muscles aching that she didn't know she had, and she felt sorely tempted to just stay curled up there all day and do nothing very much at all. Bel was surprised at how emotionally draining, shocking even, the whole thing had been. For a brief moment she wondered how Mr Supercool DI Fox was taking it. It was all very well to have someone find a body in the woods, but the pain Bel had seen on his face when she had presented him with his own notebook complete with the names of the dead girls scribbled in it made her realise that he was probably as desperate for any break to help him find Emily as she was. She wondered if he would be able to square the circle of the solid, definitive information she had given him about the dead girls the previous day, and the strange place, in his opinion, from which she had brought it. He had promised her he would take the information seriously, but in spite of that Bel also knew there was no way on earth he was going to listen to anything she told him until he had proved to himself that the information she had already given him was at least partly right. Even then, even if everything she had told him turned out to be right on the money, he still didn't have to listen to her. If he wanted he could put yesterday's events down to some massive fluke, or just decide that he didn't want anything to do with psychics. He had already made his personal contempt for her pretty clear. In her heart Bel knew that it was still up to her, and her alone, to find Emily, with or without Fox. If there had ever been any doubt in her mind just how serious this whole thing was, the discovery of the bodies in the woods had removed it forever. Bel knew in her heart that Emily only had so long, weeks, maybe just a few days or even hours, before it would be too late, and the things the other girls in the woods had shown her made Bel realise that even if she was still alive, Emily would be suffering untold horrors.

The only problem was, right now Bel didn't have a clue where to begin. She had been on the way to that little village but discovering the lay-by and the woods had derailed that plan. It was obvious in hindsight that her sub-conscious had jumped the rails to get her to that little clearing in the woods, and the thing with the map on the tablet had just been a means to a psychic end, rather than a clue to an actual place. In a way Bel was almost glad; the idea of tramping around some random village with a rucksack on her back asking if anyone knew any murderers seemed a bit flaky now. The only other thing she could think was to maybe go round to Emily's home, talk to her mother, explain who she was and what she could hopefully do to help, persuade the woman to let Bel borrow something that belonged to Emily, see if she could get a psychic hit off it. Bel started running through scenarios in her head, what she would say, how she would broach the subject. She still had the address she had found on the internet; she had written it down yesterday. Where had she put it? She started rooting through her bag.

As soon as her fingers brushed against it her heart began to pound in her throat and sour bile started to rise in her stomach. Gran's notebook. Bel knew that if she was going to find Emily, she couldn't let herself keep getting distracted like this, but the emotions she could feel coming off the little black leather book were just too spiky for her to ignore. She could feel waves of pain and fear, and a curl of guilt, but swamping everything was a wash of mournful sorrow. Bel let herself fall back on the sofa, rested her head on a cushion, closed her eyes and placed the book on her forehead. She had no way of knowing if that was the sort of thing she should be doing, but it felt right so she went with it anyway. She sat that way for more than ten minutes, willing the feelings to firm up, to resolve into voices or images in her head, anything that would help her understand what this nasty little book was all about.

Nothing.

Her coffee had gone cold. She put the book down, went through to the kitchen to make herself a fresh mug, returned to sit back on the sofa. Well, if psychic wasn't going to work, maybe she should try good old-fashioned detective skills, like Detective Inspector Super-Fox. Bel picked up the book, flicked open the black leather cover and turned to a page at random. It was just as she'd remembered; Gran's precise cursive script sitting upright on the line, taunting her in black ink, not telling some heartfelt tale of teenaged angst from the fifties as Bel had thought when she'd first found it in the cellar, not telling her anything, just that strange strings of numbers and letters, abbreviations and code words that she couldn't even begin to understand. Bel flicked from page to page, trying to find something to help her make sense of what she was reading, some recurring words or phrases perhaps. In the end she decided to start with the one thing she *could* understand. Although most of the writing was just gobbledegook, some of the numbers were obviously dates. As for the rest, Gran had written it in some code of her own making, and it had Bel well and truly flummoxed.

Grabbing a notepad from the kitchen and a pen out of her bag, Bel started scribbling notes, trying to chunk the random bits and pieces into some sort of order, find some grouping that made sense. What did make sense was to start at the beginning, so she turned back to the first page. A name, written on the top line, underlined. Anne Hardaker. Second page, Pauline Brooke. The next, Amy Shawcross. A quick skim of the others told Bel all the names were female. So, that was a start, at least. It didn't add up to anything as yet, but it was a start; she had her first clue, her first glimpse into whatever secret the book was trying to keep hidden.

What else? The dates. Bel took her time, noting down all the dates she could see on every page. The earliest was April 24th, 1926, which didn't make any kind of sense because it was before Gran was even born. The latest was October 11th, 1969. That wasn't to count the date on the last page, the date with her Mum's name against it. September 12th, 1990. She made up her mind to ignore that last name and date for the time being, rightly or wrongly. First, it was Mum's name, and secondly, although it had been written in Gran's hand just like all the others, it didn't have all the added notes and numbers that the others had, and so felt to Bel like an add-on. So, the others; there were more than forty years between the first and last. No two dates were the same. What had happened in those forty years that was so important to Gran that she had to write down these particular dates, and then hide them away, almost shamefully, from the world? Bel began to search some of the dates in Google, looking to see if she could find some string of famous events that linked together into something, anything.

Nothing.

And what about the rest of the scribblings? Letters and numbers grouped together or strung out singly. None of it was telling her anything. Bel growled in frustration. There had to be some way to make sense of this strange code. Maybe there was someone who knew the story behind what Gran had been doing all those years ago.

She knew in her heart that she really ought to go see her Mum. Mum probably knew every single person at the funeral. She had even worked with Gran in the weaving-shed at the mill one winter when she was between jobs herself as a young woman. Bel knew she couldn't approach her though. First, her name was in the book. It was obvious that the book was some sort of record of dark happenings down the years, otherwise why would Gran have been desperate to get rid of it, to make Bel promise to make it all good again for her? If that was true, asking Mum was out of the question. She would never admit anything to her own daughter. Second, Bel knew she was still in Mum's bad books, because she held her at least partly responsible for Gran's death. And to tell the truth, in her quiet moments, so did Bel. The two of them had never spoken about it directly, but it was the dark sub-text to the few stunted conversations they had had since. Bel had gone over it again and again in the days since; if she had gone round to see Gran at lunchtime like Mum had asked, she would have found her that much sooner, and, Mum reckoned, she might have made a full recovery from her fall. How was Bel supposed to explain that she suspected Gran had stubbornly made her mind up to die in hospital as much out of spite as from her injuries, without mentioning her own psychic gift, which as far as Mum was concerned, was out of bounds? The worst of it was that Bel was certain that this emotionally ugly little book was at the back of it, which brought her full circle.

Why was Mum's name there, the last name written on a page, but not because the book was full? It was as if her own daughter's name in the book had brought whatever it was that Gran had been recording to a final close. the last page? What could it mean? The frustration was like a knot in Bel's stomach. She needed to know, and what was more, she also knew she wouldn't be able to concentrate on finding Emily until she had sorted this puzzle out. Bel needed to find someone else to tell her, someone who had been a contemporary of Gran's, who had known her through the years. But who? She cast her mind back to the funeral. The people she had recognised, aunts and distant cousins, she wouldn't feel comfortable approaching, for the same reasons that she wouldn't be able to talk to Mum. Bel thought for a second of Father Jenkinson, but quickly dismissed the idea. Would Gran have made all those ominous remarks about being a good person if she didn't have some secret she was ashamed of? If that was the case, she was hardly likely to have mentioned it to her parish priest, regardless of the sanctity of the confessional. Bel pursed her lips as she realised the only other people she could think of was the gang of old women who had been sitting on the sofa, gossiping, drinking too much and eating everything put in front of them. They had kept people entertained with a string of off-colour jokes, but Bel remembered they had also recounted an equally long list of kind memories about Gran.

On an impulse, Bel searched for the number for Barrowclough's, the textile mill where Gran had worked. At first when Bel started talking to the receptionist, she could hear the exasperation in the woman's voice as she tried to explain about Gran having worked there, the funeral last week, that she was trying to trace three women who had probably retired more than twenty years before. After being put on hold for so long that she was beginning to think the woman must have forgotten about her, Bel heard a male voice, gentle and composed. 'Hello, love. I'm George Culley. Andrea tells me you're Elizabeth Briggs' Granddaughter.'

'Yes, yes, I am.'

'A fine woman, your Grandmother. She had the respect of everyone she worked with. I was proud to have been there for her funeral, to see her off, you know.'

'Oh, were you there? I'm sorry I don't know you.'

'No reason to, love, Elizabeth was thirty years older than me. We didn't move in the same circles, just worked together for a few years.'

'If you were at the funeral you might be able to help me trace someone else who was there. I'm sorry, I don't know their names.'

Well, I didn't know everyone there, but I'll help you if I can. Fire away.'

'There were three old women sitting on a sofa, whispered a lot, drank too much.'

'That would be the Three Marys. Ha, they certainly make an impression, don't they?'

'You know them?'

'Everybody knows the Three Marys. They've been around forever. They were good friends to your Gran.'

'I don't suppose you have an address, or phone number for any of them?'

'I'm sorry, no, but you could always try the Weavers'.'

'The Weavers'?'

'It's a working men's club. Have you got a pen? I'll give you the address.'

~~~~~
~~~~~

Monday, 1st November 2004
09:44

Mason parked the van in the next street, took his time, checking all around as he walked into the cul-de-sac, approached the house from the other side of the street, his hand in his pocket, reassuring himself that the thick band of leather was still there, along with the envelope. He had been planning for this moment since the day he killed the dog, more than a week before, the day he found that underground room, what he had started to call his bunker. That day he had definitely let his heart rule his head, had taken chances he knew he shouldn't, risked being caught to snatch the dog, her dog, not even understanding what he was doing, or why, driven by his hatred and his love, opposite sides of the same coin. This time, thought, he had thought it through, knew what he was doing. This time he would make her understand just how he felt, by making her feel the same. He wouldn't be able to reveal himself just yet, but at least she would know that her dog had been killed, not just stolen or escaped. He had written a letter to explain everything, how he had taken her precious Shadow, watched the animal's agony as he brought the hammer down on its back and its head, felt its bones snap and splinter with each blow. His only regret was that he wasn't able to sign his name to it. He paused at the front gate, opened it, walked up the narrow garden path towards the front door. It dawned on him that he didn't even have to worry about being spotted; she was hardly going to remember or recognise him after all this time, and he could just be someone looking for a random address. He pushed the letter through the letterbox, dropped the dead dog's collar onto the welcome mat for her to find, the dried blood in splatters and smears across it there to confirm the truth of his message. After this she could be in no doubt that the dog had not simply escaped by accident, that its death had been intentional, that the pain she felt was caused by another. After this she would start to understand his own pain. After this, it would be her turn to suffer.

~~~~~
~~~~~

Thursday 4th July 2019
14:07
Day Twenty-One

The Kirkstall Textile Workers' Club and Institute, known by one and all as the Weavers', had been typical of the northern Working Men's clubs in its day, full of ordinary working men and their families, drinking beer at subsidised prices while being entertained by a range of variety acts. Many star names had cut their teeth on the northern club circuit. Like a lot of places over the years, the Weavers' had fallen on hard times. Star names were a thing of the past. There were still glimpses of the former glory to be seen, velvet curtains and plush pile carpets, but these days there was mildew on the curtains and strips of duct tape making good bare patches in the carpet.

Bel asked at the door, feeling rather foolish, for the three Marys, and was told with a smile that only Mary was in at the moment, but Mary and Mary might show up later. She got the feeling this was in the way of a standing joke, so smiled dutifully. The doorman explained that Mary Middleton was in the snug, pointed towards a double door.

The first thing that struck Bel about this Mary was that she looked even smaller and more fragile than she remembered from Gran's funeral. Maybe that was down to her sitting on her own, tucked into the corner of the booth. The second thing was the palest wraith of smoke draped over her shoulders like a shawl, little more than a blue-grey mist that ebbed and flowed as it moved across her body and face. Bel couldn't remember noticing it at the funeral, but it was still so pale, and she hadn't been looking for it back then, so there was no reason why she should. The old woman almost certainly didn't know there was anything wrong, and there was no way Bel was going to say anything. She wondered what might be wrong with her, and how long she had left.

'Excuse me, you won't remember me, but my name is Bel, Bel Barker. I'm Lizzie Briggs' Granddaughter. Can we talk?' She made to shuffle into the booth, but Mary picked up her glass and waved it in Bel's face.

'Of course I remember you, young Isabel, I even went to your christening, though I wouldn't expect you to remember. Mine's a port and lemon, or a brandy if you're feeling flush.' Bel took her glass and went to the bar. She decided she may as well try to start on the right foot, bought the old woman both. This, she knew, was not a time for half measures, if that wasn't too cheap a pun. Bel herself stuck to lemon and lime. She had to drive back, after all.

'Ooh, that's nice of you, dear,' Mary clucked in appreciation as Bel slid the drinks across to her. 'Cheers.' Mary tilted her glass towards the younger woman in a gesture of thanks, took a swig. It was just after two in the afternoon, but Bel could see that the old woman was already swaying slightly. She smelled of stale cigarettes, alcohol, and sour perfume.

'Well, you haven't come here just to buy me drinks, so what's on your mind?' She smiled at Bel as she put the glass back on the table with a perfectly steady hand. Experienced drinkers never spill.

'I was hoping you might be able to solve a puzzle for me.'

'What kind of a puzzle?' As she spoke, she breathed out the haze that only Bel could see in a pale cloud that ballooned out towards her. She desperately wanted to wave it away with her hand, but that would have looked rude, and would have been impossible to explain. She was just thankful that it seemed to disperse before it got as far as her face; she wasn't sure she would have been able to cope if she thought there was any chance of breathing the stuff in, whether it was a figment of her imagination or not.

Mary raised the other glass in a toast, took a hit of port. She lowered the glass, looked a Bel for a second, then spoke. 'There's obviously something on your mind, otherwise you wouldn't have come all this way in the middle of the afternoon to buy drinks for an old woman who hasn't laid eyes on you since you were a baby. So, what is it that's troubling you?'

'I think Gran's entrusted me with some sort of a secret, but I don't understand what it is, and I don't know what to do about it. On the day Gran fell down the cellar steps, I found a book of hers, that she'd hidden away. I was hoping you might help me understand what it's about.' Bel reached into her bag to take out the book, held it out tentatively towards the old woman. 'It doesn't seem to make any sense. It's all just notes and numbers. Names and dates. I was hoping you could help me work out what it means.'

Mary looked at the book for a long time without moving, then took it from Bel with a hand that trembled slightly. It almost looked as if she feared to touch it. She seemed to be more alert, more sober now, as she held it open at the first page, scowled at what she saw. She turned the page, scowled again. 'Where did you get this? Did Lizzie really give it to you?' She slapped the book down on the table in front of her and fixed her eyes hard on Bel. They were sharp and clear now, no trace of booze.

'She told me where to find it,' Bel answered, a little taken back by the ice in the other woman's voice, 'after she fell down the cellar steps. She said I would know what to do. I half think she wanted me to destroy it, but I'm not sure. The thing is, I need to know what it means before I can work out what to do with it. That's why I've come here. I was hoping you might be able to explain it to me.'

Mary licked her lips, hunched forward 'The fucking bitch! She kept a record. After all her promises and reassurances, still she kept a record.' The words came out in a bitter hiss, little more than a whisper. The old woman grabbed the sleeve of Bel's jacket, pulled her close as she spoke. 'Listen, girlie, this book has nothing to tell but sorrow. My advice to you is to get rid of it. Go home right now and burn it, or bury it, forget you ever saw it.' She dropped her grip on Bel's sleeve, sat back, scooping up the brandy glass and draining it in a single swig.

Mary looked rattled, and it was obvious from the way she had started shuffling in her seat that she didn't want to talk about it anymore, but there was no way Bel could let this thing go if there was any chance to get to the truth, to unlock this secret, whatever it might be. She snatched up the empty brandy glass, though she doubted Mary would protest, headed for the bar, returning with a double, pushed it towards the older woman. 'Look, Mary, Gran kept telling me to remember she was a good woman, but you've just called her a bitch. I just want to know what's going on, that's all. What is this thing a record of? What is it all about? If you tell me, I promise it won't go any further, I'll take the book away and you'll never see it again. But if I have to find out some other way, I will. It's up to you.' After her little speech Bel sat perfectly still in her seat and waited for Mary to make up her mind, to respond.

This time Mary picked up the port and lemon and swirled the glass, watching the slice of lemon as it spun in a tiny vortex. She sighed, drank down the contents in a single mouthful, put down the glass. A decision had obviously been made. 'Get me another one, would you?' The pale cloud seemed to sit a little closer around her shoulders.

Although she knew it could only be her imagination, when she returned with more drinks for Mary, Bel felt as if the room had got smaller somehow, darker. The old woman started talking before she had time to properly sit down.

'Your Gran really was a good woman, don't ever let anyone say otherwise.' Mary gave a wry smile as the memories came back. 'She was training to be a nurse; did you know that? When she was young.'

A nurse? Bel couldn't remember anything about Gran being a nurse. She'd been working in the mill since before Bel was born, and she had just assumed that was the sum total of the old woman's life. She wanted to ask questions, but she held her silence as the old woman continued, worried that the slightest interruption would bring the tale to an abrupt end. 'She was good at it too, a natural,' Mary continued. 'She had brains, your Grandmother.'

'So why did she give it up?'

'She got herself a boyfriend, a doctor, a few years older than her. She was rather taken with him, by all accounts.'

'Boyfriend?' Now Bel couldn't even pretend to hide the look of surprise on her face. Gran and Granddad had always been together, hadn't they?

Mary gave a little smirk of superior knowledge. 'I know what you're wanting to ask, but this was before she met Arthur. Anyway, he led her astray, this doctor. Knew it all, so they reckoned. Too big for his boots, if you ask me. The sort of bloke who bends the rules to make them fit.

'They'd been going out for a few months, and everyone thought they were going to end up together, until Lizzie started turning in late for work, missing a few shifts, making silly mistakes on the ward. The management did a bit of checking, carried out an unofficial audit, on the quiet. Anyway, there were a few discrepancies with the ward dispensary records, turned out there was some morphine missing, quite a lot of morphine.'

'She was a drug addict?' This was getting crazy. Bel tried to get her head round the idea that her Gran had been a druggie.

'No, don't be silly! She would never do anything like that. No, it was the doctor. He liked to party, by all accounts, and of course Lizzie would keep him company. Too many drinks and too many late nights started to catch up with her. The problems with the missing drugs were all down to him. The inside money was on him being some sort of home-grown dealer to the local version of the jet-set,' she said, her lips thin lines, 'but none of that ever came out. Your Gran found herself caught in the crosshairs, instant dismissal, removal from the national nursing register. She became pretty much a social outcast. Her doctor friend was given a reprimand and offered a position at one of the big hospitals down south, all very cosy. He didn't even stop to say goodbye, had it away on his toes before your Gran even knew he'd gone.'

'So that's what she was worried about all these years? Stealing drugs for a bastard of a boyfriend?'

'Ah.' There was something about the inflection in that one syllable that sent a warning chill down my spine. Bel drained her own glass, wishing it was something stronger than lemon and lime, and waited for Mary to continue.

'She met Arthur a few months later,' The pensioner settled back into her seat and took another sip of her cognac. She seemed finally to be settling into her role as storyteller. 'It was at one of the tea-dances at the local baths. He was a big bloke back then, and handy with it. I watched him sort out three men in one go, once. When he hit you, you stayed hit! Arthur fell for her big-time, but Lizzie wasn't so keen. Anyway, he put word about that anyone who said anything about what had happened to Lizzie at the hospital would have him to answer to. He got her a job at the mill where he worked, and they were married within the year. Proper smitten with her, he was.' Mary smiled again at some personal recollection.

This was all very nice, thought Bel. So it turned out Granddad loved Gran and he was her knight in shining armour. Maybe that would explain some of the feelings of love and devotion Bel had felt wash over her in the cellar. She licked her lips, watching in envy as Mary raised her glass again and took another drink. By this time Bel had already promised herself that she would catch up just as soon as she got home. Right now, she needed to sit quietly, try to ignore the pale wraith that seemed to be caressing the old woman's shoulders, as she waited for the story to be taken up again.

Mary's head dropped to her chest. For a second Bel wondered if maybe she had been taken ill, affected somehow by the smoky shawl on her shoulders, but then the old woman took a deep breath and lifted her gaze again to meet Bel's own. 'You've got to remember; it was a different world back then. There were no mobile phones or interweb. A car coming down the street was a bit of an event. Ha, most of the streets were still cobbled. And there was certainly none of this sex, sex, sex; girls flaunting themselves all over the place.' Just for a second Mary sounded jealous.

'But people did it, even then,' Bel felt she had to remind her. 'By definition, my parents were doing it before I was born.'

'Yes dear, people were doing it. If you were married, you knew you would be bringing children into the world. The problems usually happened to the un-married ones.'

It suddenly dawned on Bel where the conversation might be starting to go. 'Are you trying to tell me Gran got pregnant? That she had to get married?'

'No, not your Gran. But she did understand the problems that might arise, having been a nurse. She didn't judge, either, and that mattered, when it came right down to it. There was no pill in those days don't forget, and you should have seen the johnnies,' she smiled a thin smile and Bel could see she was talking from personal recollection, 'great big thick ugly things they were, you couldn't feel a thing with those in the way.

'Sometimes, a girl could be persuaded though,' she continued, 'all those tales about the first one being for free, and standing up didn't count, that sort of thing. Promises of eternal love helped, of course. Sometimes, later, afterwards, that's where your Grandma came in.'

The woman picked up the little journal, gripped it so tight in her hand that her knuckles blanched. In that instant Bel knew, knew this woman's pain and sorrow, carried down the years, knew Gran's part in it, for good or bad.

Mary slowly opened the scruffy little book, casually glanced at the passing words as she flicked through the pages. Bel could only hold her breath, fearful that she knew the words to come. 'That's me,' Mary whispered, 'before I was married.' Her voice trembled with emotion as she pointed at Gran's carefully written notes on one particular page. Bel took a couple of seconds to make out the name upside-down. Mary Roberts gave the woman opposite her a resigned look.

'I was nineteen. Gerald, his name was. He was in the Navy.' A long sigh escaped Mary's lips, betraying a whole lifetime of sorrow in a single heartfelt sob, as her memories took her back to a different world. 'He was the biggest, strongest, most handsome man you ever laid eyes on. Of course, I went weak at the knees as soon as I saw him, all the girls did. He attracted quite a following in the few short weeks he was here, did Gerald,' she took a slug of her brandy, as if it would wash away the pain of recollection, 'but for some reason he only had eyes for me.

'I couldn't believe my luck; I thought the gods had destined me for eternal romance and bliss. So, when he asked me, when he begged me, when he told me he would love me 'til the end of time; well, you would, wouldn't you, for a man like that.

'A week later his shore leave was over, two weeks more and my period was late. A lot of people would have been happy to see me caught out like that, jealous, I don't doubt. Your Gran didn't judge though. She helped me. Helped me put it all right again.'

Bel looked Mary Middleton, nee Roberts, up and down. The shock of white hair, the lines of life etched deep around her eyes and mouth, the feeling of a 'what if' never recovered from, struggled to hold back a tear that threatened the corner of her eye.

'So Gran was carrying out abortions?' That explained why the cellar looked like it did, stark white with a bright light over a big table. She would have needed to keep it clean, sterile, if possible. Questions lined up in Bel's head. 'Wasn't it wrong, though? Illegal?'

'Illegal isn't always the same as wrong. Some girls had been known to kill themselves rather than face up to the shame of being pregnant.' Mary took another sip of brandy, stared to one side, looking at another time. Bel could understand exactly what she meant. Boys will be boys, but girls end up being called whores and slags, and usually for doing the things the boy involved persuaded them to do in the first place. Talk about displaced guilt. There wasn't a woman in the world who wouldn't recognise the scenario.

How difficult must it have been, all those years ago? Taking a gamble every time you had sex; the gamble that you wouldn't fall pregnant, or if you did, the man would stand by you, and the stigma of being labelled a harlot, or worse, an unmarried mother, always hanging over you.

And even if you were married you were still in the thrall of the gods. Making ends meet would have been a full-time challenge for too many families. What if you were faced with another un-planned pregnancy, while the small children around your feet cried with hunger? How bad would things have to get before you would take a chance on a life-threatening, un-regulated operation carried out by some back-street quack rather than bring another mouth into the world? Reputation would be everything in a world like that; the knowledge that things would be done with care, compassion. Word would have got out, whispered on a women's grapevine. Gran and Granddad would have been providing a service, albeit at a price, to their friends, neighbours, people in the area, who knows, maybe even further afield.

'Your Grandparents would have been ruined if word ever got out what they were doing, Mary stated. 'A prison sentence would have been the least of their worries.'

'How did Granddad get roped into all this?' Bel couldn't actually think of any world where the stolid, upright, almost righteous man she had known all her life would have got involved in this sort of thing.

'Ah. Your Grandmother knew she could help, but she needed somewhere to work from, and someone to guard over her in case mistakes were made or things went wrong. What she was planning was still dangerous, after all. Your Granddad filled that need. Lizzie had seen the aftermath of back-street abortions a couple of times as a nurse and was determined to make a difference. That's what drove her in the end, her compassion for the poor girls. She told me once that she knew she would have to answer one day for what she was doing, but she was going to do it anyway.'

Gran's panicked expedition down into the cellar on that fateful day began to make sense now. Obviously, the whole idea of answering for her actions had started to weigh on Gran's mind as she approached the end of her days.

'That was why they got married.'

'You make it sound like a business arrangement,' Bel cracked a smile, trying to inject a spark of humour into the conversation. It didn't work.

'It was, at least at first. Lizzie told me as much. Arthur was an overseer at the mill, and the job came with a tied house. Lizzie told him what she wanted to do, and he agreed to help her, on condition that she marry him. She accepted. Your Gran let it be known that a girl in trouble could find the help she needed. She helped me, when I needed it, and I always knew there were more like me. That book proves it. If you have any love for your Grandmother, you'll destroy it and forget you ever had it.' Mary seemed to shrink in on herself as she picked up her brandy glass and stared into it, seeking comfort, memories, answers. It might just have been her imagination, but to Bel it seemed as if the inky shroud around the old woman's shoulders seemed to darken a shade and wrap itself closer as she sat before her.

A shudder ran up Bel's spine on icy toes. She could feel the turmoil of confusion about her grandparents roll over in her stomach, the conflict between what they had been doing, and why. She felt as if her brain had jerked inside her skull. She gently took the book out of Mary's unresisting hand. 'The only question is,' she said as she thumbed to the last written page, 'why is my Mum's name here? This date is only a couple of years before I was born, way after terminations were made legal.' She looked down at the handful of words on the page, written for sure in Gran's copperplate hand. 'Why? What does it mean?'

'I can't help you with that, I'm afraid,' Mary locked watery eyes on hers. 'You'll have to talk to your mother about that.'

Bel took a deep breath to try to break the spell that had fallen on her, pushed the black leather book deep into her bag and stood up. She didn't want to be here a second longer. She whispered a hurried thank you to Mary Middleton, walked out of the Weavers' without a backward glance.

~~~~~
~~~~~

Date and time unknown.
Sometime between Friday 14th June 2019 and Saturday 6th July 2019

She couldn't tell if it was day or night. Time was measured in the breaths she took. She tried to work out how long she had been here, but thinking was more difficult, almost as if she had grown softer inside her head somehow. It must be the water, she reminded herself, taking another sip. He'd put something in the water. It didn't taste drugged, though.

She pulled the duvet around herself, hugging her knees tight. Maybe she could work out how long she'd been here if she counted the bottles, the empty bottles. Then she realised she didn't know how many she drank in any day, five or six maybe, and anyway, she was fairly sure the man cleared away the rubbish sometimes. At least she assumed he did. Most times when she woke up the chemical toilet had been refreshed and there were fresh sandwiches and bottles of water.

She decided to try to work out how long she had been held captive here, how many days, how many nights. She had no way to know. Maybe if she counted the bottles, the empty water bottles. She looked around. All the empty bottles had been taken away.

She wondered how long she has been here.

She pulled the duvet close to herself, hugging her legs. She felt so tired. She rested her head against the cool of the wall. After a while she fell asleep.

~~~~~
~~~~~

Wednesday 24th November 2004
14:53

He watched from the van for twenty minutes, observing the occasional comings and goings, before he got out and walked towards the house. He smiled to himself, deep in thought, as he checked all around, lifted the latch to open the gate, walked up the garden path. He'd been thinking about his, decided he was going to check out how easy it would be to break into the house, so that when the time comes he could snatch Mandy away, take her to his secret little room, where he would be able to keep he until he made her understand just how much he had loved her, and just how much that love had turned to hatred. He slowed. Something wasn't right. He stuttered to a standstill, looking back towards the gate and the road, then looking across the garden and up to the house, as he tried to put his finger on the thing that jarred in his head. Curtains. There were no curtains. He walked more slowly now, up the path, peered into the front window, not knowing what to expect.

Empty. No furniture, no carpets, nothing. He stared through the smeared window, searching for clues he knew weren't there.

'Interested in buying the place, are you?'

Mason spun round. 'What? he asked, blank-faced.

A middle-aged man leaned on the adjoining fence; eyes screwed up as he took a drag at an un-tipped cigarette. 'It's for sale. Interested in buying it, are you?' Mason looker around. There was a "For Sale" sign planted next to the gate. How could he have not seen it?

The man flicked ash onto the vacant garden. 'I'm not one to gossip,' he glanced around, fostering conspiracy, 'but there's a tale to be told there, if you ask me.'

'Why? What happened?' Mason was only half-listening, his mind still on the empty room.

'They just upped and offed one day, a couple of weeks ago. Someone stole their dog about a month before, they said. Then a couple of weeks later there was something to do with finding out it had been killed, I don't know what happened exactly, but it was enough to make them leave the next day and not come back. They sent some firm to clear all the stuff out of the house, and the next thing anyone knew, it had been put up for sale. All that for a yapping bloody dog. For me, I wouldn't have been that bothered, but some people get proper attached to their pets, don't they? She hadn't been well, the mother, and I think the dog was the last straw. It was a stroke, by all accounts, the mother. They moved her into a nursing home somewhere, the daughter got a chance of a job there too. I think she lives in, but I don't know.'

'But where, though? Where did they go?'

'They never said, but we didn't speak much anyway, except when I had to complain about that bloody dog of theirs.'

Mason stood looking at the pinch-faced man. His head dropped and he tried to fight back the tears of frustration that burned behind his eyes. When he looked up the man at the fence smiled. 'Still, I hear they're open to offers, so you might get the place at a knock-down price.' Mason didn't hear him as he walked away.

He didn't remember how he got back to Manorgrove. He drove without thinking, his mind a blur. Turning off the engine, he listened without hearing as birds called the close of the day, watched without seeing as the sun dropped out of the sky. After dark he cried his frustration into his fists, before exhaustion overcame him and he fell asleep in the van where he sat.

The next day brought no respite. He clenched his jaw against the anger and frustration that bubbled up inside him. She had done this on purpose, to spite him. There could be no other explanation. One thing was certain; he couldn't allow her to get away with it. He would find her, punish her for what she had done.

On his days off he began to drive around the area where she had lived, knowing she wasn't there but searching all the same. The hot anger inside didn't cool. Days passed, weeks, months. The season turned, then turned again.

And then he saw her. He was driving through Leaside. It was June, warm.

He had passed her before he realised. His head snapped round to check in the rear-view mirror. He couldn't believe his eyes.

Mandy Armitage.

A torrent of pain and anger jarred through him. He spun the van round, bumping up the kerb, tyres squealing, headed back towards her.

There she was, walking down the street, smiling at the world as if she was something special, swinging her violin as she walked. The very sight of her filled him with rage.

He stamped on the brakes, jumped out of the van, his breath coming in heaving snorts, fists clenched.

She started screaming as soon as she saw him running towards her.

He grabbed her by the arm, started dragging her towards the van, his lips a thin line of determination. He clamped his hand over her mouth to stop the noise, but she bit down, hard. With a yelp he pulled his hand free. He grabbed her hair, twisted a handful in his fist, yanked her head backwards and down. She somehow managed to slip out of his grip, lashed out, swinging wildly with the violin. It caught him on the face just below his eye, the heavy case making him blink in pain. His head jerked back from a second blow. His grip on the girl slipped. He lifted his hand to his face, his reward a smear of blood.

She wouldn't stop screaming. How could he get her to stop screaming? She was stronger than he had expected, kept struggling against his grip. This was all going wrong. He had to get away before someone saw what was happening, came to help her.

He shoved her away from him, pushing her to the ground, ran back to the van, his heart pounding in his throat. He gouged the van into gear, glanced in the rear-view mirror, gulping for breath, rigid with panic. She was sprawled on the kerb, sobbing into her hands, the violin case on the ground next to her. He drove hard, determined to put as much distance as he could between them before she could call the police.

Eventually, miles later, he pulled over, pounding his fists against the dashboard, cursing himself for being so naive. He shouldn't have assumed he could just snatch her up and carry her away without a struggle. Next time he would be ready. Next time she wouldn't get away. Next time he would make sure she paid.

~~~~~
~~~~~

Thursday 4th July 2019
17:58
Day Twenty-One

He was sitting on the floor with his back against the apartment door. Bel almost walked into him as she struggled to dig her apartment keys out of her handbag. Too late she decided she should have pretended she hadn't seen him for an extra couple of steps; given him an "accidental" kick. This, he, Nigel, was the last thing she needed after the day she'd already had. 'You finally plucked up the courage to come for the rest of your crap, then?' Bel put maximum sneer into the words, so there was a good chance that even Nigel could understand that she wasn't pleased to see him.

'Hello, Bel,' he had a sheepish grin on his face as he rolled out of the way and got to his feet. Bel twisted the key in the lock, opened the door. 'How have you been?' Nigel asked. Sheepish, she well remembered, was his default expression. 'You're looking good,' he continued. Bel didn't bother to answer. To be honest, she was past pretending to be interested in his small talk, just wanted to get him out of her home, her life, as quickly and permanently as possible. She left the door open and went inside.

Bel had spent less than an hour talking to Mary Middleton, but she came away feeling shattered, physically and emotionally drained by the things the woman had told her. There was a bottle of Moscato in the fridge and she had planned to flop on the sofa and spend an hour or so moving the wine from the bottle to a glass, and from the glass to her mouth. The stuff Mary Middleton had told her was going to take some getting her head around, and she was hoping the wine would help her take it all in. Nigel turning up was going to delay the plan, but she was determined to make the delay as short as possible. 'Well, don't just stand there, come in, and shut the door behind you.' Bel pointedly ignored his feeble attempt at a compliment. The last thing she needed was for Nigel to start getting all chatty on her and think that the two of them still had some sort of relationship.

Bel moved through to the kitchen. Nigel followed. Following her like a mindless lapdog was one of the things about him that Bel had had found cute in the beginning, but she now realised was a bit tedious. 'You haven't changed anything, then,' he commented as he walked in behind her.

'It's only been four fucking weeks, Nigel, I haven't even changed the air fresheners.'

'How have you been?' He risked another shy smile. The one that used to endear him to Bel so much. Today it looked childish and twee.

'You mean how have I been since I dumped you for shagging some random bird in your living room in the middle of the afternoon? I've been fine, Nigel, top of the world.' Bel took the bottle out of the fridge, unscrewed the cap. That was when she made the mistake. This was no silly slip-up, this was "def-con 5" level stuff, though at the time she just shrugged it off. She did it out of habit, she told herself later, rather than any subconscious desire to get him in the sack. She looked down to see herself pouring two glasses of wine. By then, of course, it was too late. She winced inside as she slid one glass across the worktop towards him. 'Here, you may as well have a drink while you're here.' Nigel snatched up the glass and took a hurried slurp, obviously worried that she might change her mind and ask for it back. 'But don't think it means I've forgiven you, because it doesn't.' Bel knocked back her own wine, then filled the glass right to the top. She pointedly didn't top up his glass.

'Wait here, I'll get what's left of your stuff.' Bel went through the lounge into her bedroom to get the last of his bits and pieces.

When she came back, he had wandered into the lounge. Wandering was another of his so-called endearing qualities; he never seemed to go anywhere in a straight line and had no concept of elapsed time. 'We had fun that day, didn't we? Remember?' He was holding a plate that Bel remembered decorating at one of those "make your own pottery" places they had visited a couple of months previously. She had drawn a goofy, short-legged giraffe on hers. His had been a sketch of an eagle. He had dropped his before they got back to the car. It wasn't that good, anyway.

'Yeah, it was fun,' Bel replied. 'That was back when you weren't cheating on me, remember?' Nigel put the plate back down, shuffled where he stood. She passed him the bin bag. 'You'd better have a look through, because if there's anything missing you can kiss it goodbye.' She turned, walked back into the kitchen to retrieve her glass.

'Don't be like that, Bel.' He had slouched down on the sofa now and was rummaging through the bag's meagre contents. 'It was good while it lasted.'

'It could have lasted a whole lot longer if you'd been able to keep it in your pants.'

He found the smelly socks, held them out in his fingertips, then dropped them back in the bag, rummaged some more. 'Here, this is yours.' He held out a CD, "Tapestry" by Carole King. As old as forever, but still one of the best.

'No, you bought it, I don't want it.'

'Are you sure? I bought it for you, a gift, remember?' Bel just shook her head. She didn't need any lingering reminders of their time together. Nigel stood up, scooping his things back into the bag. 'I suppose that's that, then. A hug good-bye?' He opened his arms. It would have been churlish to refuse. He hugged Bel tight, and as they separated, kissed her on the cheek. The kiss lingered for a couple of seconds, soft, breathy, warm. Bel couldn't work out exactly how it happened, but his lips somehow drifted until they were kissing her on the mouth. She was surprised how much she had missed this. Being kissed is always nice, but he was particularly good, very good. It must have been the wine that made her do it, she tried to convince herself later, because it had never been part of any plan, but she found herself responding. She somehow allowed him to kiss-walk her into the bedroom, where they began to pull at each other's clothes.

Bel was already wondering to herself if this might not be a good idea as Nigel lowered her onto the bed.

~~~~~
~~~~~

Date and time unknown.
Sometime between Friday 14th June 2019 and Saturday 6th July 2019

Emily dreamed.

She was standing in a bedroom. A large bed with pure white sheets stood in front of her. She took a step towards the bed, touched the covers, white satin, felt the soft warmth of the bed, longed to lie down.

Someone was already lying there. A young woman, restless, turning in her sleep.

Emily leaned towards her. She recognised the face, though she knew she had never seen the woman before. The woman turned again. She was speaking, muttering to herself as she slept, the same phrase, a pattern of words, a hurried whisper, like someone in a fever-bed. Emily looked at the woman's skin, pale in the light that seems to drift down from above. She leaned forward, trying to catch the words. The woman sighed, rolled away from her, started to mutter again, a fractured sob in her voice.

Emily wished there was something she could do to help the woman sleep peacefully. She looked down, discovered the violin in her hand. Of course. She should play to the woman to soothe her, something gentle, a childhood lullaby, perhaps. She lifted the violin, tucked it under chin, set the bow to strike the first note.

She knew this piece, it was her favourite, though she couldn't remember what it was called, or where she remembered it from. Music swelled behind her. An orchestra picked up the theme, carried it as she was lifted into a vortex of sound, the bow gliding under her fingers. Tears filled her eyes. She couldn't work out why. As Emily played, the woman sat up, climbed out of the bed, her nightgown a mere whisper of silk, walked towards, then past Emily, not seeing her. She went to the wardrobe, flung open the door.

Emily looked over the woman's shoulder. The inside of the wardrobe seemed to go on forever. Inside sat Emily's orchestra. As the door opened, they stopped playing, looked at the woman.

'I'm sorry,' the woman said, 'I'm looking for Emily.' The orchestra simply sat and looked at the woman. She closed the door, turned to go back to bed. 'Looking for Emily.'

'I'm here, I'm Emily.' She took a step towards the woman, but she was already lying down, whispering Emily's name, the word a sigh.

Behind her the orchestra picked up the refrain. Emily lifted her violin, started to play.

The woman slept on.

~~~~~
~~~~~

Friday 5th July 2019
07:49
Day Twenty-Two

Bel awoke with a start. She was thankful to find the bed empty beside her. She knew she wouldn't have been able to cope with the cringe-making conversation if Nigel had still been there, especially if he took it into his mind that this was the start of some crazy reconciliation. So, all in all not a good end to not a good day. Next time, Bel promised herself, she would make sure the wine stayed in the fridge. Even better, next time there wouldn't be a next time. She sat up and swung her legs to the floor.

She felt so tired. The drink and the sex weren't the only reasons. She'd had the dream again. It felt like it had gone on for most of the night. Emily on her violin, sobbing, an orchestra playing, the full works. With a sigh Bel hauled herself to her feet, headed for the shower. Water as absolution. After drying off she made herself a strong coffee to claw back some of the lack of sleep, scanned the local newsfeed for any new info on Emily. No hits. Unfortunately, it was nothing more than she expected, really. If Emily had been found; alive, dead, rescued, or just wandered in off the street, Bel knew the dream would have been different somehow. For some perverse reason she half-expected to see something about Gran in there too, a revelation of her lifetime of secrets, but she knew that that would be down to her subconscious mind trying to process what Gran had done. Bel wished she could tell herself that what had happened had all been some sort of fantasy, that the old woman in the Weavers' had lied to her, told her a tale; but she knew that the pain she had seen etched on Mary Middleton's face and the sorrow in her voice as she told her own sad story meant that she had been telling the truth. All of her life Bel had known that Gran was a sweet little lady who used to work in a mill and had been ready with a kind word or helping hand when needed. Now Bel had to get her head round the fact that a helping hand hadn't been the half of it. Gran, that same sweet little old lady, had in fact carried out dozens of illegal abortions over the years, from even before she was the age Bel was now. She could understand the service Gran had been offering, a life-changing or even sometimes a life-saving service, but right at that moment she couldn't get her mind past what must have been at times a savage and brutal operation. If there had been an open fire in her flat Bel could have quite happily thrown the book onto it and raked over the ashes rather than open it again, but it wasn't easy to make that kind of gesture with a combi-boiler and high output radiators, so she took a frothy slurp of her coffee and stared at the book on the coffee table.

In spite of everything, Bel knew what she had to do. Before she could find any peace, before she would be able to put this whole crazy episode behind her, she knew she would need to speak to Mum about why her name was written on the last page and to do that she would need to know for certain exactly what the book said, every word, every letter, every symbol, so there would be no doubt in her mind when she did speak to Mum. She hit the internet connection on her phone, picked up the book, opened it at the first page. She tensed herself, mentally preparing for the same jolt of emotion that had hit when she had touched it in the cellar, but this time it didn't happen. That was one of the things Bel had never been able to work out. All that psychic stuff sloshing about inside her, but no on-off button. She never knew if she was going to open a portal onto a wild winter storm or a damp day in Doncaster. This time it was Doncaster.

She worked methodically through the little black book, taking each piece of information in turn, typing it into the internet, adding the words abortion or termination, then trawling through the results, gathering a collection of notes for herself on a pad of paper. After a while, the book began to give up its secrets. Each page had a name at the top, obviously the poor, desperate woman involved, and her date of birth, which explained the early dates, including the ones before Gran was born. There was also what Bel worked out could only be an expected date of delivery, along with the date on which the abortion had taken place. Some of those dates were a bit too close together to make for comfortable reading. What was more disturbing were some of the other notes; if the heartbeat could be heard, or if the baby's movements could be felt, or worst of all, how the termination had been carried out. She couldn't help but wonder again about the tiny points of bright light that she had seen coming out of the book that day in the cellar. Now that she had begun to understand the details in the book, she wondered if they might somehow represent the trapped souls of those poor unborn children, their lives cut short literally before they had begun. She hadn't realised how emotionally exhausting the decoding of the words would be; she could feel the fatigue spreading like a sponge through her brain. Only a few more pages to go, she turned to the next. A montage of images began to play out again in her head; a scared woman sobbing, begging for help, whispered conversations arranging a secret appointment in the cellar, followed by the pain and the fear and the sorrow and the guilt, none of which could be numbed by any anaesthetic, or eroded by the passing of the years. She tried to stay calm, to keep a distance on the emotional turmoil that roiled around inside her, but now that the feeling had been unleashed it quickly started to slide out of control. She could feel the nauseous cramps biting at her stomach again, the tears welling in her eyes, tears of frustration and second-hand guilt. She pushed the book to one side, feeling wiped out, surprised to find that she had been chasing clues in the cryptic words for more than two hours.

There was a buzzing noise coming from somewhere. It took a few seconds for her to realise it was the intercom for the apartment. She stood up, feeling the fatigue of concentration spread across the muscles of her neck and shoulders, ran her fingers through her hair in an effort to clear her head, then snapped the button to answer it. 'Yes?'

'Ah, hello, I hoped you might be in. I was just passing; thought I'd call round to see you. I wondered if you might have gone to work or whatever, but your car's parked up, so I tried the bell.'

Bel frowned. Her head was jangling from what she had put herself through that morning, and the tiny speaker reduced the voice to a crackly squawk, so she didn't recognise it. 'Who is this?'

'I'm sorry. It's me, Ian. Detective Inspector Fox. Can we talk?' He sounded sheepish through the crackles.

'Fox?' Bel was so surprised that she could only stand staring at the intercom, a slack-jawed frown on her face.

'Hello?' Fox called again. The static silence strung out for so long he must have begun to think the intercom has some sort of fault.

She found her voice at the same time she found her sense of indignation. In spite of herself, or probably because of herself, she couldn't resist having a dig. 'Come to apologise, have you?'

'Actually, yes. Yes, I have.'

'Oh.' His response took the wind out of Bel's sails. 'I suppose you'd better come in, then.' She hit the button to let him in, made her way to the apartment door, unlocked it and left it ajar. After a few seconds she could hear a hesitant, almost apologetic tapping on the open door as Fox announced his presence with a timid hello, and walked in. And there he was, holding a bottle of rose wine in front of him like a shield. 'I know it's a bit early, but I thought I'd bring a peace offering,' he said in that soft, slightly gravelly voice of his and offered a small smile.

Bel had to quickly remind herself that she was supposed to be deeply upset and offended at his off-hand, even rude, treatment of her in the past few days, but when she saw him, blond hair slightly tousled, faded, slim-cut jeans and pale blue three-stripe trainers, coupled with a baby-blue pullover that looked so soft and was probably cashmere and perfectly matched his eyes, She could feel the familiar blush starting to creep up her throat. It deepened into a shade of embarrassment as it dawned on her that he was probably gay. Now she felt as if she'd made a fool of herself again, on top of everything else.

She took the bottle; she reckoned that after everything that had happened it was the least she deserved. She snatched a glance at the time on her phone. It wasn't even eleven, yet. As much as she wanted to, she resisted the temptation to crack the bottle open and start drinking it in front of him. She knew that he already saw her as a waste of space, and she didn't want to give him any more ammunition. No doubt in his social circles rose wine was served chilled, an accompaniment to tapas delivered from the restaurant around the corner, at a reasonable hour in the evening. Bel was willing to bet he didn't live in any part of Leaside. She blustered him into the living room and went to make fresh coffee. Besides, if she was going to speak to this guy, she wanted her brain to be firing on all cylinders, not befuddled by booze.

When she came back from the kitchen with two mugs, he was doing that classic thing of checking the bookcase to see if he could tell what sort of person you are by the books you like to read.

'Ah, thank you,' he took the mug in his big, finely manicured hands.

'See anything interesting?' Bel asked. She found herself eager to meet with his approval in spite of herself.

'I'm not sure.' His forehead creased in a frown. 'Vampires and werewolves I sort of expected, but Buddhism? String theory? "A Brief History of Time"? And what exactly is Eternalism? It sounds like some weird religious cult.'

'It's a theory that states that time is multi-layered, not a single stream, and that it doesn't necessarily run in a straight line like we all think,' She smiled inside as he offered her the look of a man out of his depth. 'Think of it like this; everything happens everywhere, all at the same time. We just see different bits at different times, but it's not compulsory to see the first bits first and the last bits last.' She could see that he was still struggling to take in what she was saying, but she couldn't help but feel secretly pleased that she'd given him something about herself to think about, instead of him dismissing her out of hand as he had done up until now. Bel casually scooped up Gran's book from the coffee table as she put her own mug down, dropped the little leather book in her bag. The last thing she needed right now was for him to get curious about that book in particular. Some things were not for sharing. 'Oh.' Fox seemed a bit non-plussed at her answer. She could tell by the way he spoke to her that he had never given any thought to her level of intelligence, and it was good to see that he was taken aback at her answer. He gave a quizzical look. Bel decided to take it as a challenge for her to expand on her statement.

'It's sort of a philosophical extension of membrane theory, if that helps,' she responded, keeping her face poker straight.

'Er, you'll have to explain it to me sometime,' he mumbled.

She smiled inside at the flustered look on his face, gave a mental fist-pump. Score one for Bel. 'So,' she dropped into her favourite chair, 'you mentioned something about an apology?' She indicated the sofa. Fox sat down, perching on the edge rather than relaxing back into it.

Bel took a studied look at the man as his face came up and his eyes locked onto hers for a second. He looked drawn, weary. He breathed in deeply, started talking. 'Look, I'm sorry I was so abrupt at the station.'

'And in the woods,' Bel pointed out, none too gently.

'Yes, and in the woods. The thing is, I've come here because, well, because I need to ask, first, is it true, what you do, and if it is, how do you do it; all these dreams with dead people, your visions.' He seemed sheepish, embarrassed. Bel could see in his eyes and his posture that he would rather be anywhere else right now but here, talking to her.

'What's up? Have you changed your mind? It doesn't all seem so far-fetched now that you've seen the bodies, does it?' Bel wasn't going to let him off the hook easily. 'You were only too happy to kick me out onto the street when I came to the station to try to tell you about Emily, weren't you, but now you're not so sure.' Bel could feel the anger beginning to rise in her stomach as she recalled the feelings of contempt and rejection that he had instilled in her, but she managed to rein it in. She picked up her coffee, took a sip. 'I'm guessing you've started to check out the girls' names, and some of the things I said are panning out.'

'Well, we've not made any definite identifications yet,' Fox replied, 'but we've started to run through the names you made a note of.'

'And?'

'There really was a Chelsea Ambrose living in Harrogate who went missing in April 2002. She would fit the age profile of the girl you mentioned.'

'What about the others? Suzanne? Kimberley?'

'Some of the things you told us are beginning to look like they might stack up, to fit with actual missing persons reports, some of them going back years.' He trailed off, almost as if he could hear himself, and didn't want to admit the truth of what he was saying. Bel looked at him. Finally. The whole saga was sad, no doubt about it, but from her point of view she had just been proved to be valid as a person, not some random nutter. Fox continued, 'We've started to get in touch with family members, but until we can take DNA samples to make comparisons against, we can't actually be sure. To a certain extent it's a waiting game.'

'But you can't wait, can you?' It was a simple statement of his position.

'No, we can't. I can't. Emily Phillips has been missing for nearly three weeks now. We've run out of time and we've run out of leads. To be honest, there are no leads, never have been. All we know for sure is that she arrived at the College of Music that morning. She was seen by one of her friends parking her car a couple of streets away, and we found her handbag lying on the floor in a corridor at the college. After that, nothing. As far as this investigation goes, she's just vanished off the face of the earth.'

'Which brings you here to see me.' In her quieter moments since their first meeting in the police station those few short weeks ago, Bel had day-dreamed more than once that Fox would be forced to grovel an apology on his knees in front of her, preferably in some spectacularly public place, but now that he was here, now that she could see how heavily this thing was weighing on his shoulders, her cheap glass of small revenge didn't taste as sweet as she had anticipated. She realised that the payback might not be worth it.

'Yes, I suppose it does.' There was a long pause as he drank his coffee, looked around the room, ran his fingers through his hair, licked his lips, took another drink of coffee. 'The girls in the woods,' his voice was little more than a whisper, 'the one's you found, the dead girls.'

'Yes?'

'Up until now we've been working on the assumption that Emily's disappearance was a one-off. Mostly, we've been hoping for a ransom demand, but it hasn't happened. One or two of the team have been holding out that she's had a breakdown, hopped on a train to Bristol, or Aberdeen; somewhere, anywhere, just to get away from all the pressure for a few days, and that she'll turn up safe and sound, and pick up her life where she left off.'

'I can hear the "but".'

'All that changed in the woods, when you found those bodies. We're having to start again. There isn't going to be any ransom, we realise that now, she hasn't wandered off for a bit of a break. We think the dead girls are all victims of the same man. I hate to have to tell you this, but it looks like you've found yourself a serial-killer. The pathologist has been looking at the bodies, the bones, and he says that all the girls had signs of torture, broken bones; some more than others.'

'Chelsea showed me what he did to her mouth,' Bel replied. 'He'd pulled out some of her teeth. And there was the thing with Kimberley's thumbs.'

'I saw the autopsy reports. Look, I know this might sound sick, but all these signs of torture are probably our best hope. It means that Emily might still be alive. If he's torturing them before he kills them, she might not be dead yet. We might still have a few days before he decides to get rid of her.'

'She's not dead,' Bel answered, the words coming out almost like a stab. Fox looked at her, his eyes searching her face, she guessed her was looking for some sign to convince him she was telling the truth, that he would be able to believe her. 'Emily. She's not dead,' she repeated more quietly, looking straight at him.

'How do you know? That's the bit I don't get! How can I take your word for it that she's still alive? That you can find her?'

'If you're asking me to explain what happens, and how, I can't, because I don't know myself. I just know that Emily is still alive. Look, sometimes I see ghosts, sometimes I have dreams. I can sometimes pick up information from photographs, and sometimes I get impressions from objects. It works best if the object belonged to the person, or they used it a lot, and the more emotionally involved they were, the stronger the images.' Exactly like the book in her bag, she thought, Gran's book, but she wasn't going to tell him anything about that. 'Apart from that, your guess is as good as mine. It's just a thing that happens to me.'

Fox looked down at the floor. Bel sipped at her coffee, waited for him to respond. When he did, she decided to not take offence; his answer was more or less exactly what she had been waiting for him to come out with, sooner or later. 'Are you really psychic? I'm sorry, but I just don't understand. I've read about this sort of thing, and like I said at the police station, we get one or two of...' he hesitated, licking his lips again.

'"My sort" is the phrase you used; I think.'

'I did, didn't I? Sorry. It's just that I have to work in hard facts, provable pieces of information. To be honest we don't have the time or resources to follow up every...'

'Crazy-Flake?' Bel suggested.

'You're not making this any easier.' He ran his fingers through his hair again.

'Remind you of anybody?' Bel could see the pain behind his eyes that her jibe had made, finally relented. 'I'm sorry, go on.'

'Well. I suppose I've come to ask you if it's true, that you're psychic. I know you found those bodies, but that might have just been some kind of a fluke, and I need to know for sure, for Emily's sake. To be honest, I'm desperate. I need to know if you really can help us.'

'Wow. Desperate. I'm flattered.'

'I'm sorry, this is all coming out wrong. The thing is, no-one else knows, about you, about how you ...'

'And you'd rather keep it that way? Again, thanks.'

'I'm sorry, Isabel,'

'Bel. I don't like Isabel. Call me Bel.'

'Bel, right. You need to understand how difficult a position I'm in. Can you imagine what would happen if I told my boss that I was following a tip-off from a woman who has dreams about where the bodies are buried? He'd laugh me off the case in an instant, and probably out of my job.'

'What do you want me to do,' Bel shrugged, starting to feel a little annoyed, 'prove it to you?' And then the penny dropped. Looking back, she knew she should have seen it coming. 'You bastard. You low down, dirty fucking bastard. You've brought something with you, haven't you? Something to check me out!'

He lowered his head, apology writ large. 'I'm sorry. What was I supposed to do? Emily's out there somewhere, and right now I'll do anything to find her.'

'Right now, Emily is the only reason I'm not throwing you out on your ear. Okay, out with it. Let's see what you've got.'

At least he had the decency to look embarrassed and shuffle in his seat a little. 'I've got this. It belonged...'

'No!'

He stopped in the act of reaching into his pocket, looking confused, as if he had done something wrong and been found out.

'Don't tell me. Don't tell me anything about whatever it is you've got. If I'm going to do this, I'm going to do it properly. I don't want to know who it belongs to, or when they were born, or what they do for a living. If you tell me anything, you'll be able to say later that I didn't really do it, that I picked up clues from what you said.'

He silently took the object out of his pocket and leaned forward, placing it timidly on the coffee table.

It was obviously a padded jewellery box, about four inches square. The fact that it was a jewellery box didn't of course mean it contained jewellery. There could be anything inside, that was the whole point, part of the test. Bel looked at the once dark red velvet plush, now faded to pink, scuffed bald on the corners, knowing as she looked that she had no choice but to pick it up. This was her chance to prove to Fox once and for all that she was genuine, that she did have access to sources of information that were somehow barred to others, that she really was psychic. She glanced at Fox, wondering if this was some particularly cruel set up he'd devised for her, to bring her crashing down in ignominy. She half-expected him to have a condescending smirk on his face at having outwitted her, but to be honest, he looked pale around the gills, as if he was getting ready to throw up. Lines of concentration and worry were etched deep across his face.

Bel snatched up the box and opened it in one swift movement. Inside was a pocket watch, roman numerals, the gilding on the crown and bow rubbed away over the years. So, it was obviously old. The casing bore a million tiny scratches. She took the watch out and rested it in her hand. She knew without looking that Fox was watching her, she could feel his eyes boring into the top of her head as she concentrated on the watch. Fox licked his lips, leaned forward in his seat.

For one brief second as she waited for some sort of connection to happen, the thought flashed across that mind that knowing her luck this would be the day her gift decided to desert her, to not turn up, to leave her feeling empty, worthless, in front of Fox. One thing was for certain though; nothing was going to make her fake it. Either it was there, or it wasn't. The instant that certainty settled in her head, the first image hit.

She blinked in surprise and looked around.

The blinding white light of the overhead sun beats down on me, bites into my eyes. I squint against its power. I feel myself wrapped up in an intense heat; a sticky, humid, relentless heat, like being thrown into the oven on regulo seven.

I feel a thirst grab at my throat, a thirst that pounds inside my skull, bites deep into my bones. It feels as if I haven't had anything to drink since the dawn of time, and every slow, brackish drop of sweat I feel oozing out of my pores is a tear of sorrow for the thirst inside.

My legs are leaden and weary under me, weak from fatigue and hunger. I would give anything right now to be able to stop walking, to find some shade from this relentless sun, to sit down and rest, if only for a moment.

But I am not allowed. There is only one rule, one imperative: to keep walking at all costs, keep putting one weary foot in front of the other, mile after slow mile, day after hot, hard day. To fall is to die.

We, I suddenly realise I am one of many, surrounded on all sides by others just like me. I can feel the slow, stumbling pace of hundreds of tired legs and feet shuffling alongside me, forced to march.

The steps already number hundreds of thousands, and still we march. No pause, no rest.

To fall is to die.

Bel put the watch down on the coffee table a little harder than she had meant to, winced, hoping that she hadn't broken it.

'Are you okay? You look like you're going to be sick,' Fox asked.

'I'll be alright. It just took me by surprise, that's all.'

'Let me get you another coffee.' He stood up and walked towards the kitchen.

'Tea, please,' she called after him, 'no sugar.' Her stomach was starting to feel sour from all the coffee she'd had over the last few days. Grateful for his offer, she let him get on with it. She just needed a minute to get her shit together, and right at that moment she wasn't sure she could trust her legs to work.

By the time Fox got back from the kitchen she felt composed enough to explain what she had seen, what she had felt. For a second Bel wondered if the vision she had had was accurate, then decided she wasn't going to do it like that. Why should she worry whether he believed her or not? No, she was just going to tell him what she had seen, and he could either accept what she said as being genuine, or he could just leave, it wasn't going to alter who she was and what she did. Fox brought the drinks, sat back down on the sofa opposite. Bel took a sip of hot tea to steady her nerve, then started to tell him. To his credit, Fox didn't say anything, just leaned forward in his seat, his gaze focussed, intense, as she spoke, as she told him of the impressions she had got from the watch; the heat, the hunger, the despair. When she had finished, she folded her arms to quiet the slight tremble she could feel threatening to break out in her hands and waited for his response. A strange twitch crossed his face and he cleared his throat.

Fox told her about the watch. It had belonged to his Dad's uncle, who had been taken prisoner by the Japanese forces in World War

Two, and put to work in a labour camp, somewhere in Burma. The climate had been fierce, high temperatures and even higher humidity. Food, when it was given, was meagre; thin gruels and rice, supplemented with cockroaches or other insects the men could find to add to their diet. As prisoners they were considered to be lower than nothing, already dead in the eyes of their captors and treated as such. There were long marches from site to site, where the prisoners were put to work building a railway across the country.

More than half of the men he was captured with died in the two years he had been there before he was finally liberated by the Allies, and although he survived to live another thirty years, he never really recovered. 'I have a photograph of him,' Fox said in a hushed voice, 'in an old family album somewhere. You can see he's still a prisoner, deep down inside where it matters, even years later. He looks empty.'

Minutes passed in silence, Bel sipping tea, Fox's untouched on the coffee table, each of them wrapped in their own thoughts.

'So, do I pass the test?' Bel asked at last. 'Do you believe me? Can you accept that I'm psychic, or do you need me to tell you which horse will win the first race at Kempton Park tomorrow? No, I can't do that,' she held up her hand when she saw the look of surprise in his eyes, 'I was joking.'

'Sorry, of course you were. I do believe you,' he said. 'I believe you've got something. Don't ask me what it is, and I'm not even going to try to understand it, but there's no way you could have known about that watch, about my great-uncle, unless you really are psychic. It's just not possible!'

'So, are we going to work together, you and me; to find Emily? Before it's too late?'

'On one condition.'

Bel caught a slightly shifty look in his eye. 'I think I know what it's going to be, but tell me anyway,' she said.

'No-one gets to find out about all this,' he gestured at the watch lying on the coffee table, at the two of them sitting there opposite each other. 'This is strictly between me and you. No press, no publicity, not a word to anyone!'

'I'm not in this for publicity, I just want to find Emily, before it's too late.' Bel shrugged, secretly relieved. 'I was going to ask the same of you. The last thing I need is my name in the papers. Imagine the headlines; "Police Witch Solves Missing Girl Case."'

'I don't need it any more than you do, believe me.' He picked the watch up off the table and stood up. 'Come on, then. Let's get going.'

'Why? Where are we going?'

'The College of Music in Leeds. We're going to find Emily Phillips.'

'There's something I have to do first.'

'Why? Where do you need to go that's more important than finding Emily?'

'I need to see my Mum about something, something that happened a long time ago.'

'I'll take you,' Fox said.

'What?'

'I'll take you. To your Mum's. You do what you need to do, I'll wait in the car for you. Then we can go straight round to the College.'

Bel looked at him, turning the scuffed old jewellery box over in his hands, unable to keep still. 'I don't know how long I'm going to be. This is not something I can rush.'

'I'll wait all day if I have to.' He turned and walked towards the door. Bel grabbed her phone and door-key, hurried after him. She could almost see the trail of energy follow him down the stairs to the ground floor.

~~~~~
~~~~~

Friday 17th June 2005
16:28

Mason drove like a man possessed, putting fast miles between him and the scene of the attack. Eventually, he pulled to the side of the road, sat, hands clenching the wheel to stop them shaking, adrenalin punching sweat through his skin. After a while his heart began to slow, and he made his way back to Manorgrove, hugging the speed limits, parked the van outside the workshop. Over the next few days he made excuses to not drive. Convinced that someone must have seen him, or that the girl had made a note of the registration number and reported him, he waited with taut nerves for the police to appear. That first night he couldn't sleep, lay with eyes wide open for the knock on the door, ears straining for the siren sound of approaching police cars. He finally managed to fall asleep as the sun came up, snatching a couple of hours before he had to start work. The next night was a little better. When a week has passed without him being arrested, he started to hope that perhaps nobody would call his name, stop him, interview him, arrest him. After three weeks he began to relax.

He started driving again, and his mind turned once more to Mandy. He had seen her once; he knew he would see her again. He had allowed his excitement and surprise to get the better of him last time, making him hurry and panic. He wouldn't make the same mistake again.

The next time he found her he would be ready. The next time he would be prepared.

He found what he had been looking for in a pawn shop near the Kirkgate market in Leeds. Mason struck up a conversation with the watery-eyed old man behind the counter, showing passing interest in the sovereign rings and old medals. The conversation meandered as they checked each other out, established some sort of rapport. After almost half an hour the man offered to show him the "special" items that he kept in the back. With the shop door locked, he led

Mason along a narrow, cluttered corridor to a small, musty room. A table held the centre, with three tarnished mugs, an overfull ashtray, a kettle and sugar bowl. The spoon was crusted with congealed sugar.

After Mason had waved away a selection of lock-knives and bayonets the man held out a black plastic rectangle. 'This is special,' he said with a smile.

'What is it?'

'Let me demonstrate.' He flicked the switch on the side. A blue-white arc of energy danced in front of Mason's eyes. He was mesmerised in an instant. He took the object from the man. It was heavier than he expected but felt good in his hand. He gazed in fascination at the living spark that danced between the metal spikes.

He paid the asking price without haggling, pushed it deep into his jacket pocket, walked out of the shop, a soft smile on his face.

Henderson's had been in business in Malton for almost half a century. Dr Henderson was a vet of the old school, which was why, when Mason broke the glass in the back door there was no alarm and he was able to reach in and prise off the bolt and hasp with a nail-puller. He stood in silence for a minute, letting the jagged sounds he had made be absorbed back into the small noises of the night, before pushing open the door, walking in. Once inside he kept the beam of his torch low, under the line of the windows, as he moved from room to room until he found what he was looking for.

The drugs cabinet was just that; a steel, free-standing cabinet, almost five-foot-tall, painted a dull red. There was a serious lock on the front. That would have been a problem, but Mason smiled to see the cabinet wasn't even bolted to the floor. If he had wanted, he could have rolled it out of the building on a parcel trolley. He rocked it back and forth, turning it until the back was no longer lined up against the wall. Sure enough, the back was much less sturdily constructed. He stabbed at one edge of the panel with the nail-puller, causing a dent. The dent left a gap in the seam where the back had been spot-welded in place. It was easy for him to push the pry-bar in the small gap and begin to peel away the metal sheet.

Once inside, he knew what he was looking for; He had done a bit of browsing on the net, not sure at first what his searches might yield, but knowing he would recognise it when he saw it. Random strings eventually led him to a particular chat site. He feigned interest, struck up a couple of conversations that pointed him in the right direction.

The vet's vials of ketamine were in a drawer on the bottom shelf. He scooped all ten into the rucksack on his shoulder, along with forty or fifty sterile-packed, single-use syringes he found in the next drawer. He checked the rest of the stock and was rewarded with dozens of packs of diazepam. He added them to his stash. After he pushed the back panel more or less into its original place and turned the cabinet around again it didn't appear to have been touched. He wondered how long after they discovered the break-in, they would realise just exactly what had been taken.

Dr Henderson called an electrician to have an alarm fitted the next morning. The damage to the drugs cabinet wasn't spotted until lunchtime

Mason began driving around, searching once more for Mandy.

He finally spotted her on a Saturday in September, walking, skipping along in the warm, late-morning sun. She was wearing a summer dress and the light bounced burgundy highlights from her auburn hair. She looked younger than he remembered her.

He pulled to the side of the road, tried to stay calm as he watched her walk past the van. She didn't recognise him, didn't give him a glance.

He drove a couple of hundred yards further along the lane, away from the houses, waited nervously for her to come towards him.

As she passed the van he jumped out, lunged at her with the stun gun, catching her on the neck. Her eyes rolled up as he hit the button. She dropped to the floor like a ragdoll as the charge pulsed through her. In a second he had scooped her up, bundled her into the back of the van, dumping her onto a thin mattress covered with a pile of old bed sheets. He could feel his breath catch hot and dry in his throat as he started the van, drove away. A glance in the rear-view mirror, checking he hadn't been seen. Nothing. It had all been so easy. He looked over his shoulder at the girl lying unconscious in the back of the van, the beginnings of a smile on his face.

He knew he had to move fast, before she came to. After less than a mile he found a deserted lay-by, pulled in, killed the engine, clambered over the passenger seat into the back. The girl fluttered her eyes, began to stir. Deftly, he opened a plastic box and took out one of the small syringes loaded with ketamine, jabbed it into the meat of her thigh, watched in fascination as her muscles relaxed under the impact of the drug and she slumped soft on the floor. He rolled her quickly onto her front and tied her hands behind her back, working efficiently, strapped her ankles together to stop her kicking out at the sides of the van if she woke up before they got back. Tearing off a strip of duct tape, he put it across her mouth, taking care that she could still breathe through her nose. Satisfied, he threw a musty old sheet over her, climbed back into the front, and set off towards Manorgrove.

Nobody paid the slightest attention as he made his way up the drive, past the mansion house itself, then followed the old track that led up into the woods. The track petered out after about two hundred yards, far enough for him to be out of sight to all but the most curious of eyes. He stopped the van, sat there for a few minutes, listened as the pinking of hot metal from the cooling engine and the regular deep breathing of the girl in the back were absorbed into the quiet sounds of the woods that drew in around him. With a quick glance around to confirm he was still unobserved, he climbed out of the van, walked round to the back door. Leaning in, her draped her easily over his shoulder, snatched up her violin case, and strode into the woods, towards his lair.

He had made sure the entrance was well concealed, weaving skeins of still-growing ivy and long grass through a willow hurdle, so that when he rested it across the mouth of the tunnel, the foliage continued to grow, a living barrier that only he would ever be able to find. At one end he had pinned it into the hillside with half a dozen of his rabbit snares, so the whole thing swung open in one easy movement. Inside the short tunnel, he had worked steadily over the last few months, scavenging discarded bits and pieces from around the estate, making items when he needed to, stealing when there was no other choice. He acted cautiously; the last thing he needed was to lose his job for some petty infringement. One room he left empty, the larger one he had kitted out as a cross between a bedroom and a dungeon. The telling difference was the padlock on the outside of the steel door.

The girl, his new Mandy, was waking up. He could feel her starting to tremble as he dragged her in through the tunnel and bundled her into the little chamber, rolling her onto the mattress. He cut the plastic ties he had bound her with, showing her the sharp blade as he did so, relishing the fear it induced in her eyes. He snatched the tape from her mouth in a single sharp movement, his reward a long squeal of pain.

'Hello, Mandy,' he stood over her, smiling down at her tear-streaked face as the girl trembled before him. 'Surprised to see me again?'

'Please don't hurt me,' was the only thing her brain could find to say as she looked at him through her tears. She would repeat this every few seconds for the last moments of her life, as if she had become locked in a loop of fear, as if she couldn't comprehend what was happening to her.

'How does it feel, to be scared, hmm? To know that your fate rests in my hands. That I can make the pain worse,' his hand shot out and grabbed her arm, squeezing hard into the soft flesh just above the elbow, squeezing and twisting until she bent and hunched to try to escape, 'or I can make the pain go away, if I choose.' He let his hand drop, and watched the tears form in her eyes.

'Please don't hurt me.'

'First,' he smiled a broad, sardonic smile, 'I want you to play for me.' He picked up the case and flicked it open. Only then did he register how slim the case was, how light. Inside was a silvered-chrome flute. He stared at it, trying to understand.

'You bitch. You fucking bitch! You did this on purpose, didn't you? All this time I've been looking for you, waiting for you, and this is how you repay me? With a flute!' Red heat filled his mind. He threw the case across the room, the metal parts of the flute squealing as they bounced off the walls. He grabbed her by the hair, pulled her head back. The punch swung round and landed with a crackle in her throat. She collapsed breathless as her knees gave way. Swinging his leg back, he kicked in the stomach, listened with excitement as the air gasped out of her lungs in a strangled whimper.

'Please, don't hurt me.' She could only mouth the words now as he twisted a hank of hair around his fist, tugged upwards so that she had to scramble to her knees, leant towards her to snarl in her face.

'Hurt you? Hurt you?!? Do you want to know what it's like to be hurt, to be picked on, made fun of? Do you? Do you?' He hit her on the ear so hard her head snapped sideways, and her chin rammed into her shoulder. Her eyes were wide open in shock now as they searched out his own, silently begging.

He ignored their pleading, punched her in the face again. Her lip split, blood spilling, two dark, heavy drops, down her chin. He knelt down beside her. 'Let me tell you what it's like!' His hand tightened in a claw around her throat, squeezed. Her eyes were still looking at him, but all confusion was gone now. Her eyes filled with fear. For the first time, she fully realised that she was going to die. For the first time a tear of sad realisation traced a salt-streak down one cheek. She watched as his snarling face drew closer, until with a snap of his jaw he leaned his face into hers, bit her in the lip. She squealed in agony, jerked her head back, but that only made the pain sharper. After that she could only watch, feeling lost, detached, as he tugged and cut and tore at her clothes, as he climbed on top of her, as the world turned red and loud in her ears. She felt the beat of her heart growing faster and stronger in her chest until she thought it would burst. With a final wrench she tried to escape from under him, then watched, curious, as the pitiful scene played out below her. She stood looking down on the body of the girl as the man raped it.

The name-tag inside the instrument case read Jessica Curtis.

Friday 5th July 2019
11:51
Day Twenty-Two

Bel knocked on the door. She hadn't had her own key since the day she moved out. She could still remember Mum standing with her hand extended, waiting for her to hand it over as she carried the last of her bits and pieces out to the car. What upset Bel most was seeing the front door closing behind Mum before she herself had even driven off.

'Hello, love,' Dad opened the door, broke into a smile as he greeted his daughter. It always cheered her up to see Dad, he was a genuinely nice person. He hugged her tight, waved her in. 'Nice to see you. Your Mum's out the back, she'll be glad you came.' Bel knew that wasn't true, but Dad seemed to believe it. The house had a special smell all of its own; equal parts furniture polish and the Panache perfume Mum had worn for as long as Bel could remember. She began to breathe in her childhood as she followed Dad along the hallway through the kitchen and into the conservatory. Sarah, Bel's imaginary friend, stood at the bottom of the stairs, glared at her as she walked past. Sarah looked about ten or eleven years old, as if she had been trapped in time somehow, not allowed to leave, not allowed to grow.

Mum was working on a jigsaw, "The Gardens at Balmoral". She didn't look up as Bel entered. 'What brings you here?' She picked up a blue piece, stared at it for a few seconds, then clicked it into place in the sky.

'I thought I'd drop by to see you,' Bel replied quietly. 'How have you been keeping?'

'As well as to be expected, I suppose.' Bel could see how tired Mum looked, hollowed-out, almost. It had only been five days since the funeral. Too soon. Bel so wanted to hug her, but daren't ask.

'I'll make the tea then, shall I?' Dad tried to lift the mood with the pitch of his voice alone, went back into the kitchen to fill the kettle.

Mum scanned the pieces for the next fit.

'It was a nice service, wasn't it?' Bel offered.

'We need to start clearing the house out soon.' Mum responded in a monotone.

'Okay. I'll get in touch with one of the contractors we use at work, if you like.'

'And I assume you'll be handling the sale.'

'Yes, mum, of course.'

'We'll leave the money side of it to you.' Bel already knew in her heart that her parents were never going to touch any of the money from the sale; it would go into a separate account, and Bel would inherit it herself when they both died. She didn't think she wanted it.

'Is there anything you want to keep, anything special, before they clear the house?'

'Your father and I stayed behind after the funeral, brought a few things home with us, a couple of photo albums, a brooch she loved. There's nothing more we need.'

Bel stood for long seconds, listened to the beat of her heart as the hard silence rolled on. 'Can we talk, Mum? About Gran? Please?'

'Yes, let's talk. Let's start with why you left your Gran to die at the bottom of the cellar steps!'

'I didn't "leave her to die", Mum. I had somewhere to go. You said she was ill, in bed. I didn't think it would matter if I went around to see her later than I said.'

'She had a broken hip, Isabel. She was lying on the cold floor for hours, all alone, scared, in pain.'

'I know. I'm sorry, Mum.'

'Where did you have to go, anyway?'

'That doesn't matter, right now. I want to ask you something about Gran. Did she ever talk to you about what she did when she was younger?'

'There's not much to talk about. When she left school, she trained to be a nurse. She did that for a few years, then married your Granddad and got a job in the mill. Why?'

'I went to see Mary Middleton yesterday. She was at the funeral, she worked with Gran, back in the day.'

'Yes, I know Mary, vaguely.'

'She told me about Gran's cellar, what Gran did there.'

'You're making this sound a bit ominous, Isabel. What on earth are you talking about?'

'Gran used to carry out operations there. She helped women, Mum. Women in trouble. She used her nursing experience to give women terminations, in the cellar, back in the nineteen fifties and sixties, before it was legal.'

'Stop it! What are you saying? Why are you lying? Wasn't it bad enough that you left her alone and in pain, without making up these evil lies about her?'

'I'm not lying, Mum. Gran kept a record of what she did, a sort of diary, or ledger, with the names of the women she helped. That's why she'd gone down into the cellar that day. She wanted to get rid of the book while she was still able, to destroy it. This book.' Bel dug the book out of her handbag.

'Stop it! Stop it, right now!' Mum stood up, almost screamed at Bel. The slap stung Bel's cheek; made her head snap round to the side. 'How dare you? I'm not going to listen to another word of this nonsense,' she hissed at her daughter. Bel blinked back tears, felt the spread of warmth on her cheek.

'Ask her about me.' Sarah shimmered into sight beside Bel, spoke inside her head. Bel tried to push her away with her mind. Be quiet, Sarah. I'm talking.

'Okay, don't listen if you don't want to, but it's still true, it still happened.' Bel tried to keep her voice calm, steady, as she spoke to Mum. 'There's a name at the top of each page, a woman's name. They're the names of the women Gran helped.'

'No! That's not true. Why are you telling me these lies?'

'It is true, Mum. Gran wrote it all down. It's all in here. Look.' Bel started turning pages. 'The only thing I don't understand is why your name is on the last page, here, look, with a date a couple of years before I was born.'

'Me. Ask her about me!' Sarah's voice was louder, more insistent. Bel felt a pulse of sorrow dig into her mind as Sarah stood between the two of them. She seemed to be wrapped in a pale, yellow glow.

Realisation hit Sarah as she looked at her mother. 'You had a termination too, didn't you? That's the only reason Gran would have written your name in the book. But Gran didn't do it, did she? Terminations were legal and safe by then, weren't they, so you would have been able to go to a clinic, wouldn't you? Did Gran arrange for you to go?'

'Stop it. Stop it. Stop it!' mum was talking over Bel now, her voice getting louder with every word. 'Get out of my house! Get out!' She stood up and started pushing Bel backwards, forcing her towards the door through into the kitchen. With a gasp of revelation, Bel felt a wave of images punch into her mind, and she suddenly understood. 'Oh, my God! It's Sarah, isn't it? Sarah is the baby you had terminated. No wonder you got so angry whenever I played with her.'

'It was evil, the whole thing. Her coming back here to torment me. And you! You were evil, too, playing with her all the time. Don't think I didn't hear the two of you, always talking, laughing. "Sarah says this. Sarah said that. Sarah did the other. She was supposed to be dead, gone to heaven, not come back here to haunt me.'

'She's still here, Mum. She's standing right next to me.'

'No. Stop it. You're doing it again. It's evil. Just stop it.'

'Is that why you got so upset when I tried to tell you about that friend of yours, that lady, Angela? Do you remember? When I was a girl. The day her husband died.'

'It's not natural. None of this is. Spirits. Talking to the dead! It's the work of the Devil!'

'I'm not the Devil, Mum. I'm just your daughter. The only thing is, I'm psychic. I didn't ask for it, but that's what happened, and it keeps happening, whether I like it or not. Sarah is here, Mum. She's right next to me, and she's crying. All she's ever wanted was for you to acknowledge her, explain to her why you did what you did, and if you can, tell her that you loved her.' Mum's face lost its fierce scowl. 'If ever you want me to help you, just let me know.' Bel turned to walk out.

'Wait!' Mum grabbed her arm. Neither of them moved for long seconds. 'Is she really there? Can you really talk to her? To Sarah?'

'Yes, I really can. I can talk to her, and see her too, sometimes.'
'What does she look like?'
'She's about ten or eleven years old, fair-skinned, with wavy blonde hair and pretty blue eyes that sparkle when she laughs.' Bel could feel Sarah come to stand beside her. 'She's standing right here, if you want to talk to her.'
'Is she?' Mum held out both hands. 'Can I, can I touch her, feel her?'
'I don't know, I'll ask her. Sarah, Mum wants you to touch her.' Sarah looked at Bel with tears in her eyes, reached forward, brushed Mum's cheek with the back of her fingers. Mum let out a gasp, brought her own hand up to the spot. Tears ran down, falling over her fingers.
'I need to explain. I need to explain to her about what happened, why I had to do it.'
'So, tell her, Mum. Sit down and start talking. She loves you and she just wants to know that you love her too.'
'I do love her! I've always loved her. I love both of you. That's always been part of the problem, I felt guilty about Sarah, what I did to her, and every time I looked at you it reminded me of her, and how she wasn't here with us. Please forgive me, Sarah. I've been such a terrible person.' Mum broke down in tears, dropped into the little cottage sofa that she sat in to watch summer birds. Sarah draped herself around her shoulders.
'Sarah's sitting with you right now, Mum.'
'Is she? I wish I could see her.'
The light flickered. 'I think that's Sarah letting you know.' The light dimmed again, for almost a full second, before brightening again. 'She'll always be here, as long as you want her to be.'
Bel stayed more than an hour, listening to Mum talk to Sarah, passing on Sarah's replies. She dropped the book into her handbag, said nothing more about it. When she finally left it was to the sound of Mum crying. It felt like a good sound.

~~~~~

Friday 5th July 2019
13:06
~~~~~

Day Twenty-Two

Bel felt emotionally washed out after talking to her Mum, but, in the end, she felt happy. She felt as if she had made some sort of a breakthrough. They had talked together for more than an hour, the three of them; Mother, Daughter, and the other one. Mum explained that she had felt overwhelmed by the fact of being pregnant, not sure she had wanted a baby at her young age, and when the quad test showed a high probability for Down's syndrome, Gran had taken charge. Mum had been swept up into a course of action that had led to an appointment at a discreet clinic, followed by a couple of weeks to recuperate. Afterwards, she had been filled with guilt, and then, when Bel had been born, and worse, started talking to the ghost of the little girl she never had, Mum had turned against Sarah, against Bel, the whole situation, as a defence mechanism, more out of guilt than hatred.

'Okay?' Fox leaned across to open the passenger door.

Bel nodded in response, climbed in. Fox started the car, pulled away.

He drove well, managing to find gaps that Bel wouldn't have risked going for, and in less time than she thought possible, they were pulling up outside the College of Music. Bel's nerves began to fire in jangly little spikes. It had already been a big day and it was only going to get bigger whichever way things worked out here. Bel had been insisting that she could find Emily, and now, after discovering the bodies of the girls in the woods, and Fox testing her with that watch, she was finally going to be let loose on the last place Emily had been seen alive. If ever Bel needed her gift to deliver, this was it. Her stomach turned a fluttery flip-flop as she got out of the car and looked up at the grand building.

It had originally been a Victorian maternity hospital, but closed in the 1960's, standing empty until a speculative bid for European City of Culture in the nineties had persuaded the city to invest in such things, and the building was re-conceived as a centre of musical excellence. The granite facades had been sand-blasted clean of more than a century of mill-chimney soot and grime, and today shone white in the summer sun.

'Emily parked down there, just around the corner,' Fox gestured along the street as they climbed out of the car. 'Come on, I'll show you.'

Bel looked down the street to where he pointed. It was busy, lots of people passing and re-passing. She doubted that any impression Emily may have made would still be there after all this time and all those people. More than ever before, Bel knew she would need a focus, some place or event where Emily would have been emotionally highly charged, and she didn't think parking her car around the corner was going to cut it. No, all the trauma the girl had suffered, the fear and panic, all that had happened inside the college. Bel started up the wide entrance steps. 'Let's go inside.'

'But I thought you wanted to re-trace her steps, pick up some vibes.' Fox fell into step beside Bel, a puzzled look on his face.

'I'm not going to get any "vibes"', Bel air-quoted, 'from the street,' as she pulled open the large, glass-panelled, pale oak door and walked into the cool of the building. Suspended from the ceiling was an abstract representation of music staves and notes. Right under the treble clef sat the reception desk, and to one side, a tiny cafe-lounge area with a machine in the corner that promised "the instant that's just like ground". Some wag has added "That's why it tastes like mud." underneath the logo.

'Fancy a coffee?' Fox offered. Bel smiled her thanks, found somewhere to sit. Her headache seemed to be lifting at last, but she was beginning to wish she'd had something to eat. She was surprised but pleased when Fox came back with the coffees, and a couple of muffins and croissants. Bel nodded her appreciation as she wolfed down a croissant in two bites, took a mouthful of coffee, which tasted flat and tepid but washed down the pastry anyway, and started to feel better.

'Eat them all, I got them for you,' Fox stirred sugar into his coffee. 'You're looking a bit peaky, and I'm starting to feel guilty about asking you to do this.'

Don't be,' Bel replied as she helped herself to another croissant, 'I'm just grateful that you're giving me a chance to help.'

'Well, let's just say that based on what you showed me in the woods, and that thing with my Great-Uncle Roger's watch, I'm open to anything that you can offer that might help us find Emily.'

Bel looked at him across the tiny table as he spoke, the frown lines on his brow, the tense set of his jaw as if he was permanently clenching his teeth. She chewed on the last of the croissant and started drumming her fingers on the table, wondering if she could get away with taking the blueberry muffin. Fox made no attempt to eat, just sat nursing his coffee, and he had said they were all for her. Bel let her fingers walk across the table to casually collect the cake, dragging it back like a spider with its prey, gulped it down in lumps, washing it down with the last of her coffee as she looked around at the busy swirl of people, so young, so vibrant, so full of life. The air seemed to dance to the music in their minds. There was something else though, a dark undercurrent that maybe only Bel was aware of. It felt to her as if the building itself knew that Emily had been taken and was holding its breath, waiting for news, anxious for her return.

'So, have you got any, impressions. Is that the right word? Impressions? Or is it too soon?' Bel came back from her people-watching, back to the now. Fox's voice sounded exhausted, his drawn features reminding her just how much he too had invested in this. Bel watched as his eyes moved about, constantly searching, it seemed, for something, anything, that might help him locate Emily Phillips.

'It's getting to you, isn't it?' Bel asked.

'If you mean by getting to me no sleep and seventy hours a week with nothing to show for it, yes, it's getting to me.'

'Why don't I buy the coffee this time, and then you tell me what you know about Emily's disappearance?'

Fox was frowning when Bel returned with fresh cups, small curls of steam rising from the sipping lips. 'I thought you didn't want to be told anything in case it compromised your psychic powers.'

'No. I just didn't want to be told anything about that watch this morning so that you could be sure in your own mind that I was telling the truth, that I was genuine, that was all. Right now, I don't care what information I get, or where it comes from, as long as we find Emily.'

'There's not a lot to tell, to be honest. Most of it's already been in the papers. She came here, got as far as her tuition studio, then just disappeared. Her handbag was found in the corridor, the contents strewn all over the place. That was how the alarm was first raised.'

'What about CCTV?'

'Apparently it's against the artistic and nurturing ethos of the college.'

'In that case, there's no point putting this thing off any longer. Why don't you show me where her tuition studio thingy is, where it all happened?' Bel took one last slug of the too-hot coffee and stood up. Fox covered his own cup and pushed it towards the middle of the table, then made his way towards the double-doors opposite the reception desk.

'Do you really think she's still alive?' He asked as he held open the door, his voice little more than a whisper.

'Yes, I do. She keeps asking me to help her, in my dreams, and daft as it sounds, I think she would have told me if he had killed her. I just have to keep hoping that I'm not missing something.'

'I want to be optimistic,' he replied, 'but in spite of what you did last night I don't have your faith, or your inside info, if you see what I mean. If I'm honest, I worry that we're running out of time, that it might already be too late, that she might already be dead. It's been three weeks now with no news. The kidnap we were all secretly hoping for early on turned out to be a no-go. There's been no contact of any kind. No word, no sightings, nothing. And then you go and make it worse by finding the bodies of those other girls in the woods. I don't want to put you under any pressure, but if you can't give us something to work with, I personally don't hold out much hope for Emily anymore.'

As they made their way down the corridor, Bel paused to look into a side-room through the glass-panelled door. A young woman with thin shoulders and wearing a floral summer dress caressed a cello as she coaxed music out of it. Three others nursed their instruments between their thighs and waited their turn as she played. An older man stood behind her, swaying as he listened with eyes closed, a baton that nobody was following marking time in his raised hand.

Fox stopped at the third door on the right, pushed it open to reveal a small, stark room. Bel followed him in, stood just inside the room as the door swung closed behind her, looked around, trying to get a feel for the place. A sash window at the end of the room let in the summer sun, causing dust motes to swirl in the air, and ripe orange clouds of colour to bounce off the burnished parquet floor. The room had almost no furniture. There was an old upright piano against one wall, its mouth open to show black and off-white teeth. A semi-circle of music stands took up the space in front of an old stone fireplace, a plastic stackable chair behind each one. The nearest stand held a manuscript in its tiny brass fingers. Bel glanced at the score; "Adagio for Strings" by Samuel Barber. She'd never head of it. She shrugged and turned away.

'This is where Emily had her tutorials most days,' Fox said, pursing his lips.

Bel looked around, wondering where to begin. Everything looked so benign, so ordinary. It was difficult to imagine that Emily had been taken from this twee little room.

'She was doing extra practice for a concert in a month's time,' Fox was still speaking, 'it was going to be her first big performance, broadcast live on the BBC and everything.' He gave a brief shrug. 'I guess it's over to you.' Bel could see the tension drawn taut on his face. 'So how do you want to do this? Shall I wait outside?'

'You can stay if you want, just try not to make too much noise.'

Bel turned to face the room, took a deep breath, closed her eyes, waited.

Nothing.

She called the Mendelssohn to mind, started humming the opening passage in her head as best she could remember it. She walked over to the window, looked out onto a small courtyard, wooden benches hidden in the shade of broad-leafed trees and bushes, students lounging and chatting in the sunshine. She wondered if they had been sitting there three weeks ago when Emily was snatched, had heard sounds, a scream maybe, looked up to this window, curious.

Bel moved on, past the music stands, brushing a finger against each in turn, all the while calling in her head for Emily to talk to her, to come forward and let Bel see what had happened. A series of images bounced across her mind with every step she took, each one playing out for a second in front of her eyes before fading. She could see and feel a stream of students fretting and stressing as they worked their instruments, worrying about relationships, money, food, the music, before they drifted away, to be replaced by the next. She could feel Emily trying to catch her attention, but when she paused and tried to concentrate, the feeling evaporated as quickly as it had come. In less time than she had hoped she found herself back at the door, back beside Fox, who stood, pinch-faced in anticipation. Written in his eyes as large as life, the single word, the only question; 'Well?'

Bel could barely bring herself to look at him. 'Sorry. It's not working. I don't know what it is, but I can't seem to grab hold of Emily's vibe.' It felt so frustrating. Bel began to wonder what might be causing the flatness inside her. How had she been able to see Jessica's mother at the house, find the girls in the forest, and yet here, now, when she needed it more than ever, she wasn't able to connect to Emily, the girl who needed her most? Bel played the various scenarios through in her head, trying to think if there was something different she had done this time. She recalled how Mrs Curtis had ambushed her at her house, and that she had found the lay-by by chance, where the ghost dog had turned up to lead her to the girls, which all meant that she hadn't actually done anything to make those contacts happen, had she? In fact, the only time she *had* tried to force a contact she'd had that surreal vision where her computer had filled with blood and the whole thing had turned weird and freaky on her. She turned to Fox. 'I'm sorry, but I don't think it's working. It feels as if too many people have left too many impressions for me to pick Emily out.'

'What if I gave you something of Emily's to hold, like you did with the watch earlier?'

'Such as?'

'Strictly speaking this is off limits, but I've got an evidence bag in the boot of my car. This needs to stay strictly between the two of us, okay?' Bel nodded and Fox left the room, returning a couple of minutes later, slightly out of breath, carrying a large clear plastic bag, official red police adhesive tape sealing it along one end. 'Here, try this.' He handed it across. Inside was Emily's make-up bag.

'Am I allowed to open it, to take it out?' she asked.

'Best not. Will you still be able to, you know, get anything?'

'Let's find out, shall we?' Bel let it rest on her hand, determined not to force the issue, to let it happen, let it flow.

Taking a long, slow breath, she looked around the empty room again. The whole place felt blank, sterile, empty of energy. The only impression she got was that she was wasting her time, that this wasn't where she was supposed to be. She turned to look at Fox. 'You said Emily was attacked in the corridor?'

'We're not sure exactly,' he shrugged. 'Her bag, phone, make-up, were all found scattered on the floor just outside, but she might just have dropped them there.'

'I think that's where I need to be, then. Come on.' The plastic bag made a sharp crinkling sound as she gripped it tight to her chest, pulled open the door and took the three small steps that put her in the middle of the corridor. Two girls were walking past, deep in gossipy conversation. Bel didn't bother to listen, turned to speak to Fox, standing just inside the doorway.

The light was different; brighter, clearer somehow, like a twist of light scattered through a prism. There seemed to be an electricity in the air, a charge that popped and tingled on Bel's lips. She was standing in the corridor, the studio door now closed beside her. She couldn't see Fox anymore, and the giggling girls who had brushed past a second ago were nowhere to be seen. She felt a frisson of cold fear as she realised she was alone. A frown creased her brow as she looked up and down the softly lit corridor.

Emily appeared, seeming to drop out of the air without falling, a few yards along the passageway. She was walking towards Bel, wrapped in concentration. Bel could feel the spikes of thought in Emily's head as surely as if they were in her own. The girl was looking forward to getting the piece nailed, especially the double-stop finger-work in the first movement. Bel could feel the notes in her own fingers, hear them in her head. Emily walked right up to her, looking right through her without seeing, pushed one hand through Bel's stomach to open the door, walked into the room. Bel turned to follow, the door an insubstantial smear as she passed through.

Bel heard a hoarse whisper from somewhere behind her, a voice she didn't recognise. 'Mandy'. Bel stopped dead in her tracks, feeling the hairs on the back of her neck spring up in a cold rush of adrenalin. Who is Mandy? She didn't understand. She could feel the puzzled frown growing on Emily's brow as sure as the one on her own. Bel echoed Emily's movements, sucked in a sharp gasp of breath, turned towards the voice.

'Hello, Mandy.' The voice was deep, gruff. The man sounded almost like he was out of breath. Something punched into Bel's shoulder and a cold fire erupted in her bones as a hard numbness flashed across her back, a thick pain that seemed to swell inside her brain. She couldn't hold her head up anymore, her teeth begun to chatter with effort, and her legs didn't seem to have the strength to keep her upright.

Bel tried to take a step forward, but she couldn't understand why she was lying on her side on the floor. She couldn't work out what was happening; she wasn't even sure which way was up.

One arm waved about until she finally found the floor, and she pushed hard to try to get back onto her feet.

An electric noise filled her head.

Black.

'Are you okay?' Fox jumped forward, a worried frown on his face, as Bel turned towards him, pale and shaky. He put his arm around her shoulder as she dropped the evidence bag on the floor, leant against the doorjamb. She squinted, trying to force her eyes to focus on the real world, pushed the vision to one side, tried to put something like a realistic smile on her face. Judging from the look on Fox's face she wasn't sure she completely succeeded. 'You scared the shit out of me. I swear I saw your eyes roll back in your head like you were going to pass out,' he said.

Bel just gave him a weak smile as she played for time, tried to sort out the bits that were real and all around her from the bits that had only ever been inside her head. She stood upright, even though that meant letting go of Fox's arm. 'I'm okay. I just saw Emily. I saw who kidnapped her. I saw it all. I just watched it happen.' Bel took a deep breath, tried to settle her breathing. 'Sorry, it all got a bit intense.'

'That's incredible. What did you see?'

'It's just like you said. He attacked her as she walked into the studio. I think he used some sort of stun-gun; I remember seeing blue sparks. That's how he overpowered her. He was hiding somewhere, waiting for her. He watched her from the corridor, then came into the room after her. He had this all planned. He was waiting for her. Shouldn't you be writing this down?'

'Never mind that. Did you get to see what he looked like; the man? Would you recognise him if you saw him again? I want you to come back to the station, look at some mug-shots, do a photo-fit, maybe.'

'He looked older, forty, maybe fifty, with dark, wiry hair. He was dressed in dungarees or a boiler-suit, brown, I think. He's thickset, stocky, a bit on the fat side. He needs a shave, but he didn't have a beard, just scruffy. He has a bit of a limp, I think.'

As she told Fox the details of what she'd seen, Bel picked up the evidence bag, held it close to her chest, watched as the images swim like pale shadows in front of her again.

Emily lay in a heap on the floor. Bel felt as if she was looking down on her, almost as if she were looking out through the eyes of her assailant. Bel could feel a growl of anger, no, hatred, form in her head.

'Mandy.' He spoke the name again. Bel could feel the man had done this before. In spite of his anger he was calm, organised. She thought back to the

poor girls buried in the wood, realised this was how they had been taken, this was the way they were snatched away from their lives.

There was a backpack on the floor by the man's foot that Bel hadn't noticed before. He reached inside it as she watched, took out a syringe, pushed it into the rubber seal of a tiny bottle that she could now see in his other hand, then swiftly stabbed the loaded needle deep into the meat of Emily's thigh. The girl didn't flinch, she was still out for the count from the stun-gun that had left Bel sprawled on the floor, disorientated.

The man rolled Emily onto her front, quickly binding her hands behind her back with a thick black cable-tie. It buzzed like a wasp as he zipped it tight. Bel watched as the plastic bit into the girl's wrists.

The man stood, and with a grunt of effort scooped Emily up into his arms, draped her over his shoulder like a sack of spuds. He picked up his backpack, retrieved her violin from where it had fallen, pulled open the heavy, sound-proofed classroom door and turned right. The door fell closed behind him. Bel watched as he moved away from her along the corridor, surprisingly strong under the chubby belly.

Bel felt her focus shift, could see Fox as a pale shadow to one side now as she watched the man walk away with the unconscious Emily draped over her shoulder. She felt a panic roll through her stomach as she watched the scene play out before her, almost as if she daren't let him out of her sight, as if that would mean she would never see Emily again. 'He's taking her down there,' she heard herself shouting at Fox. 'Come on, quick!' She grabbed the door, pulled it open. She could sense Fox fall into step behind her as she too turned right to follow the image that only she could see. The corridor was already empty in front of her, the only thing visible now a soft shadow just disappearing round the corner at the far end. Her heart leapt in her chest and she let out a gasp, scared that she wouldn't be able to keep up. She dashed forward, turned left. The shadow was already starting to fade. 'What's down this way?' she called back over her shoulder as Fox hurried to keep up.

Fox frowned. 'I don't know, a staff car park, I think.' Bel nodded, set off again to chase the shadow. She was running as she rounded the next corner and then watched as the insubstantial shadow dissolved through a barred fire exit.

'Open it,' Bel snapped as Fox caught up. 'Hurry.' He didn't even break stride, brushed past her, kicked the bar with the full force of one foot. The door slapped back on its hinges so hard Bel thought he must have broken it. She squinted out into the sunlight, so bright after the subdued lighting in the corridor. The car park seemed bleached, with pale coloured hard-core compacted down and already starting to form ruts, tinder-dry bushes along the sides suffering in the summer heat. Bel scanned around the car park, searching for some sign, some clue. Her eyes were drawn to a dark-coloured van over in the far corner.

Bel knew as soon as she saw it that the dark-coloured van wasn't really there because its front half was parked inside a blue estate car that occupied the space in the real world. Bel watched as the thickset man walked towards it, Emily slung loosed-limbed over his shoulder like an American Ragdoll. He seemed to be carrying her almost without effort, her head flopping down over his back, her long auburn hair brushing the back of his trousers as he walked. He moved across the car park towards the dark-coloured van. Grey? Green? A logo on the door. Something like a crest, or coat of arms. The van looked boxy, new, just another van. Green. The van was definitely green. The man opened the cargo door and rolled Emily into the back, dropping her violin in after her. Bel hurried to get closer, desperate not to miss anything.

The man stood, looking down at his prize, a smile on his lips. He slammed the door, moved to the front, climbed in, fired the engine into life.

A new fear rose in Bel as she realised what was happening. 'He's getting away!' She turned to scream at Fox, but he just stood in the doorway staring at her, a puzzled frown on his face.

Bel could feel the frustration well up inside her as the van moved off. She tried to read the number plate but couldn't seem to make out any of the numbers. The vehicle paused at the entrance to the car park, turned left, then evaporated in the unforgiving light of day.

A sob of despair escaped Bel's lips. 'She's gone, she's gone.' She turned to Fox, tears in her eyes, trembling as the adrenalin of the chase started to wash out of her. She wiped away a tear with the back of one hand. Her chest was raw with emotion. It was as if Emily's abduction had just happened, right now, right in front of her. She clenched her fists, growling as much as sobbing as she stamped her feet, looked around the car park. She wanted to destroy something in her frustration, or throw something; not at anything or anywhere, just throw. A strange crinkle of light caught her eye, somewhere off to the right. She turned, trying to work out what it might be. A charcoal smudge appeared out of the hedge at the far end of the car park, a dark blur that darted past in hot pursuit of the departing vehicle. As it ran in front of her, Bel heard a low growl. It was the black dog, the same black dog that had led her to the clearing in the woods. As soon as it passed it dissolved into pale mist under the bright morning sun.

Bel spun round to look at Fox, blinked the remainder of the tears from her eyes and smiled. When she spoke, her words came out slow, deep and sure. 'I know where we need to go. I know where to find Emily.'

~~~~~
~~~~~

Date and time unknown.
Sometime between Friday 14th June 2019 and Saturday 6th July 2019

He held her left hand, but this was no lover's touch. His fingers dug into her wrist, pinning her hand to the cold concrete floor. She tried to resist, to struggle free, but he was too strong. His grip tightened like a vice. She could see the beads of sweat standing out on his forehead.

It was only then that Emily saw the hammer.

An icy bolt of fear slammed into her heart. 'What, what are you doing?'

He brought the hammer up slowly, held it in front of her face, gloating at her fear. She watched wide-eyed in dread fascination as he slowly moved it from side to side, watching as the dull, yellow light bounced off its metal head.

'Please. What are you doing?' Emily renewed her struggles, pulled harder, desperate now to free herself. His hand held tight; his steel grip unmoving.

'Scream as loud as you like, no-one can hear you,' his voice a breathless whisper close to her ear. She could feel the moisture on his breath, smell the sour, curdled odour of stale sweat. He smiled, a long, slow, sardonic smile as she fought to free herself, struggled with a wailing, sobbing strength she didn't know she possessed. In vain. Still his grip held tight.

She could feel her stomach turn over as he raised the hammer above his head, feel the breath escaping from her lungs in stuttering gasps of anticipation as it paused above her. 'No, no, no, no, no!' she begged, her voice a no more than a trembling whimper.

The hammer came down, smashed into her knuckle, shattering the joint into a thousand fragments. She had never known pain like it. Her head reeled, her stomach heaved, her bladder emptied warm down her legs. She screamed at the top of her voice, her face a rictus mask of pain. He lifted the hammer again, took fresh aim. She watched, fascinated, as it came down for a second time, marvelled at the strange spray of blood as the bone flattened to a pulp under the blow. The pain when it hit was so much worse this time. She couldn't remember anything after the hammer rose for the third time.

Her lonely screams were swallowed by the walls, by the trees and the hills; unheard, unheeded.

~~~~~
~~~~~

Friday 5th July 2019
Day Twenty-Two
13:55

The crosshair trembled slightly as he brought the air-rifle to bear. He breathed out, taking his time, then snatched a breath and held it. The tremble ceased. He let his finger squeeze the trigger, feeling the slight recoil against his shoulder. There was a puff of yellow as the pellet hit. The bird fell from the branch.

Mason walked over to where the bird had fallen, retrieved the body, not because he wanted it or needed it, just to hold the warm lifeless thing in his hand, feel the soft downy feathers as it cooled to become just another object.

With the almost weightless body of the greenfinch clutched tight in his hand he walked casually on. He remembered this part of the forest. He was close to his glade, that tiny circle of tussocky grass among the trees where he had hidden those first few bodies, so long ago. On a whim Mason turned towards it, started walking through the trees. Maybe it was time to visit the glade one more time, add this tiny yellow bird to the bodies already buried there; a salute, a remembering.

He swung the corpse of the bird by a wingtip as walked, found the track that he had used so many times in the past, the route that was burned on his memory. A sound made him pause; a voice, then a second in answer. People. The sounds were coming from up ahead, from the direction of the glade. Whoever they were they were making no effort to be quiet. Any sounds he made would have been lost under their own. He moved a few steps to one side, walked in a long arc, staying out of sight, spiralled closer until he could see the tape strung from tree to tree, encircling his secret place like bizarre bunting, saw the inflated blue tent, watched the figures in white moving backwards and forwards in their own slow methodical dance. He knew in an instant why they were there. It could only mean one thing; his private graveyard, that first one from so long ago now, had somehow been discovered, un-covered, found.

A flutter of fear ran through his chest, caught hold of his breath, pinned it to his throat. He dropped to his haunches. There had been no out-of-place sounds to bring his mind into focus, no shouts of surprise to show he had been seen. He knelt there for long minutes, focussing his ears to the sounds around him, sector by sector, like an auditory radar, listening, waiting.

Nothing.

They would have arrested him by now, wouldn't they, if they knew? If they knew. He would have to be more careful from now on, just in case they really were on to him rather than just somehow stumbling across the graves in the clearing, just in case they were following him, watching. He stood up, waited, then turned slowly to look in each direction in turn, watching for that tiny glimmer or movement, that mis-placed patch of colour that would give his enemies away. Minutes passed in silence. When he was sure he was alone he walked quietly away from the glade, headed up into the hills, towards his dungeon, where Mandy waited for him. He increased his pace, his breath thick with anticipation.

A jangle of ice up his spine made him freeze mid-step.

What if they had found it already, the dungeon? What if they had already snatched Mandy away from him, were waiting now in hiding for him to appear, to arrest him, take him away, lock him up?

He beat clenched fists against a tree trunk in frustration. He knew he wouldn't be able to risk going there now. He had no choice but to stay away, at least for a few days, until he could be sure, until he knew it was safe again.

He tried to remember how much food he had taken up there when he had last visited two days ago, how much water. He couldn't remember for sure, but there was nothing he could do about it now. He looked down at his hand, remembered the cooling, yellow body of the greenfinch he had killed so carelessly moments ago. He let it fall to the pine-carpeted ground, turned away, made his circuitous way back down to Manorgrove.

~~~~~
~~~~~

Friday 5th July 2019
14:51
Day Twenty-Two

Bel couldn't sit still, fidgeted in her seat, checking the speed again as Fox carved his way through the suburban traffic, willing him to go faster. 'It's okay, calm down,' he glanced over to smile at her agitation as he cut out onto the opposite side of the road to pass a bus that had pulled into traffic without indicating, 'we'll be there soon enough.' Bel frowned in reply, tried to relax back into her seat. He was good to his word, and soon they were heading out of town on the road towards Harrogate, and the country lane where she had first stumbled across the lay-by from her vision.

There was no doubt in Bel's mind anymore that the black dog she had just seen at the college car park was the same one that had led her into the clearing in the woods, which meant that Emily had been taken by the same man who had killed the other girls. The problem with that thinking was that the dog had taken her to find bodies, dead bodies, so that would mean that they were now going back to the clearing to find Emily's body. If she was already dead and Bel had been fooling herself that she was alive all this time, where did that leave her psychic intuition? A hypnotic flutter of weariness began to creep up on her as she watched the scenery flick by the car window. Everything seemed to have happened so fast these last few days. At this rate she was going to be a basket case before the end of this. She cracked open the window an inch, let the wind push cold vigour into her face. She needed a drink, or at least a strong coffee. She let her head rest against the glass, cool on her forehead, closed her eyes. She didn't open them until the car slowed and Fox pulled into the lay-by, the tyres scuffing up the dusty earth as they came to a halt.

Bel climbed out of the car and stood for a moment to look around, letting the feel of the place wash over her again, a sombre world of dust and monochrome. The bleached-out lay-by was just as before, the dark tarmac serpent of road flicking its tail as it disappeared around the corner, the regiment of trees stood lined up to the very edge of the road. Today though, the trees didn't seem so close to each other, so tightly packed.

She stood looking up and down the road, willing the black dog to leap out, to lead her to Emily, to find her, alive hopefully, and put her dark fears to rest. Nothing. Fox stood beside her, waiting for her to make her move. He glanced across; eyebrows raised. He didn't need to say anything, there was only one question on both their minds. Bel couldn't put the moment off any longer, so she shook her arms loosely to try to release the tension building in her muscles, then walked towards the gap in the trees.

She could feel her breath begin to rasp dry in her throat as she pushed through the undergrowth, Fox close behind. She looked down at the muck and dust of pine needles that she kicked up with each step. The smell caught in her throat, adding to the thirst that had already started to take hold. The place was just as she had remembered it, but felt different in her mind somehow, as if she were approaching from a different direction. Perhaps she was, perhaps the passage of time itself meant she had no choice but to visit the forest from a different mental direction, like the old proverb about not being able to cross the same river twice. After a few steps more Bel pushed through a scissored overhang of branches to stand looking again across the barrier of blue and white tape into the tiny clearing.

The circle definitely seemed to have shrunk since she had last been here, like when you go back to your first school and marvel at the small desks. In reality the clearing was probably less than twenty yards from one end to the other. She knew that this little place should have struck her as beautiful, but the natural serenity only seemed to scrape against her soul. The light felt brittle, the air itself too hard, too dry, too dusty. The pale pink flowers that grew in a clump to one side had been trampled into the earth by the passage of dozens of pairs of feet. She had thought that after the bodies of the girls had been found the place would have been deserted, but three forensics officers clad in grubby white paper boiler suits were still working away. The young one she remembered from last time wasn't there though. Maybe he had been invited to a picnic after all. The three of them looked up as Fox and Bel approached, then turned back to their digging after acknowledging Fox.

Fox reached the tape, hunched down under it, held it up for Bel to follow.

'So, how do you want to do this?' Fox gave a pensive smile.

'I don't know, I guess I wander up and down until something happens. That's sort of been my game plan up until now.' Bel started to move about the clearing, stepping sideways when she came to a patch where the soil had recently been scraped away to recover the body of one of the girls. She knew that she was stalling for time, waiting for the dog to appear, to take her to Emily's body, which her deepest fears told her must be here.

All the time she paced up and down she could feel Fox's eyes fixed on her. 'Can I ask you a question?' he asked.

Bel stopped and turned to face him. 'Go on.' She prepared herself for some sarcastic remark.

'How do you do it? I mean, do you get some sort of a flash of light, or a voice, or what?'

Bel treated him to her second-best old-fashioned look. 'I'm not sure you'd believe me if I told you.'

'This isn't where you come clean and admit it was all some sort of a trick, is it?'

'No. There is no trick. I only wish there was. You must have you heard how some mediums have a spirit guide?'

'Go on.'

'Well, the spirit that keeps coming to me, keeps guiding me, is a dog.'

'What? Hang on. Your guide is a dog? A guide dog? Like a blind person, you mean?'

'No. I keep seeing a dog, a big black dog. A ghost dog, I suppose.' Bel watched his face as she spoke. Nothing. He passed her a bottle of water she hadn't noticed he'd picked up, nodded for her to continue. She took a tepid swig, ploughed on. 'It's important, the dog. It means something. It's connected to the girls we found in the woods, I don't know how, it just is. It keeps appearing. It was here when I came here before, the first time. I couldn't tell you, obviously, but it led me to the clearing, to the girls, to the graves. Then I saw it again today, at the College of Music, in that little car park at the back when I saw Emily being carried out to that truck in my vision. I think it means Emily is here, in this clearing. I think in the end I was wrong. I think she might be dead, that I've missed her somehow.'

'So, you decided to come back here because of the dog?'

'I had to. I guess I'm hoping the dog will be here, that it will show me where her body is. I don't think this is going to be fun.'

'It will confirm that Emily has been taken and killed by the same man.' A statement, not a question.

'The more I think about it, the more sure I am. Why else would the dog show up at the car park like that?'

'Shit!' He growled.

'What? What's wrong?'

'We're no closer, are we? You keep finding the bodies, but we've not got a clue who's doing this, or where they are. As far as I can see the killer himself might as well be a ghost.'

Bel took another swig from the bottle before handing it back to him. Fox drank from it without wiping the neck; she felt an incongruous frisson of intimacy as she watched him. 'So, what do you want to do now?' Fox asked.

'I just want to find Emily.'

One of the crew in the paper boiler suits rustled towards them. 'Sorry to interrupt, Inspector. You'll want to see this.'

'What is it?'

'We've just found another body. It's over there.' He gestured towards another part of the clearing where a woman in a matching paper suit knelt, leaning forward to scrape at the soil in a shallow depression. Bel felt her heart sink. Emily's body was here, after all. And there had been no trace of the dog.

'Shit!' Fox pushed his fingers hard through his hair as if he was trying to scalp himself.

Boiler suit man was still talking. 'We've got the long bones of the legs exposed. This one looks a bit smaller than the others. She must be the younger. Jackie's tracking through, trying to find the skull.' He nodded towards the kneeling woman. He sounded as if he was almost rejoicing in the discovery, which made Bel want to punch him in the face, wipe the smirk off his face, but her bottom lip was trembling, and she knew she was on the point of tears. Fox started walking to where the other man stood pointing.

Bel followed on unsteady feet. She noticed that Jackie looked up as they approached, a broad smile on her face; she too was obviously pleased with her day's work. The first tear began to roll down Bel's cheek. She turned her face away to brush it off. 'Just in time,' Jackie was saying, 'I've got an edge of the skull. I'm just going to lift it now.' She scraped out soil from under a piece of exposed bone, pushed a small trowel into the gap, began to prize it up. It came free with a jerk.

Somewhere just outside the ring of trees the dog barked.

Bel spun round. He had turned up after all. One last goodbye for Emily.

'What's wrong?' Fox spared Bel the merest glance, anxious to concentrate on what was going on in the hollow in front of him.

'Nothing. I thought I heard something.' But Fox wasn't listening. He'd already turned back to the skeleton in the ground.

The dog barked again. Bel took a single step towards the sound. A black shadow seemed to form out of the ground, just beyond the treeline, grew, thickened. There was a long, low, blood-dripping growl, and a rush of movement. The dog burst through the undergrowth, ran into the clearing, aiming straight for Bel. She flinched back, scared that it might be attacking her, even though she knew it wasn't real. It leapt into the air, dived through Bel's chest in a fire of ice, ran on, heading straight towards Jackie. It lunged at her, trying to bite the skull in her hand. Jackie stumbled, a puzzled frown on her face, almost as if for a second she could feel something, some force, some power even though she couldn't see the dog that was attacking her, let the skull drop to the ground. The dog gave a long howl, a mournful cry, full of wolves and tundra and loss that nobody but Bel could hear. She shuddered as a frozen wind rattled through her without stirring the leaves on the trees.

The howl echoed away. Silence. Inside her head mainly, but Bel could feel it spreading through the trees in a widening circle. She stared at the dog as it began to fade out of sight in front of her eyes, felt a hard sense of loss, that bit deep into her heart.

'Ah, fuck!' Fox wiped the back of one hand across his dust-smeared chin.

Head reeling as she turned towards him, still trying to take in what she had just seen, Bel finally found her voice. 'What's wrong?'

'It's a dog. The skeleton. It's a dog. Just a dog.'

Forensics man shrugged his shoulders somewhere in the depths of his boiler-suit. 'Sorry. What can I say? I guess we got it wrong.'

Fox turned away, cursing all the idiots it had ever been his misfortune to work with. Bel stood, trying to work through everything. Back at the College of Music she had been so sure that the dog was going to lead her back here to find Emily, to find her body. Instead, the dog itself had disappeared right in front of her eyes when its own body had been uncovered. Maybe that was it. Maybe this whole thing had been nothing more than the spirit of a dead dog trying to lead her to its body and finding the girls had just been a co-incidence. No, Bel knew that wasn't true. The dog had led her to the exact spot where the remains of Jessica Curtis had been buried. It had wanted Bel to find her, and the other girls. So what had it been trying to show her this time? That this was the end? That it could do no more?

Bel made her way across to the shallow grave where Jessica had lain, looked down at the pitiful scrape in the soil. She waited for the hairs on the back of her neck to bristle up like last time, when she had made contact and that lurch of raw emotion had rolled through her. Nothing. This time as she looked at the spot, it felt more like she was trying to piece together fragments from a half-remembered dream. She could recall the images, but they didn't seem quite real anymore. Where her heart had thumped wildly in her chest, it now beat sedately, barely registering any reaction, because she knew Jessica wasn't there anymore.

This was getting her nowhere. She needed to stop thinking like this. She had to concentrate, bring her thoughts to a tight, bright point, lock onto Emily. Emily was what this was all about. She reached out with her mind, forced herself to relax as she imagined herself standing among the surrounding trees, tried to listen for meaningful sounds in the branches, or perhaps the little yellow bird that had sung its bright, brittle song last time. Everything was quiet. She brought the Mendelssohn to the top of her thoughts again, screaming the notes out as loud as she could inside her head. No effect. Now that their bodies had been taken away there was no reason for the girls' spirits to stay. Each of their life-forces had left. As soon as she formed the thought, she realised Emily couldn't be here, and the reason she couldn't be here was that she must be still alive. The dog really had brought her back here just to watch its own remains being dug from the ground. Bel realised that everything she had done so far had been about the past, about recovering the bodies of the dead. She was all out of ideas, all out of inspiration. She wondered what she would have to do to find a girl who was still alive.

She tried to pull herself out of her blue funk, went to stand next to Fox, a grunt of frustration escaping through gritted teeth. 'I'm sorry, it's no good. I was wrong. She's not here.'

The two of them stood in silence for a few seconds, looking at the scruff of trees in front of them. 'Hey, don't beat yourself up about it,' Fox gave a thin smile of resignation. 'That's a good thing, no? We came here expecting it to be all over, to find Emily's body, remember? Well, we didn't find it, did we, so I'm going to assume she's still alive. We need to re-group, that's all, start again.'

Bel wiped itchy dust off her sweat-smeared brow with the back of one hand and took a swig from the bottle of water Fox held out for her. It tasted just like the rest of this crazy, stupid excursion felt; flat and tepid and unsatisfying. 'Maybe you're right. To be honest, I'm knackered. Right now, I just want a long, hot shower, and a long, cold drink.'

'Come on then, let's get back.' He turned to walk out of the clearing, back towards the road. Bel was only too happy to fall in behind him. She looked at the back of his shirt, not so much a plain white T now as a grubby, sweat-streaked rag. Every tiny branch that flicked in Bel's face made her feel worse. As if he was reading her thoughts, he spoke as he unlocked the car. 'The stuff you've done so far, finding the girls, has been fantastic. Look, we'll go back to Leaside, I can get back to some old-fashioned policing, knocking on doors, asking questions. Something's bound to turn up sooner or later.'

'We both know there are no more doors to knock. And Emily doesn't have time for later. You know and I know that time really is running out for her. We either find her soon, or it's going to be too late.'

'Maybe something will turn up when we trace the girls you found in the woods, talk to their families. We'll find Emily, I promise.' He rested his hand on Bel's forearm, the first time he had shown any proper concern for her. 'Let's get back to civilization, we'll call it a draw for today, start again nice and fresh in the morning. I'll buy you that drink if you like, my treat.' He straightened in his seat, turned the wheel to pull out onto the road. Maybe Bel had been wrong, maybe Fox was straight, and he was making a play.

Bel slumped back in the seat, stared unseeing as the landscape slipped by, her mind empty, wrung out.

~~~~~~
~~~~~~

Friday 5th July 2019
18:05
Day Twenty-Two

Fox brought the car to a halt. Bel jerked her eyes open, looking around as she tried to get her bearings. She recognised the door to her apartment block. 'I thought we were going for a drink.'

'You've been asleep most of the journey back. I figured you'd just want to get home and get some rest. We can maybe get a drink another time, when we have something to celebrate.'

'Or you could come up with me anyway and we could open the bottle you brought this morning. Just for the hell of it.'

'Sounds nice, but look at me, I'm filthy. I should get home, get a shower.'

'I've got a shower too, you know. My washing machine will sort your clothes out in about ten minutes flat, and while you're waiting you can try on my biggest, pinkest dressing gown.' Bel tried to make the words as casual as she could. In the couple of seconds before he answered she could feel her heart doing flip-flops in her chest.

'I'm tempted, I must admit. It's not often I get a chance to try on a fluffy pink dressing gown.'

'That's settled, then.' Bel climbed out of the car, opened the foyer door. She heard the clunk of the car door closing behind her, held the door open for Fox to follow.

They walked up to the first floor in silence. Bel spent the few seconds checking in her head that all traces of Nigel had been removed from the apartment. As she turned the key in the lock she had completed her mental tour and was confident Nigel was out of her life; not that she was planning for anything to happen with Fox, she reminded herself.

'The bathroom's through here,' Bel opened the door. 'Throw your dirty clothes out onto the bathroom floor and I'll put them in the washer. There's a couple of spare toothbrushes in the cabinet if you feel the need and I'll put glass of wine on the vanity unit for when you've finished, next to the dressing gown.'

'Er, okay, thanks. Just one thing,' Fox smiled as he pulled open the shower door, 'is it just me, or does this seem a little bit weird?' He pulled the t-shirt over his head, let it drop to the floor.

Bel looked at the lean cut of his body, tried not to stare, tried not to let her mouth fall open. 'What's weird about inviting a man into your home to try on your clothes?' She smiled and turned away, resisting the temptation to look back as she walked out of the bathroom. She went through into the kitchen, took the bottle of rose out of the fridge and poured two glasses. A small part of her was disappointed to find that the shower screen was opaque with steam as she went back to pick up his dirty clothes from the bathroom floor. She left his wine, and the dressing gown, then moved through to the tiny utility room next to the kitchen. In a few seconds she had shrugged off her own clothes, bundled everything into the drum, hit the button to start a fifteen-minute wash-and-dry cycle. She walked naked through to her bedroom, relishing the frisson of knowing that Fox could appear out of the bathroom at any second. She wondered what he would say, what he would do, if he did. In the bedroom Bel wrapped herself in a silky dark green dressing gown before making her way into the living room. After a few minutes Fox came into the room, seeming bigger crammed into the pink dressing gown, towelling his blond hair dry, a shy grin on his face.

'The bottle's on the coffee table if you want to top up your glass. Now it's my turn in the shower. I'll be back in a few minutes.'

Bel stood under the stream of hot water for a few seconds, letting the spray hammer on the top of her head. She could feel the water begin to ease the tension in her neck and shoulders. When she stepped out a few minutes later she felt altogether more human. Clean made such a difference.

Fox was sitting on the sofa nursing his glass to his chest as Bel walked in. He shuffled more upright. Bel picked up the bottle from the coffee table, leaned over Fox to top up his glass. Looking back later Bel wondered if she had been subconsciously planning this right back to this morning when Fox had given her the wine. If she had, her subconscious was far smarter than she was, right down to having her put on the chiffon dressing gown, which, as she leaned forward to pour the wine, slipped an inch. Bel watched Fox's glance move to her cleavage. She was definitely showing some serious bosom.

'Sorry, sorry, I shouldn't have…' Fox became flustered as he realised Bel had noticed his quick glance. He leaned forward to put his wine glass on the coffee table.

Bel's body acted without her permission. Her fingers tugged at her dressing gown, letting it fall open to reveal a strip of flesh a few inches wide that ran from her throat all the way to her thighs. She stepped forward, the flesh of her stomach less than an inch from Fox's face; she could feel his hot breath on her belly. Bel put both hands around Fox's head and pulled him towards her until his lips were touching her skin. Fox didn't move for almost a whole second; Bel began to panic that she had made a terrible mistake. Then Fox's lips parted slightly, and he breathed in deeply as he began to taste the soft sweetness of her skin. Bel felt the breath catch in her throat. In one powerful movement Fox stood up, lifting Bel effortlessly in his powerful arms. The bedroom door was open. He carried her through, opened the pink dressing gown, let it fall to the floor as he placed her on the bed as if she were a delicate flower.

~~~~~
~~~~~

Date and time unknown.
Sometime between Friday 14th June 2019 and Saturday 6th July 2019

She could feel the hot waves of pain pulsing through her hand even before she opened her eyes. It felt as if she was wearing some strange, thick, heavy glove. The blood pounded in her fingers as if her hand was going to burst.

Emily drew herself up onto her knees and held her mutilated hand up in front of her face. She couldn't stop it trembling, no matter how she tried. She looked at the damaged, distorted knuckles on her left hand, at the ragged splits in the skin, the clots of blood around the wounds. Bruises covered the whole of her fingers and climbed all the way to her wrist, clouds of purple pain writhing under her skin.

Emily's head flinched back as she replayed in her mind's eye the hammer coming down, the spray of blood that erupted from the first blow, the sight of the hammer as it slowly rose for a second time. After that, nothing. She must have passed out, or maybe her mind simply ran away and hid from the true horror of what was happening.

She stared at her hand, turned it to examine the other side. Straightening her fingers was impossible. When she tried to move them, slowly, gently, carefully, with the fingers of her right hand, there was a disturbing, grating feeling under her skin, as if her whole hand was filled with a million shards of broken glass.

Her eyes filled with tears as the thought she had been hiding from herself finally bubbled to the surface, and she rocked backwards and forwards on her haunches, keening in grief at the realisation of her loss. The damage to her hand was so bad she couldn't imagine how she would ever be able to play the violin again.

After a time, her wailing sank into fitful sobs, and a gut-deep weariness gouged into her stomach, overwhelming her. She crawled back to the mattress and curled into a foetal ball. Sleep crashed over her in a dark tsunami.

Time was the thing she had never been able to keep track of. She had thought she would know instinctively deep down inside herself, but everything seemed to be wrapped in an amnesiac fog. Part of her had worked out that she must have been here more than a week, from the number of times she has eaten, and, laughably, been to the toilet. She never imagined that her life would be measured in bowel movements. On the other hand, she hadn't started her period yet, so she couldn't have been here more than two weeks. It felt so much longer. Maybe the stresses and traumas she has been through had caused her period to stall on itself. She gave up trying to keep track of individual days after she realised the bottles of water she was forced to drink from had all been opened before she got them. At least that would explain the permanent fatigue that surrounded her, the wooziness that made her thoughts stutter inside her head. In the end it didn't really matter; she slept, she woke, she ate, she suffered. The minutes followed each other, composed of long, sorrowful seconds, and the only release was when exhaustion dragged her under again, and sleep returned to comfort her.

She didn't dream anymore.

When she woke again, she tried to gather her thoughts, to concentrate above the current of pain that ran through her body, to come up with some plan of action to help her cope with the terrible mutilation of her hands. She had to get a grip, because if she lost focus for a second, allowed the fears she held in check deep in her stomach to escape, to bubble to the surface, she knew she would never be able to come back from the edge of that precipice.

Being in control was the only answer. She looked again at the mutilated mess that was the remains of her hand. The blood and crust had solidified while she slept, and her hand itself had swollen to more than twice its normal size. The pain was always there, but now that she had got over the initial horror, it had settled into a rolling, throbbing ache that she had managed to push to the back of her mind.

Some instinct told her she had to clean the wounds. Things were bound to look better once she cleaned things up, she told herself. Besides, she worried about getting an infection. Without medical help that was something she really didn't want to have to think about.

She opened a bottle of water, no longer expecting the crack of a breaking seal, and poured a splash over her hand. Drugged or not, she knew the water was going to be better than nothing. It felt icy cold as it washed over her hot swollen skin, soothing where it touched. She dabbed at her wounds with wet wipes, gently brushing at the crusted blood, until her hand was more or less clean.

The open wounds looked better now, but still a mass of ragged, bruised flesh, and the whisper of fear rose again inside Emily's head.

She remembered when she first woke up to find herself in this place, how everything had seemed strange, bizarre, unreal. It wasn't until the man had appeared and the beatings and rapes started that Emily realised she wasn't travelling in some gruesome dream, that this was real, this was happening.

And now this.

Up until this moment she had held a slim, secret hope in the depths of her heart; that something would happen, that the man would have an epiphany of conscience and let her go, or the police would work out what had happened, trace her movements, find this secret place, rescue her, take her home, to her Mum, her life, her world. She sobbed at the burning, acid thought as she realised anew that she would never see her Mother again.

Emily looked once more at her twisted, broken hand, the swelling under the skin, the heat the wounds gave off. She knew that she desperately needed medical attention, and she was equally sure she wasn't going to get it any time soon. She finally started to accept the fatigue in her heart with a sigh, and the realisation that all hope had gone, that she was never going to escape this place, that she was going to die here.

Now that she was honest with herself, she could admit that she had always known what this whole sick episode was about, right from that first moment when she had struggled to wake up and take in her strange new surroundings, from the first time she had seen the man standing in the doorway. Not the specifics, those would be locked forever inside her captor's mind, but she had known there could be no escape.

Then he had raped her.

Nothing that bad was ever going to end good.

He would keep coming back to beat her and choke her and rape her, and mutilate her, again and again. She wondered how long it would be until he got angry or bored or carried away and killed her as he was choking her, going just a little further to get his kicks each time until he made a mistake. Or killed her anyway, as part of his thing. It might be his whole thing. He might come back next time to smash the fingers on her other hand, then a foot, a leg, her back, her skull.

She wondered if he had done it before. He must have done, she realised with a chill certainty. How many times, how many girls had woken up in this strange, terrible place to realise they were being kept alive in a small hell? How many had he raped, killed?

Or maybe he wanted to get her pregnant, rape her again and again, force her to have his baby. Maybe he has some perverted need to be head of a family, even if it was only one he had created in the sick depths of his twisted mind.

There had been that case in the papers, she vaguely remembered, years ago when she was a little girl. Some weirdo somewhere in Europe had kept a girl in a cellar, and she had brought up a child there, the child of her rapist, her captor. Emily couldn't remember how it had ended, if the girl had escaped or died and the bodies of her and her child were not found until years later.

She wondered how it would end for her, and when. A hot anger grew in Emily as she realised she didn't want to be at the mercy of this nasty, creepy little man anymore.

She knew she wouldn't be able to cope, kept here forever, an object to be used and abused again and again until her willpower crumbled to nothing and she accepted this as normal, this became her world, her life. She would rather kill herself than allow him to have that sort of control over her. The still, small, part of her brain that she kept hidden deep inside realised, understood, the part that she told herself was normal, pushed forward an idea. If she killed herself it would somehow mean she had won, that her death would be her escape, her victory over this evil man. She started to laugh as she realised this was her "normal" part doing the thinking.

Would she be able to do it though, now that she came to actually think about it? Could she really kill herself, if she needed to? When she needed to, she corrected herself She wondered when she would know; what final gasp of despair would finally force her hand? At what point would she abandon her last forlorn hope of rescue, of escape, of home?

She didn't even know how she would do it. What could she use for a weapon? It wasn't as though she was surrounded by sharp knives, just lying around for her to snatch up and start hacking at her flesh, or his, she wished. Without a weapon the only thing she could think of was to dash her brains out against the walls of this prison that he had her kept in. She was pretty sure she remembered seeing it in a film once. Some prisoner in olden times was being repeatedly tortured, until he knew he was going to reveal all his secrets, or betray his king, or something. He had run at the wall of his cell with his head down and killed himself. That was all very well in a film, but was it true, would it work in real life? Would she be able to do it? Would she really be able to hit her head against the wall hard enough to kill herself, without flinching, without pulling back? And then a new idea formed in her head, and she knew instantly what she was going to do.

Toilet roll.

She would screw up a ball of toilet paper and stuff it down her throat. Not swallow it, but ram it down into her windpipe, deep enough and hard enough to make her choke. She just had to hope she would be able to control the force that was sure to rise inside her, that she would pass out before her desperate survival instinct urged her to pull it out.

It wasn't much of a plan, she knew, but it was the only one she had.

If she could commit suicide, she could escape, stop him abusing her, using her, treating her like a piece of meat, like an object, a possession. In fact, it would be the most real escape possible; an escape from everything.

That was what it was really about, she knew. He may think her owned her, had her in his power, under his control, but she was determined to not relinquish herself, her inner identity, she would not be a possession. Nobody owned Emily Phillips except Emily Phillips.

A strange joy filled her heart. Now she had a plan, something to focus on, a source of comfort in the depths of her despair. Now she could take control, with one last wilful act. Her head spun, she rejoiced inside, knowing that she had stolen back the whole game from him. She knew she could hold on now a little bit longer, now that she knew she didn't have to.

Her head filled with music, unbidden, the Mendelssohn. She looked across the dank little room to the shattered remains of her violin, broken on the cold, hard floor. Her parched lips cracked in a smile. She would have to use the other violin, the one she kept in her head.

She knelt on the mattress, gritting her teeth against the pain in her shoulder, the scratches and bruises on her arms and legs, ignoring the frozen bar of agony across her throat, the mutilated mess that was her hand. She held her hands just so, felt the crushed fingers of her left hand settle gently on imaginary strings, balanced the unfelt weight of the bow in her other. She held her breath for a second, bringing the music to a pinpoint focus in her mind, then struck the first note with a confidence and power that came from the depths of her soul, rose in her head, in her heart.

The sound of music filled the tiny room, and for a brief moment Emily Phillips escaped her prison.

~~~~~
~~~~~

Saturday 6th July 2019
07:55
Day Twenty-Three

Bel was making her way along a dank, poorly lit corridor. The walls were bare brickwork, dripping moisture. Bel's head throbbed as she passed under a flickering old fluorescent light that only seemed to throw the shadows around her into sharper relief. There were rusty metal doors on each side of the passageway, all closed and padlocked. There was a sign on each door. Bel slowed to read them as she walked past. The first one said credenza; then, Mr Murdoch; next, Nigel's flat. She was puzzled by one that read; Sarah's funeral. Bel knew she needed to read each sign, knew she was searching for a particular one, but couldn't remember what it would say, though she knew she had seen it before. She hoped she would know it when she saw it. At the next door Bel read the word croissants. She took a deep breath, smelled the warm, just baked aroma. She frowned, moved to the next door. As she turned her gaze to read the next word, a fresh coffee smell added itself to that of the croissants.

Bel opened her eyes.

Fox was standing by the bed, the pink dressing gown too tight around his lean frame, a tray in his hands and a sheepish grin on his face.

'Good morning,' he said. 'I figured I would make breakfast; I hope you don't mind. No sugar, right?'

Bel sat up, rubbing her eyes, grateful for a chance to cover her face for a second while she dragged her thoughts together.

Fox rested the tray on the bed, sat down next to it, picked up a mug to pass to Bel. 'Listen, about last night…'

'Thatcher's Hamlet!' Bel felt an electric jolt as her brain caught up with what she had seen in her dream. She jumped up, scrambled to get out of bed.

'What the hell!' Fox hastily tried to steady the cup and scoop up the tray at the same time. It didn't work. A stain of coffee spread on the duvet.

Bel didn't even notice. 'Thanks for the coffee. I'll be right back. Shower.' She took a slurp, passed the mug back to Fox, and hurried out of the bedroom.

'That's okay, I'll just wait here.' Fox sat on the bed again, took a drink of his coffee.

'Run it by me again, but this time remember to breath while you're talking.' Fox was driving as they headed along the county roads that would take them out through Otley and on towards Swinsty reservoir.

Bel turned sideways in her seat to face him. 'I had a dream, this morning, just as I was waking up; one of my visions, if you like.'

'Which explains why you threw coffee all over the bed.'

'I'd let myself get distracted by the dead girls in the clearing and the ghost dog. I should have been thinking about Emily. She isn't in the woods because she's not dead. He buries them in the clearing when he's finished with them; it's his private graveyard if you like, but before that, he has to have somewhere to keep them prisoner, to rape and torture them, to play his twisted games.'

'And that's why we're going to Thatcher's Hamlet?'

'That's where I was going when I first saw the lay-by,' she continued, her voice starting to go squeaky as she tried to contain her excitement. 'There was this thing with a map and my laptop. Anyway, I was going there when I pranged my car at the lay-by. Once we found the girls the how and the why I got there got pushed to the back of my mind. The only reason I was anywhere near the other girls is that I was on my way to Thatcher's Hamlet. That's where Emily is, I'm sure of it.'

Fox concentrated on driving. Bel just sat there, hugging herself. She began to feel cold, some sort of emotional shock maybe. Her earlier euphoria at remembering about Thatcher's Hamlet had evaporated, and now she swam in a tidal pull of brackish self-doubt. She was still worrying about the ghost dog. The dog had guided her to the clearing to find the girls, but now it was gone, disappearing for good after they had found its own body in the clearing. So now she was worried that the whole thing might fall apart around her and she would find herself in Thatcher's Hamlet with no clue as to where Emily might be, and no way to find her.

'Here we go.' Fox nodded towards a signpost, slowed to a crawl, turned off the road. The sign was covered in a scummy layer of green mould, half hidden behind a scrub of weeds. Bel wound down the window, craning her neck to look around as they drove down what she guessed must be main street. The flat, drained, feeling that had built up in her on the drive over began to melt away, and he could feel the adrenalin start to bubble and fizz in her veins as she peered from side to side, anxious to not miss anything.

In the back of her mind she had been expecting the place to be full of chocolate-boxy cottages with roses and wisteria around the doors, and a cricket pitch on the village green. What she hadn't been expecting was the smell. It scraped across her sinuses, a combination of heat, dust and the sour stink of cow shit and piss. After a few minutes her nose gave up trying to cope and shut down. After that it didn't seem too bad. It turned out there was no cricket pitch and no village green, but main street seemed nice enough, apart from the smell; a few well-kept little houses, hanging baskets overflowing with flowers, neat little lawns, a tiny church just around one corner. It wasn't all pretty-pretty, though. There was a run-down farm on the right that Bel at first thought was derelict until she saw the dog chained up in the yard. It seemed to be mostly guarding a rusting old tractor that looked like it hadn't moved in years. The dog sat up and sniffed the air as they drove past, reserving the right to bark.

Main street ended at a T-junction. The church was to the right. Fox turned left. They passed another row of cottages, these less well-kept, with paint-flaky window frames and shabby lawns. After the cottages there were a couple of run-down old barns and a few lean-to buildings before the road petered out to become a country lane again.

Fox pulled the car to a gentle halt at the side of the road. 'Did you get anything?'

Bel could hear the desperation in his words, hoping against hope that she had got something. She stared down the lane as it narrowed into the distance, featureless apart from one wide drive with a dark green sign on the right, shrugged her shoulders in mute response. She felt so frustrated. Just for those few seconds, when she had remembered about this place back at her apartment the hope had welled up in her so fast, she had felt almost winded with anticipation, but now they were actually here there was just nothing. The ghost dog was nowhere to be seen. 'No. Not a thing, sorry,' she said.

'We can drive around a bit more, if you think it will help,' Fox said. Bel didn't know how to answer, shrugged again.

Fox eased the car a bit further down the lane, reversed into the drive to drive back up the lane. 'I'll arrange for a team to come and have a poke around, get them to check over some of those out-buildings, interview whoever lives in that stinky farmhouse and the cottages. You never know, we might get lucky.' He looked across at Bel, but Bel had stopped listening. She was staring at the sign at the side of the driveway. Fox followed her gaze upwards, then back to her face. 'What is it?'

'The sign.' As she spoke, a scruffy dark green van turned in, headed up the drive. Bel grabbed Fox's arm, her fingers digging deep. 'That van. It's just like the one from the College of Music. The one that I saw in my vision.'

'Fuck.' Fox gripped the wheel, pulled it hard over, bounced the car up the grass verge as he struggled to turn it round in the narrow space. He stamped on the gas and the gravel kicked up as they set off in pursuit.

The van had already disappeared out of sight around a bend in the long drive. As he took the bend Fox had to slam on the brakes. A red and white barrier barred there way. Sitting primly next to it was a tiny cabin. A pale-faced girl with "invisible" dental braces seemed to have a genuine smile on her face as she leaned out of the cubicle window. 'Welcome to Manorgrove. Admission is two pounds fifty per vehicle, and last entry is at five pee em.'

'We're not here to visit,' Fox returned her smile with one that almost matched but was empty of emotion. 'I need to speak to whoever's in charge.' The warrant card appeared in his hand, hovered in front of the girl's face while she read it and her mouth started to fall open.

'If you stop in front of the main house, reception is through the big doors and on the right,' she pointed towards the large house at the top of the rise. The barrier rose, Fox threw the clutch, and the vehicle skittered up the drive.

It was supposed to be some sort of a stately home from what Bel could see, but it wasn't massive, and although it must have been nice in its day, she could see it badly needed a lick of paint around the windows. A piece of guttering hung down from the roof, pointing back down the drive. There was a stripy lawn and a small ornamental lake at the front, but the view to the other side was obscured by shrubs and fence panels. A few dozen people were wandering about, family groups mainly. To one side was an 'Olde Worlde' signpost, indicating the way to among other things a bird garden, hedge maze, picnic area and petting zoo.

Fox locked up the wheels and was out of the car almost before it had stopped moving, striding up the stone steps towards the huge heavy wooden doors at the top two at a time. Bel followed as quickly as she could. She could see the look of impatience on his face as he waited at the top, holding open one of the doors. He walked through as she caught up. Bel followed. In spite of the place being slightly tatty, there was no disguising the fact that the house belonged to somebody with serious wealth, the sort that's not only wide in the wallet, but deep in heritage too. Two huge staircases defined the entrance hall, sweeping down in wide arcs from balconies on either side of the first floor to arrive exactly facing the dark oak double entrance doors. A suit of armour stood in front of each of the newel posts at the bottom. There were flags and banners displayed on every wood-panelled wall, trophies from what Bel guessed must have been every battle of every war in the last five hundred years, along with sweeping displays of longswords and pikestaffs. An enormous coat of arms dominated the wall above the granite fireplace that itself must have been at least six feet tall. 'Et non esse timorem' the motto offered in a pale blue ribbon under a white boar squaring off against a lion. Bel's heart skipped a beat as she saw it, and she felt a cold claw drag down her spine. It was the same emblem that Bel had seen hidden in the dirt and grime on the side of the van in her vision at the College of Music, the same emblem on the sign at the bottom of the drive, and again on the van that had passed them as they sat there wondering what to do next.

Fox didn't seem to have noticed any of this, walked straight to the reception desk. 'Detective Inspector Fox. I need to speak to whoever is in charge. Now.' He wasn't loud, but his voice had a penetrating timbre that was impossible to ignore.

The girl behind the desk was beautifully made up, had probably come to work this morning expecting nothing more exciting than a little light manicure and some gentle web-browsing for handbags and shoes. No-one who looked that good expected to be exerting themselves. Bel looked at her, knowing that she would never be able to put in the effort needed to maintain that standard, even if she had nothing more taxing to do than sit around all day eating peeled grapes. The girl looked at Fox, a flash of lust in her eyes, until she spotted the warrant card. She jolted upright, then jumped off her high stool and hurried to a glass-panelled door. She tapped nervously before opening the door and poking her head into the room.

'It's the police, Mr Matthews,' she said, sounding flustered. Fox pushed past as she spoke, walked into the room, Bel hurried along behind, swept up in his wake.

The room was a cramped, dishevelled space with a small desk and chair, and a couple of filing cabinets that took up most of the rest of the room. Mr Matthews turned out to be pale and chubby, with a receding hairline and a sheen of sweat covering his brow. He was squeezed in behind the desk, his legs overhanging both sides of the small chair, and he looked hot and bothered as he glanced up from the computer screen, peering at the interruption over thick-rimmed glasses. He stood with a sheepish smile, held out one podgy hand to shake with Fox. He had a diamond-cut signet ring on one finger, fat bulging out on either side. 'Nicholas Matthews. I'm the estate manager. How can I be of assistance?'

Fox ignored his outstretched hand. 'DI Fox, West Yorkshire Police.' He produced his warrant card again, allowing Matthews to see it for less than a second. 'We're investigating the kidnap of a young woman and we have reason to believe she is being held somewhere on these premises.'

Matthews let his hand drop to his side. 'But that's not possible. I mean... how?' He raised his hand again for his fingers to twitch at the knot of his tie, smooth his receding hairline, back to the tie, before finally coming to rest on the corner of the desk, a look on his face as if he had just lost a pound and found a penny.

'We've just followed a van onto the estate,' Fox continued, 'dark green, a large logo on the door.'

'Yes, that would be part of the fleet based here at Manorgrove. You're referring to the Standale crest. We have almost a dozen liveried vehicles on the estate, Brunswick green. They're for the maintenance team, mainly, and the animal welfare staff. There's a large workshop at the rear.'

'Take me there.'

'Are you seriously suggesting that this kidnap of yours has something to do with the estate, with one of our vehicles?'

'That's exactly what I'm suggesting. Now, take me to where the vans are kept.'

'I'm sorry, Detective Inspector, but as I understand these things, don't you need a search warrant, or some such?'

'Yes. You are, of course, quite right.' Fox seemed to have slipped into a copy of the other man's speech. Bel looked on, trying to work out if he was empathising, or if it was a display of mockery. She should have known. 'I shall phone my Chief Superintendent. The warrant will, unfortunately, have to be in the name of the owner.' He started to take out his phone. 'How are we spelling Standale?'

Fox's words hit the spot. 'Perhaps you could give me a moment, Inspector.' Matthews turned his back, picked up the phone on his desk, spoke for a moment in hushed, almost inaudible tones, then listened for several seconds, before replacing the handset. He ran the tip of his tongue over his lips, plump, moist, sent his fingers to do another circuit of his tie, his hair and the corner of the desk. 'His Lordship requests that you obtain a warrant as soon as reasonable, but in the meantime, I am to offer you any assistance you may require.'

'Splendid,' beamed Fox. 'Lead on.'

As they swept back out through reception, Matthews, Fox and Bel, the receptionist stared, open-mouthed, the envy of exclusion etched across her face.

All the way on the long walk up to the workshop Matthews kept up a kind of low-grade monologue under his breath about the prospects of a crime having been committed by someone in his lordship's employ. Fox ignored him, lengthened his stride, forcing Matthews to skip and hop every few steps in an effort to stay ahead of the man he was supposed to be leading.

The workshop wasn't just a building, it was huge, a space the size of a hangar, tall roller doors open at both ends letting in the warm summer breeze, work benches along the sides strewn with machine parts and tools. Bigger machines, ride-on lawnmowers and mini diggers awaited repair in bits on the floor. Bel tried to take it all in, her eyes tracking the length of the workshop to where, near the far entrance, stood a row of car-sized vans, painted in that dull dark green. As soon as she saw them Bel felt her chest tighten and she knew they were in the right place. As she watched, the driver's door of one van began to open and a man in brown dungarees eased himself out. Fox was on his toes in a second, bumping Bel's shoulder as he rushed forward, hurrying towards the man, hollering at the top of his voice. 'Police! You! Stay right where you are! Don't move a muscle!'

The man stared open-mouthed as this growling beast in jeans and a T-shirt pounded towards him. He gripped the driver's door, cowered behind it as Fox hammered on the bonnet of the van. 'Get out here, now!'

'What's wrong? What's happening?'

Fox leaned across, grabbed him by one strap of his dungarees, almost lifting him off his feet as he dragged him around to the front of the van, pinning him on the bonnet. 'Is this him?' he shouted across to Bel as she hurried to catch up. A single glance told her all she needed to know; the man was too thin, too stooped, too wiry to be the killer. She dismissed him with a brief shake of the head.

'Matthews.' The single word almost a bark as it escaped Fox's lips. He reluctantly released the man with a shove. 'Are these all of the vans? You said there were other vans on the estate?'

Matthews' head nodded as he counted off the vans in front of him. 'There are these, and another four in the team. They'll still be out working.'

'Get it in touch with the drivers. Tell them to stop work right now and come back here. Don't say anything about my investigation.' There was a pause as Matthews stared at him. 'Go on, then. Do it.'

Matthews fingers fluttered towards a pocket, pulled out a mobile phone and he started dialling.

Fox draped an arm over Bel's shoulder, pulled her head close to his, spoke in a low voice. 'I'm going to phone for the forensics team. They'll get here as soon as they can.' He walked her around to the other side of the van, opened the passenger door, 'but it might be an hour or two before they turn up. If you're up for it, I reckon you and me can crack this thing before they even get here.'

Bel saw a sharp glint in his eye. There was a hunger there that she had never noticed before, and she knew then that she would never want to cross him. 'What are you wanting to do?'

'We need to move quickly on this, before people here find out what we're doing and start trying to cover their tracks. I want you to stay close to me while I take a look in these vans. If you see anything, or feel anything, it doesn't matter how small or insignificant it might be, sing out. It just might be the one thing that makes all the difference, okay?' He smiled a confidence in her that she didn't feel herself. For a fleeting second, she suspected that if they had been standing a bit closer, he would have hugged her, or again it might just have been her mis-reading the jumble of signals after the previous evening. The moment passed and Fox turned back to the van. Bel did as she was told, moved in to stand close behind him as he opened the passenger door, leaned into the cabin, started going through the door pockets, glove box, running his hand over the grubby fabric of the seats and carpet. Bel checked out the muscular shape of his back as she watched Fox work. He settled into a focussed silence as he moved methodically through the space, skipping nothing.

More than a minute passed, then, with a sigh he stood up, gave a slight shake of his head, moved round to the back of the van and swung open the cargo doors. 'Shit!' Bel stood next to him, stared inside, looking for something to call a clue among the mess of tools, bags of sand and lengths of wood piled in there. After a few seconds scowling Fox hunkered down and started moving bits and pieces out of the van, piling them on the concrete floor. She watched intently, hoping for something to light up as Fox dragged it out, but nothing offered even a spark of intuition. When he had finally emptied everything out of the van, he looked across to her, eyebrows raised in hope. She could only shrug, shake her head. He nodded in acknowledgement, moved to the next van, leaving the contents of the first strewn on the workshop floor, no longer his concern. Twice more he made his methodical way around a vehicle, opened each door, carried out the same fingertip search. As he started to wipe his hand across the seats of the fourth van there was a small catch of sound in his throat. He paused, then slowly stood, keeping his movements under rigid control. He turned to face Bel, held one finger to pursed lips, a reminder to not break the silence. Only his blue eyes were alive, guiding her to look at his other hand, clenched, white-knuckled at his side. Slowly, he held his hand out towards her, uncurled his fingers. There, resting on his palm, a green and gold scrunchie. 'I've just found this in the passenger side footwell,' he said, his voice little more than a murmur. 'It's got to be Emily's. Tell me if you can see anything.'

Bel took the little curl of fabric gently from his grip. At the first touch she let go a gasp.

The light was softer, the sun shining from a different direction, lower in the sky. She was standing in front of the van. The van was on a rough track, but there was no clue as to where she was. Bel took a step back, tried to compose herself. She shivered as she saw the man she'd watched at the College of Music climb from the driver's seat, walk to the rear of the van. She had no choice but to watch, to follow. He flung the doors wide, leaned inside. Bel struggled to see over one shoulder, but his bulk took up most of the opening. She moved a little closer, and the man evaporated in front of her as she stared into the van. There was a thin, grubby mattress thrown on the floor of the van, strewn among the tools and parts, and on the mattress the figure of Emily Phillips, curled up, looking cold, scratched and bruised, slumped unconscious. The man leaned in, his hands and arms sweeping right through Bel, reached down to scoop up the frail sleeping girl, carried her out of the van, towards the trees. Bel turned to watch but he faded from sight. A voice whispered from somewhere far away, as if carried on a phantom breeze, 'Help me.'

Bel pushed the scrunchie back into Fox's hand. She had touched it for less than a second, but that had been more than enough. She leaned towards him, whispered her response. 'Emily was here, in the back of this van. I've just seen her.'

Fox pushed the scrunchie into the pocket of his jeans, turned to Matthews. 'Whose van is this?'

'Er, I don't know, I'll have to check. The logbooks and maintenance records are kept in the workshop office.' Matthews pointed to a little shed within the shed, tucked into one corner. Fox hurried over, emerged a few seconds later from the poky little room, thumbing through a tattered old ledger. As he got closer, Bel could make out the letters and numbers written large in black marker pen on the front cover. Even upside-down, she was able to make out the registration number of the van, this van. Written underneath, a name. 'Who,' Fox asked as he stood toe to toe in front of Matthews, 'is David Mason?'

'He works here on the estate. He's one of the groundskeepers.' Matthews almost stuttered in his haste to answer, shuffled backwards under the power of Fox's scowl.

'And does he always drive this van? Does anyone else get to drive it?'

'As far as I know the men generally keep to their own vehicles. Some of them take a personal pride in their vans, they keep their own tools and bits and pieces in them, so they're not going to let just anyone drive it.' Bel looked in at the grubby state of the driver's cabin, wondered about this man Mason's definition of personal pride.

'And where's Mason now?' asked Fox.

'I don't know, exactly. The men work shifts, early starts, weekends. There's a rota. You could try his cottage. The staff are free to come and go when they're not working. From what I understand he spends a lot of his spare time up in the woods. I don't know what he does up there. It's none of my concern.'

Fox shot Bel a glance, his eyes on fire, then looked back at Matthews. 'Mason has a cottage? Here on the estate?'

'It's a tied property,' Matthews replied. 'A few of the un-married men have them. They generally move out or move on when they get married.'

'So, Mason is single. Does he have a girlfriend? Or a boyfriend, maybe?'

'Not that I'm aware of, but I don't take an interest in the personal lives of the workforce.'

'Take me to his cottage.'

Matthews led the way, again muttering to himself all the while. As Fox followed, his phone made a pulsating buzz. He put it to his ear, grunted a small thank you. 'The warrant to search Manorgrove has been processed. The whole of the estate and everyone on it now answers to me.'

~~~~~
~~~~~

Saturday 6th July 2019
11:12
Day Twenty-Three

It turned out there were three cottages sitting in a quaint little courtyard tucked away at the back of the big house. They must have been at least a hundred years old, roofs dipping where supporting beams had bowed under the relentless weight of thick sandstone roof-tiles, random stone walls with thick layers of mortar, uneven windows, and not quite straight doors. In different circumstances Bel would have relished a chance to draw up a blurb; any one of them would have been sure to sell in seconds. 'It's this one,' Matthews almost bowing in subservience to Fox as he pointed at the first cottage.

Fox thumped on the door with the heel of his hand. He hit it so hard the windows rattled. A bird, not heard until now, stopped singing, listened to the hectic noise. Fox thumped again. Nothing. He rubbed at a grubby window with the flat of his hand and looked into the kitchen. 'It looks like our friend Mr Mason isn't home.' He turned, smiled that cold smile again, spoke to Matthews. 'Thank you for your assistance, we can take it from here.'

Matthews looked indignant, opened his mouth as if he was about to protest, but Fox just looked at him coldly. Matthews lowered his eyes, turned and walked away, head down, back towards the main house. Fox looked up at the sky, stared at clouds, almost as if he was counting under his breath. When he reached a total that only he knew, he bent down, picked up a fist-sized rock, hefted it in his hand as if somehow judging its relative charms, turned, and casually rammed it through the glass window of the kitchen door.

'Are you allowed to do that?' Bel asked as Fox reached one hand through the newly made circle of glass daggers and unlatched the lock.

'I've got a warrant, remember. Come on, let's take a bit of a look around.' The heavy wooden door scraped on the uneven stone floor slabs as he pushed it open, reminding Bel for a second of the scrape of Gran's cellar door, so long ago now.

She followed Fox into the kitchen.

It was obvious that Mason didn't have a girlfriend. To judge by the state of the place he hadn't been in anything approaching a relationship for years. Everything in the kitchen carried a patina of grime, deeper than dust. Some sort of machine parts sat on the draining board next to a pile of dishes that hadn't been washed for so long the food had dried and started to flake off.

'So,' Bel pulled her gaze away from the encrusted dishes, turned to Fox. 'How do you want to play this?'

'We've got some time before the forensics team gets here,' he replied, 'I thought we might have a quick look around. This might be the only chance we get, and like you said, time is running out for Emily, and fast.'

'So, what are we waiting for?' Bel moved to a cupboard, opened the door. A quick glance inside, looking for she didn't know what. She found cups, plates, nothing special, moved to the next one. Tins of food, biscuits, dry goods. This was stupid. She gave up on cupboards, scraped an old chair out from under the table and sat down, began to look around the room, hoping for something to psychically wave at her, then ran her eye over the shambles of stuff strewn on the table, wondering where to begin, not knowing what she should be looking for. A couple of spanners and a screwdriver sat on a plate with a grubby knife and fork, next to a bag of bolts that seemed to play the part of an hors d'oeuvre. A strange-looking object lying on the table at the side of the plate caught her eye. She leaned forward to look closer, shuddered as recognition lit in her eyes. The skull of some small animal, bare-bone-teeth smiled up at her, stripped of all flesh but still showing brown streaks of dried blood. She tried to work out what animal it might had been, finally settled for guessing that it might have been a rabbit, but secretly worried that it could just as easily have been a cat. It looked fragile, delicate, too precious a thing to be discarded with the scraps of dinner, a life discarded. Two deep scrape marks had been gouged into the bone. Bel inched out a finger to touch the skull, as if she needed to prove to herself it was real, then changed her mind at the last minute and let her hand drop. She glanced across at Fox, who was still making his methodical way around the room. He returned her gaze as he saw her hesitate. 'What's that you've got there?'

'Nothing.' she answered, returned to scanning the detritus on the table. 'Hey, have you seen this?' A folded newspaper had been left open at page ten.

'What is it?'

'Last night's Evening Post. There's a paragraph about Emily.' Bel picked it up to read, noticed a copy from a couple of days before sitting under it, open at page five, showing a more detailed article. 'There's another one here.' She held the paper out towards Fox. There was yet another underneath, this one open at page seven, another short article. 'Looks like our friend Mason has been reading about Emily. Seems he's been following the case.'

Fox took the paper from Bel, scanned it in a second. 'Come on, let's keep going.'

They kept looking, but the kitchen held no secrets that they could find. After a few more fruitless minutes they moved through to the living room with a shared nod. At first glance it didn't hold any more promise than the kitchen. A wide stone fireplace dominated one side of the room, a stack of logs in the hearth and cold ashes in the grate waiting for the first chill of winter. The curtains at the window, threadbare and semi see-through, waited to be pulled across windows that were themselves semi see-through, un-washed for years and covered in grime. Rugs large and small were spread on the floor, covering the cold stone flags. No books, Bel noticed, but there was a pile of magazines about fishing, game, woodsmansy outdoor things, sitting on a coffee table in front of a saggy old sofa. A too-large sideboard on one side of the room looked promising. Bel made her way over, quickly started to rifle through the drawers. Nothing more than the usual stack of legal papers, birth certificate, TV licence, gas bill. A collection of part-full bottles of spirits; whiskey, gin, cognac, grubby glasses, half a bottle of flat tonic, sat inside a glass-fronted cabinet. The next drawer offered vinyl records, LP's. She flicked through, staring at names from before she was born; Human League, Gary Numan. There was just one classical piece. The Mendelssohn. Bel picked it up, hoping to get something from the physical contact, but nothing sparked. She slipped it back into place.

Bel looked across at Fox. He was holding one end of a large rug, had started dragging it to one side. 'What are you doing? I mean I can see what you're doing, but why?'

'His dungeon, his safe place, where he keeps the girls prisoner. It's got to be near here.' A frown creased his forehead. 'I was thinking it might be right here in his cottage, a cellar maybe, or some sort of holding room dug out under the stones. I'm trying to see if any of these flags look like they've been disturbed.'

'Sounds like a plan.' Bel grabbed the other end of the dusty rug, began to pull and roll it to one side with him. They looked carefully at the stone slab underneath, checking the joins and edges, looking for scrapes and scratches. None, but to be honest Bel wasn't surprised, the slab looked like it weighed about ten tons. The two of them spent the next ten minutes dragging rugs from one side of the room to the other as they checked every gap, every join, every edge. It was a waste of time. None of the stones looked like they'd been moved since the cottage was built. Together they slid the coffee table to one side, moved the sofa backwards and forwards. Nothing. Time to move through to the bedroom.

The bedroom smelled foisty, too foisty to be healthy. Bel wished she had held her breath, but it was already too late. She searched as best as she could, trying to work methodically like Fox, hoping to find some sick little item that Mason might have kept to amuse himself with at the end of the day. Fox uncovered Mason's stash of old porn mags and DVD's in the bottom of the wardrobe, but that was about it. Bel pulled the bedroom door closed as they left, happy to be out of that mildewed little cave.

The bathroom was cold, blue, stark. If she hadn't seen the toilet roll and toothbrush, she would have said the room had never been used.

As they moved back towards the kitchen Bel and Fox both froze at the sound of the kitchen door scraping open, followed by a growl of a shout from the threshold. 'What the fuck! Who's in here?'

'It's him!' Fox whispered, spinning round to face Bel. He lifted a finger to his lips in conspiracy.

'What do you want me to do?' she whispered back.

'You stay here. Things might get ugly.'

'What am I supposed to do if they do?'

'I don't know. Phone the police?' He stood up, marched into the kitchen. Bel followed, stopped just outside the kitchen door so she could listen at the gap. Her heart was pounding so loud in her chest she was certain she would be heard, certain Fox would turn around, say something about the noise she was making. Bel moved a few inches to one side, changed her field of view.

In the next second she forgot all about Fox. Standing in the kitchen was the man from her visions, the man she had watched overpower Emily Phillips then drag her out of the College of Music, the man who had captured and killed the girls in the clearing; Jessica and poor Kathy and the others. It was obviously him, even though he looked shorter and older than he had seemed in her dreams, about fifty she guessed, squat and broad, only a couple of inches taller than her. His heavy cotton check shirt was open like a jacket over a grubby vest. He had too much belly to carry the look off. Bel hated him the instant she set eyes on him. She wanted to scream at him, run into the kitchen and spit in his face, shake him until her arms fell off, until his arms fell off, hit him with all her strength until she could hit him no more. She was so angry she could feel her legs begin to shake. She could hear her own breath hissing out, snapped her mouth shut. The man was shouting at the top of his voice, stabbing out a stubby finger at Fox. 'Who the fuck are you, and what are you doing in my home?'

'My name, Mr. Mason, is Detective Inspector Fox.' He flourished his warrant card, looking for all the world like some ham actor about to take a bow, then took two quick steps forward and was suddenly right up in Mason's face. The set of his face seemed to change in an instant; his voice was hushed now, but he looked focussed, in complete control. 'Let's not beat about the bush shall we, Mr Mason? Or may I call you David?'

'What's going on? What's this all about?' Bel looked at the man from her secret vantage point. He didn't seem to be upset at all, but stood still, not backing off even with Fox in his face.

Fox smiled at him again, as if anticipating some soon to be shared joke, 'In a moment I'm going to arrest you for the kidnap of Emily Phillips, but before I do, I'm going to give you a chance to redeem yourself and tell me where she is.' Mason opened his mouth to speak. Fox held up one hand to ward off any protest of innocence. 'And don't say "Emily Phillips" as if you don't know who I mean.' Mason's mouth slowly closed. He looked into the scowling eyes of the policeman, held them for a second, before a dark scar of sick glee etched itself across his face as he broke into a smile. 'You'll never find her; you do know that.'

Bel stared at the tableau, the breath in her lungs refusing to leave, as Fox's eyes narrowed to slits, his hand clenching into a fist. She waited for the blow to land, the fist to ram into Mason's face, teeth to fly, nose to break. She knew it was going to happen, wanted it to happen. She screamed inside her head, willing Fox to hit the bastard, hit him hard, hit him now. She gasped in surprise as Fox's hand struck out like a snake, locked around Mason's wrist. The older man winced, tried to twist away, but Fox flowed with the movement, turned, spinning Mason on his heels, forcing his arm up his back. At that instant Bel saw the handcuffs in Fox's other hand for the first time, heard the metallic snap as one closed around a wrist. Mason was caught off balance. A shocked realisation dawned on his face as the second cuff snapped shut with a very final sounding click. Fox leaned close to his face; Bel could almost feel the hot anger of his breath from behind the door as he whispered at Mason. 'I can't punch your lights out, because my boss might start asking awkward questions,' Mason smirked as he saw the frustration in the detective's eyes. Fox stood in front of him, his breath spitting out through clenched teeth as he fought to restrain the anger inside. A flicker of a smile twitched across his lips, then his knee came up like a piston. It took a long second before Mason folded around his own small world of pain, 'but I don't think he's going to start looking for bruises on your bollocks, is he?' smiled Fox as he looked down on the other man.

'Oh, by the way,' he leaned forward to growl in the gasping man's ear, 'you're under arrest for the kidnap of Emily Phillips.'

~~~~~
~~~~~

Saturday 6th July 2019
12:23
Day Twenty-Three

Fox dragged Mason and man-handled him onto a heavy wooden kitchen chair.

'You bastard.' Mason tried to bring his arms round to get at Fox, even though he was handcuffed, then gave up and rested forward against the litter-strewn table. 'That's assault, that is. Wait 'til my solicitor hears about this.'

'You're not going anywhere near a solicitor until you tell me where Emily is.'

'Good luck there, then.' Mason's head came up, a smile creeping across his face in spite of the injuries caused by Fox's knee. 'I've told you; you'll never find her.'

'You're not making things any better for yourself. Just tell me where she is before things get any worse.'

'Oh, things are going to get worse alright, but not for me. All I have to worry about is getting the top bunk in my cell,' He rattled his handcuffs for emphasis. 'It's you I feel sorry for, because every minute that goes by from now on just means your precious little violin player is a minute closer to death, and there's not a thing you can do about it.' He smiled from ear to ear as he looked across the table at Fox. 'Listen. Can you hear that?' He cocked his head to one side, a moue of fake concern on his face; 'Oh, that's right, it's the seconds ticking away. Best of luck, Copper. Who's got it in the bollocks now?'

In spite of his all bravado, Mason flinched as Fox abruptly scraped back his chair and stood to leave the room. He made a beeline for Bel's hiding place behind the door. She dragged her eyes away from Mason to look at Fox, his face drip-white, his hands shaking with emotion, a mixture of anger and frustration. 'The bastard. He's not even bothered about going to prison. This can't be happening. We need to find a way to make him crack, and fast.'

'Such as?'

'I need you to talk to him.'

'And say what exactly?' Bel's voice came out as a pinched whisper. Her throat was starting to close up and she could feel the tension grab at her skull.

'I need you to hit him with the names of the girls, how they died, and when. I want you to stick it to that little bastard, make him understand we've got stuff on him, stuff that he'd never think we could have. We need to make him cough up Emily while we've still got time, while she's still got time. The forensics team will be here soon, and then it's going to get official. We're never going to get another chance like this. You've got to get him to talk.'

Bel turned away. 'I don't know if I can.' She could feel herself begin to tremble, the fear boiling up inside her, worried about having to confront this evil man who had the blood of so many girls on his hands.

'Okay, I understand. No pressure,' Fox replied. With her back to him his voice sounded calm, but when she turned to look at him Bel could see the disappointment in his face, his whole body.

'It can't be legal, can it?' she asked.

'We're not breaking any law as far as I can see. Besides, who's to know?' Fox gave a shrug.

'What am I supposed to say to him?'

'Like I said, just tell him the names of the girls we found, you found, in the woods, see how he reacts.'

'And after that?'

'I don't know, we play it by ear, I guess.'

Bel looked at Fox, feeling lost for words. The last thing she wanted was to go anywhere near Mason. In the back of her mind she knew on some level that somewhere in the future there was going to be a reckoning for this, but she also knew that if they were going to find Emily, they would have to use whatever they could find to gain an edge. 'If we're going to do this, I need you to promise that he won't find out anything about me, my name, nothing. And there's no way he can know that I'm psychic.'

'Okay, you got it.'

'There's something else I need.'

'Go on.'

'You've got to get me something of his for me to hold, something personal, something I can read. If he won't talk, maybe his possessions will.'

'I'll see if I can get you his wallet.'

'Just one other thing.'

'Yes?'

''He can't get free, can he? He can't get me?'

'He can't get you, he's handcuffed, and I'll be right there. If he tries anything, I'll soon stop him.' Fox gave her a reassuring smile.

'Okay,' Bel smiled back, 'let's do it.'

Fox pushed open the door, walked back into the kitchen. Bel followed a step behind, trying to keep out of sight of Mason as long as possible, eyes fixed on the floor so that she didn't face him until she absolutely had to. She could feel the anxiety bite hard in her stomach, the fear that came with knowing that she was going to be within touching distance of the man. How the hell had she let Fox talk her into this?

Mason looked up at Fox, then fixed his eyes on Bel. 'Well, well, well. Who do we have here? A lady copper. Come to check out the bad man?' Mason rattled his handcuffs, made as if he was trying to grab her. Bel flinched back. He laughed, a throaty cackle that upset her as much as the handcuff-rattling.

'Fuck off, Mason. Behave yourself.' Fox pushed him back down into his seat. Bel's stomach twisted in slow, cramped back flips of fear and revulsion and she gingerly slipped into the seat opposite Mason. The table didn't seem wide enough anymore. Up close the man was thick-set, scruffy, almost Neanderthal, overdue a shave and a shower, things obviously not high on your list when you're a live-alone serial killer.

'What's this, good cop, bad cop? If you think I'm going to tell you where the girl is, I've already told you, I'm saying nothing,' Mason sneered and seemed to look Bel up and down. It just made her feel dirty.

Fox leaned over Mason, his elbow "accidently" digging into the side of the other man's neck with a pressure that brought a squeal of pain, then started to go through his captive's pockets. He turned the contents out onto the table; a set of keys, obviously the door keys for this place, some small gouging tool that Bel didn't recognise, a few pence in change, an old hanky that looked like it should have been incinerated years ago, and a black leather wallet, grown soft and supple with age. Fox scattered the stuff across the table, gave Bel a meaningful glance as he tossed the wallet down; it came to rest a few inches from her hand.

Mason gave a grin. 'I'd offer to bribe you, but I get the feeling you're not the bribing kind.' His teeth looked yellowed and stained; then she saw it, hidden under hooded brows; a flicker that lasted the merest breath of time, the tiny light of fear in his eye, a spark he had been trying to bury, to push down and hide behind a jagged wall of bravado. Bel didn't fear him anymore, she could see him for what he was; a nasty, pathetic little man, locked into an everlasting cycle of evil. When she spoke her voice was strong, sure, all self-doubt gone. 'Tell me about Jessica Curtis.'

'Who?'

'Jessica Curtis. One of the girls you killed. You buried her body in the woods, in that little clearing.'

'Oh, that was you guys messing around up there, was it? Did you get them all?'

'Why? how many were there?'

'Why don't you tell me?' He grinned, settled back in the chair, with all the appearance of enjoying himself.

'Apart from Jessica there was Suzanne Foster, Kathy Whittaker, Chelsea Ambrose, and Kimberly.'

Bel had expected him to show some emotion, anxiety or fear perhaps, but he had brought himself under control again, just smiled. 'Very good, detective lady. Well done, but you missed a few, tucked away in a couple of places. Let me know how that goes.' A twisted smirk split his face.

Bel knew there had to be others, buried in other small clearings, scattered across the huge expanse of forest. Kimberley had told her, that day in the clearing, and she'd felt it too, a sadness that seemed to lay across the land, an unresolved sorrow. She promised herself she would find every single girl, even if it took a lifetime.

Bel forced an upbeat note into her voice, 'Care to enlighten me?'

Mason leaned forward again, hissed at her, 'I thought we might leave that for when you come to visit. You will visit me, won't you?'

It wasn't supposed to go like this. On the telly, the bad man admits to everything as soon as he is caught and is carted away to prison. Maybe Mason didn't watch telly. Bel needed an "in". This might be it. 'Maybe, who knows?' she shrugged, and her hand came to rest on the wallet as if it was the most natural thing in the world. A lurch of displacement inside her head, a series of stills, like a flick-flack cartoon sketched in the corner of a school exercise book.

Standing in the doorway, watching them from across the road, coming out of the pet shop, fawning over the puppy dog he has just bought her. Mandy fucking Armitage and her bastard boyfriend.

Orange knickers, with a frill. The flash of cameras.

Mason driving the van, the dog in the back.

Mason in the woods, the hammer above his head, blood dripping onto the scrub of needles.

It had to be the same dog that had led Bel to the clearing in the woods, to the buried girls. 'What's the dog called?' she asked.

A dark scowl flashed across Mason's face.

'I'm curious.' Bel shrugged her shoulders. 'It's her dog, isn't it? Mandy's. That's her name, isn't it? Mandy. The girl. The first girl. Mandy Armitage, am I right?'

'Her and that bastard dog. Shadow, she called it. Fat lump, more like. That lad thought he was well in, but she soon dumped him. Kept the dog, though, until I sorted it out. She wasn't so fucking clever after that, was she?'

'Did you kill Mandy, too? Is she out there, buried in the forest somewhere?'

Fat tears of frustration filled Mason's eyes. 'No, the bitch, she's not dead. She moved to a new house after I killed the dog. Her and that mother of hers. Upped sticks and cleared out. Good riddance to her, and the old cow too!'

This was getting Bel nowhere. Mason seemed to be locked in the past, fixated on this Mandy Armitage. Bel could feel some of his hurt, and some of the shame, but everything was stirred up in his head. She couldn't pin Emily down. She got a glimmer that Mason knew the girl was still alive. She could see plastic bottles full of water. She needed more. What was the point of all this if Emily died before they could find her? Bel snatched the wallet up from the table, pressed it against her forehead, squeezed her eyes shut, tried to search, scanning images that only she could see, looking for something that would show her where Emily was being held.

'What's going on? What are you doing? What's she doing?' Mason tried to rise out of his chair, a sneer on his face.

'Shut it, Mason.' Fox pushed him back down in his chair. 'Let her concentrate.'

Bel tried to zone in on Emily, but Mason started to laugh, fracturing her concentration. 'I don't believe it! Is she supposed to be psychic? A fucking witch? I've seen it all now. Wait 'til my solicitor hears about this. I'll be back out on the streets before the end of the week.'

Maybe it was something about being laughed at, but after that Bel wasn't able to pick up anything, either about Emily, or about Mason and what he'd been doing. He was still laughing when he was bundled into the back of the police van an hour later and driven off. Bel sat in the chair, looking around the mess of the kitchen, wondering what she was going to do next.

~~~~~
~~~~~

Saturday 6th July 2019
14:19
Day Twenty-Three

Bel walked back down to reception with Fox. A clutch of police cars and vans had appeared, the lawn already starting to suffer under the attack of skidded tyres and regulation issue boots.

The receptionist still sat there, all prim and pretty and rigidly made-up, talking to an old man, fawning at him almost, Bel thought. The old man turned towards Bel and Fox as they approached, smiling for all the world as if he owned the place. 'Ah, you must be Detective Inspector Fox, come to sort out this terrible, terrible incident. You have our full co-operation; anything you need you only have to ask. Allow me to introduce myself; Jeremy Burleigh, seventh Earl Standale.' Ah, so he did own the place, thought Bel. The only word she could think to describe him was 'dapper'. Not tall, but thin like only a very old man can be, with a weathered face, white wavy hair, a nifty little van dyke beard and 'tache. He was wearing a pink shirt under a camel sports jacket, tan slacks and pale brown brogues. A lime green cravat sat at the open neck of his shirt. The only thing that spoiled the whole effect was the wraith of pale blue smoke that sat curled around his waist and drifted upwards to sit on his shoulders. 'And I'm sorry to say we haven't been introduced,' he said, in a soft, mellifluous voice as he took Bel's hand in his. His skin felt cool to the touch, smooth but not too soft, well-manicured, in contrast to her own, which was podgy and sweaty. She was surprised when he lifted her hand, bowed, brushed the back of her hand with the gentlest touch of his lips. It was like something out of an old black-and-white movie. It should have seemed quaint, a bit twee, but it didn't, and at that moment Bel fell a tiny bit in love with the old man. She could only hope that he hadn't noticed the pink wash of a blush that had started to creep up her throat, but she felt sure that even if he had, he would have been too much the gentleman to mention it. 'My name is Isabel, Bel. Bel Barker. I'm not the police, but I'm helping Detective Inspector Fox with the investigation.'

'I'm intrigued.'

'Actually, there is something we need your help on,' Fox broke the mood, 'if you don't mind. Er?'

'Please, call me Jeremy. What is it you need?'

'Jeremy. We already suspect Mason of having committed at least five murders, but there's another girl he's kidnapped, a girl called Emily Phillips. We think he's got her in some sort of secret room, a cellar maybe, or an out-building. He's not talking, and we're running out of time.'

'Bricks,' Bel jumped in. 'The cellar, the room, it's made out of bricks. There are no windows, and it has a curved ceiling. Does that ring any bells?'

'I'm afraid not, no. I've lived here all my life, and as a child I roamed across the whole estate. There are no curved-roof cellars or out-buildings on the estate, brick-built, yes, but not curved.'

'I might be wrong about the roof,' Bel replied. 'We need to check out the brick ones, find them all, search every last one.'

'Of course, of course. I'll ask Matthews to draw up a list, show your people round, but I don't think there is anywhere that someone could be held prisoner without being discovered. At least, not that I'm aware of.'

'There's also a link to music, we think. Classical music,' Fox added. 'Did Mason ever show any interest, do you know?'

'Not personally, but the staff, all the staff, are allowed, encouraged even, to take advantage of the facilities here. If Mason wanted to study music, or history, or agriculture even, he would have had access to anything and everything on the estate. He would be able to visit the music room or library at any time he desired, within reason. There's a range of instruments, scores, tutorials available, as well as any number of recordings to help him. I'll show you, if you wish.'

Fox turned to Bel. 'That sounds like a good place to start. Bel, can you go with Jeremy, please, check out the music room? You know better than I exactly what you're looking for. I want to get started on searching the cellars. Jeremy? Is that okay with you?'

'It would be my pleasure. Shall we?' He offered his arm. Bel had always thought that sort of thing was silly, even when she'd seen it in old black and white movies, but right now she thought it felt nice, considerate. He guided her from the reception area into a plush-carpeted corridor. As soon as she took the first step Bel could feel herself becoming more tense, more agitated. There were more flags and banners displayed on both walls, more longswords and pikestaffs lined up or displayed in arcs and circles. Bel looked around nervously; she felt there must have been a million weapons in this place. The words were out of her mouth before she had a chance stop herself. 'How many swords do you actually own?'

'Ha. Hundreds, thousands, maybe. I've not actually counted. My family has been fighting and dying in battles, winning and losing wars for more than four hundred years of British imperial history. The things you see are, I suppose, the spoils, for good or bad. Trophies of victory, memorials of defeat.'

Bel watched images flash in front of her imagination, a stroboscope of the soul; men grunting with effort or screaming in terror as they fought to the death with cold steel blades. There were other images too; a man making some sort of a short stocky gun or rifle in a blacksmith's shed, the hollow thud of explosions nearby. Orders barked and secrets whispered. Wounds too horrific to contemplate. Bel noticed the gradual change as they moved further along the passageway; from bladed weapons to rifles and revolvers. The items were interspersed with photos now; sepia images of men in uniform, marching, training, fighting, dying.

'Are you alright?' Bel became aware of Jeremy's arm around her shoulder, his hand holding her elbow. She felt light-headed, so queasy she thought she might throw up.

'I'll be okay in a minute, it took me by surprise, I guess.' She took a few deep breaths, began to feel the knot of tension in her stomach uncoil.

After a few more steps Jeremy opened a door on the right. 'Here we are, the music room.' He motioned for Bel to enter first.

Manorgrove was obviously a stately home, but up until now she had thought of the place as just like an ordinary house only bigger, give or take the odd suit of armour or fifty. This room changed all that. There was no sign of careworn or shabby here. The room was ornate, palatial even. This was a room that really could have belonged in the Palace of Versailles. The walls were lined with display cases and cabinets of all sizes, some of them glass-fronted, all of them superbly made from the finest of woods. Each cabinet held some instrument or music manuscript. There was what even Bel recognised to be an Adams fireplace. On one side of the fireplace stood a delicate harpsichord. Every part of it seemed to be inlaid with pearls and semi-precious stones. It looked impossibly expensive. On the other, a beautiful, toffee-coloured grand piano, highly polished, perfect in every respect.

Sitting at the piano was the most beautiful ghost Bel had ever seen.

'Beautiful, aren't they?' Jeremy stroked his hand along the closed lid of the piano. As he did so the woman reached up to brush her hand across his shoulder. Bel couldn't resist, walked across, opened the lid on the keyboard to assist the woman. She thanked Bel with a smile. Jeremy had a puzzled look on his face. 'Could I ask why you did that?'

'Can I ask you something, instead? Do you believe in ghosts?'

'My dear Isabel, it would be impossible to have lived here at Manorgrove for all these years and not believe. Some nights, it seems almost impossible to sleep.'

Bel laughed. It was a nice little joke, and it did what it is supposed to; it put her at ease.

'Would you believe me if I told you I can see a ghost right now? She's sitting at the piano, as if she's about to play. She really is a very beautiful woman. She looks about thirty years old or so, olive-skinned, and has the most perfect black hair, tied in a loose bunch to one side.'

'Veronica? You can see her?' There was a catch in his throat as he spoke her name. Regardless of how long they had been together or how long the woman had been dead it was obvious Jeremy loved his wife deeply.

'Yes, she's smiling. She's just blown you a kiss.'

'I miss her so much. She was twenty-three when we met. Maybe she's able to show herself as a young woman. That really was such a special time.'

'She's just smiled at you, nodded her head. She agrees with you.'

'Oh, I do hope she's happy.' Jeremy gave a smile, as if recalling happy memories. 'She was a world-class pianist; that's how we met, at a recital. Together we travelled the world, her playing such exquisite music, myself just happy to be with her. I bought her this piano. She said it had such a happy tone. We were blessed with two beautiful children, Christopher and Michael. Over the years Veronica and I came to view this music room as something of a retreat, our "together" place. Whenever time allowed, we would sit here, she playing, me just loving every moment, every note, everything about her.'

'Veronica's smiling, nodding her head.'

'She can hear us?'

Bel nodded. 'Talk to her if you want.'

Jeremy began to talk, reminiscing about the small intimate nothings shared by a couple deeply in love over a lifetime. The woman simply sat at the piano, listened to every word, her eyes lovingly on him. 'Veronica, my dear, I have missed you every single day since you passed away and loved you more. It won't be long now, my love. I long to hear you play again.' Veronica smiled, stood, planted the gentlest of kisses on his cheek, then faded away.

'She's gone. She just gave you a kiss on the cheek.' Bel hesitated before continuing. 'Have you known long?' The pale coil appeared again, wrapped a tendril around the old man's arm.

'It's been with me for a few months now. I went to seek medical advice. They advised me there's nothing they can do; it's just a matter of time. I don't have any regrets, and soon I'll be with my Veronica again.' He smiled but couldn't hide the tear hovering in the corner of one eye. 'Enough of a foolish old man's reminiscences. You're here because you need to find this missing girl, this Emily. So, how can I help?'

'We think,' Bel gulped in air trying to compose herself in the face of Jeremy's obvious grief, 'that Mason took something from each of his victims. As far as we know, all the girls played a musical instrument. We think that's one of the reasons he chose them. If we can find some of his trophies, there's a chance they might lead us to Emily.'

'Ah, I see. It would make sense that he would hide these items among other musical pieces. So, you're hoping to find something with blood on, or fingerprints, something to point directly at Mason.'

'Not necessarily. My talent isn't just that I can see ghosts. I can also gain information by psychometry.'

'So, you're not so much looking for the impressions of blood and fingerprints as some sort of emotional imprint?'

'That's exactly right.'

But you've no idea what you should be looking for?'

'I'll know it when I find it. It doesn't matter what the actual object is,' Bel went on, 'it just has to be something that the person handled, preferably something that belonged to them. We reckon Mason's kept things so he can remember his victims, to gloat over what he did.'

'An imprint from a tortured soul. How sad.'

'I can't afford to think like that. I have to find Emily. She's where all this started. She's been appearing in my dreams for weeks now, and I'm hoping we might still be in time to save her.'

Jeremy moved to a cabinet close to the door. 'In that case, let's not waste any more time, shall we?' He pulled open the small, ornate door, started taking out the contents.

To be honest Bel had never given a thought to just how difficult this was going to be, up until now; now that she found herself so close. In this single cabinet alone, there was a tin whistle, a piccolo, sheet music, a couple of plectrums, and a small pile of used reeds for a clarinet or an oboe. She looked towards Jeremy for permission, then picked up the first object, the tin whistle. She felt herself poured into a honey-coloured memory. A young boy, about eight or ten years old, was marching across what could only be one of the rooms of Manorgrove, in an old, felt pirate's hat and eye-patch, the small whistle to his lips. She smiled as the memory washed over her. She would have put any money that the boy was Jeremy, or one of his children maybe, but much as she would have liked, Bel didn't have time to re-visit happy incidents, so she quickly put it to one side.

A small, delicate clock on the mantelpiece chimed the hour. Bel looked around at how many drawers and cupboards there were in the room, couldn't begin to guess how many things there might be in each. This was going to take forever. She quickly came to a decision.

'I need your help, Jeremy. How well do you know what's in this room?'

'As well as anyone, I suppose,' he shrugged.

'I can't look at everything in here, it would take a lifetime, and time's a luxury we don't have. Can you look with me, for me, pick out anything that's not right, anything that you think is out of place?'

'I don't come in here very often these days, but I can try.' He moved to a set of display drawers to his left.

Bel left him to it, moved across the room, opened a drawer at random, plunged one hand in. She was hoping that she could get a general impression of happy times at Manorgrove with everything she touched, and anything that jangled against that feeling would stand out to her. She held her hand in the drawer for a few seconds, running her fingers over objects without recognising or understanding them, then took out her hand, as certain as she could be that there was nothing of importance she needed to check on.

It was a bit of a risky strategy, she knew, but she was definitely going to be able to cover more ground this way. She moved on, taking drawer after drawer as quickly as she dared.

'Isabel?'

Bel's head came up, her mind hurrying back from an evening concert, long white gloves, tiara, the full works, all impressed in a little lace hand fan. Jeremy stood next to a tall chest of drawers. Luxuriously in-laid veneers adorned the highly polished wood. The drawer level with Jeremy's knees was open. He stood there frowning. 'Have you found something?' Bel asked.

'I'm not sure. This drawer seems to contain a collection of used strings, broken pieces of instruments, and cheap jewellery. I don't understand why we would keep such a collection of items.'

'You probably wouldn't, but Mason might.' As Bel walked towards him Jeremy dragged the drawer out, carried it to a small side-table under the window, tipped out the contents. As she touched the first piece, she instantly knew that this was Mason's sick stash.

A broken piece from a violin fingerboard, the dark wood cool in her hand, brittle. The image hit her almost before she had a chance to close her eyes, to prepare.

She walked towards Bel, cautious, unsure. 'Who are you?' she asked.

'I'm someone who wants to help you,' Bel answered.

'You can't help me. I'm dead.' The girl looked about sixteen, looked like she had stopped crying only a few seconds before.

'If you can tell me your name, I might be able to take you home.'

'My name is Natalie. Natalie Smith. I live in Ripon, near the river. I've got a dog. Pud. I miss my little Pud. He's a Yorkie.'

Bel watched as the girl dithered before her, slipping in and out of focus as if she was standing in a doorway, taking little steps backwards and forwards between this world and the next. Bel could feel a discordant thought forming in her head. Something she'd seen or heard in the short time since she'd arrived at Manorgrove was jangling away at her, trying to get her attention. Bel decided to go with a hunch. 'I can help you go home to your dog, but first I'm looking for another dog, a big, black dog, like a Labrador.' Bel knew that the dog that Mason killed, the dog from the clearing in the woods, was gone, but it felt to Bel as if it was somehow still there. She couldn't work out why, so she asked the question. 'Have you seen a dog like that anywhere?' The girl shook her head. 'Did the man who killed you have a dog like that? Another shake of the head.

Bel tried not to let her disappointment show. She managed to coax Natalie's address out of her, wrote it down in a fine notebook that Jeremy found in a desk drawer.

Bel put the broken piece down, took a moment to gather her thoughts, clear her head before she could continue. She reached for the next object, a violin bridge, split into two pieces, let the flimsy pieces sit on the palm of her hand.

'Hello. Are you dead too?'

'No, I'm trying to find someone. A girl, like you. She's about your age, plays the violin.'

'I play the violin. Played. I can't play anymore. He smashed it when he killed me. Smashed my hands, too. Look!' Bel looked, even though she didn't want to. The girl's hands were a bloody, twisted mess. Bel wondered again at how much pain and suffering Mason must have inflicted to these poor girls.

'I don't think the girl I'm looking for is dead,' Bel explained, 'not yet. She's been kidnapped but she's still alive.'

'Do you think it's the same man? The same man who killed me?'

'Yes. I'm trying to find his secret place, the place he took you before, before he...'

'Before he killed me.'

'Yes. I'm sorry.'

The girl stood looking at her, not blinking. Bel couldn't hold her gaze, turned her eyes away. 'Do you remember anything? About the place he kept you prisoner?' Bel's face still turned from hers.

'It was cold. The place was made out of bricks. Cold, wet bricks.

'What about windows? Could you see anything? Hear anything? Traffic? Birds? Voices?'

'There were no windows. The only voice I ever heard was his. Shouting. Always shouting. Except when he was raping me. He tried to be nice then, but that just made it worse, even more disgusting.' Her voice sounded flat; all emotion drained away. The girl turned and walked away, disappeared from sight.

Bel carefully placed the broken pieces of wood on the table, sat looking at them, waiting for the sorrow that had built up in her heart to fade. After a minute she picked up the next item, a tuning peg, turned again in her mind to face that special direction.

The girl was naked. She stood upright, proud, defiant.

'He never made me submit. Even when he was fucking me, I still fought him, the dirty bastard.' The girl was shouting her anger.

'He's kidnapped another girl,' Bel replied. He's holding her prisoner right now. I'm trying to stop him before it's too late, before he kills her. I need to find his secret place, the place he takes you all to, where he tortures you. Can you help me find it?'

'I don't know. I never really worked out where he was keeping me, even afterwards. I just know that I'm buried in the woods somewhere. I keep trying to walk to the road, to go home if I can, but something stops me. I keep walking back to my body. I'm stuck there.'

'I promise I will find you. I will find you and take you home, even if it takes me the rest of my life.'

'Thank you.'

'Is it far, do you know? From where he killed you to where you're buried, do you think?'

'It seemed like miles. He carried me out of the place in the middle of the night, carried me over his shoulder like a piece of meat. The sun was coming up by the time he'd finished burying me. The woods go on forever.'

'What was it like? The building where he kept you prisoner? Can you remember?'

'I just remember it was strange. Inside but outside at the same time. There was some sort of a metal door.'

'Any success? You seemed to be deep in concentration.' Jeremy had a concerned frown on his face.

It took a few seconds for Bel to bring Jeremy back into focus; in her mind as much as in her eyes.

'These are his trophies, no doubt about it. The only problem is that the girls have all been too traumatised to be able to remember where they were before he killed them. None of them have a clue where the place is.'

'Is there nothing you can do?'

'I don't think I can. When I was in the College of Music, I got images of Emily, of when she was being kidnapped. The man had what looked like a stun gun; I could see the blue sparks when he pointed it at her. I think there might have been a syringe, too. What if he drugged her? What if he drugged all of them? No wonder they didn't know where they were, they were probably all drugged up to the eyeballs.'

Which, she realised, left Bel exactly nowhere. Shit! She looked down at the evil little collection of bits and pieces on the table. 'None of these things are going to help us find Emily, after all. This has all just been a complete waste of time.' Bitter tears of frustration bubbled up inside her. Bel bit down, refusing to let them escape. After everything she'd done, everything she'd been through to get this far, for it to end like this was more than she could bear. She sagged as the weight of all her efforts came tumbling down on top of her, felt herself begin to reel under the force of all the emotions she had seen, felt, witnessed in these last few days as they crushed her heart, battered her soul. She could feel the muscles of her shoulders and neck twisted and pulled into little knots, as if she had been clenching her whole body, preparing herself for some massive action, and now, nothing.

Bel's tired fingers opened; the tuning peg dropped onto the table. It came to rest touching the broken bridge, the two items connected even now. 'I can't do this anymore. I need to get out of here.' Bel didn't know what she needed to do, or where she needed to go, just that doing this, now, in this place, was not it. What wouldn't she give for a large vodka and tonic, and the chance to not have to think about Emily, about all the dead girls that she'd burdened herself with a responsibility for. 'Enough! I can't do it! I need to get out of here.' Bel pushed open the music room door, hurried out into the corridor, left, left again, barged open the door to reception with the flat of her hand, stopped with a gasp. Something ached inside her head, a scream without sound, urging her to - what? Something was wrong. She turned, looked back down the length of the corridor.

'Is something the matter, Isabel?' Jeremy had caught up with her, looked at her, a frown of concern on his face.

'Yes. No. I don't know.' She couldn't focus her thoughts, couldn't bring whatever it was to the front of her mind. 'There's something here, something that means something. Here, at Manorgrove. Right here.' Bel felt a bit unsteady, not on her feet but inside her head, somehow. Her breath was coming in panting little gasps. She tried to calm herself, stood stock still, determined not to miss the thing that has just set her mind jangling. Bel leaned against the door frame, took a deep breath, then set off back down the corridor, retracing her steps, forcing herself to walk in slow, methodical steps, looking carefully from side to side at all the things displayed on the walls, trying to take in everything, to not miss anything, to not miss *the* thing. Bel read the placards beneath each item in turn. "Lee Enfield Service Issue Rifle." "Service issue Revolver." "Thompson Sub-Machine Gun." The ruthless efficiency of these killing machines curdled Bel's stomach; the fact that all these weapons had no soul, that a person didn't need to put any thought into killing another person, just apply pressure to a little trigger, point and squeeze. Bel moved a little further, continued to scan from side to side, the hackles on her neck bristling, her nerves jarring like a badly tuned violin. Bel looked at the framed, sepia photographs, interspersed on the wall between the weapons; black and white, so small, about three inches square, most of them, images of war, men marching, or being addressed by some high-ranking officer. The soldiers all looked so young; barely out of school, but old before their time. Bel looked closer, saw the shadows on the men's faces, the drawn expressions, harrowed stares above the forced smiles for the camera. Bel found herself cast back to the day Fox brought the watch for her to read, when he had been trying to get her to prove herself, just a few days and what felt like an eternity ago; the vision of that other group of men struggling to survive, the enforced march. It was weird, but Bel knew that this was how things worked sometimes; the universe creating a synchronicity that rippled and folded, sometimes producing a closure that happened in moments, or sometimes took half a lifetime to be resolved.

A crinkle in the light, like splinters of glass falling from a broken mirror, caught her eye. She stopped to look. On her left, about head height, an over-exposed photo taken in bright sunlight; a group of men in uniform, happy, smiling, sitting and lounging on a gentle grass bank in front of a row of mullioned windows. Lying on its haunches right at the front of the picture, the dark shape of a large dog. Bel couldn't work out what breed it might be. She stared at the animal, blinked, scrunched up her eyes, looked again. Had the dog in the picture moved? Had she just seen its wagging tail, its tongue lolling out of its mouth? Was this the thing her subconscious had been trying to show her? What did it mean? Had the ghost dog from the woods somehow come back to help her, guide her again, one more time? Or was it just a figment of her imagination, an hallucination she'd conjured up in her tired mind, thrown together in her desperation? That had to be the answer. The dog that had guided Bel in the woods had been a fat old Labrador. The one in this photo looked lean, young. Had one dog, the dog here in this old photograph, somehow connected itself to the dog in the woods, Mandy Armitage's dog? How could that have happened?

Bel turned to Jeremy, frowning. 'This picture. The one with the dog. I think it's important. I think it means something. What's it about, do you know? What's supposed to be happening?'

'I don't really know. It's just another photo from sometime during the war. It was taken here, at Manorgrove, just outside at the front there. The men are sitting on the grass bank next to the main entrance. The only reason it's there is because my uncle Edwin is in the group, just there, look. He added most of these memorabilia about the war. That's his dog, and that's him lounging on the grass at the front, but I don't know what's supposed to be happening. It's some sort of a training exercise, by the look of it.'

Bel looked closer at the old photo. 'There's something written here, in the margin at the bottom.'

Jeremy plucked the old photo from the wall with nimble fingers, flipped it over and freed the thick print from its frame. '"Two-Oh-Two Battalion, Home Guard. Special Operations training. Manorgrove. 15th-28th July 1940",' he read aloud.

'What does that mean?' Bel asked. 'Any ideas?'

'I'm afraid not. I wasn't born until the war was over, and Uncle Eddie never spoke about what he got up to, but then, few people did.'

Bel stared at the photo, willing the dog to move again. It meant something; she could feel it so strong inside her she had begun to tremble. She laid the dark image on the flat of one hand, allowed her mind to relax, to close down, tried to focus on the scene in her mind, let the grainy black and white image burn into her brain.

Hand-picked. He was telling them they'd been hand-picked.

They could walk away right now, if they wanted, without recrimination, without losing face, without dishonour.

Nobody stood. Nobody left.

They were in the library at Manorgrove. There were twelve of them. She didn't recognise any of the others.

She knows this scene has been played before, in the last few weeks, months. She knows it will be played out again.

No-one was giving away anything about who they were or what they did or where they were from. Already they'd been swept up by the conspiracy, bound in silence by the secret they don't yet know.

Training, training.

Skirmish. Disruption. Sabotage.

Take down as many as you can, before you get captured, before you get killed.

Two weeks. They were expected to be caught and killed within two weeks of the invasion.

They would be buying time with their lives. Thankless task. No glory, no medals.

After the training, the others all dispersed back to their various locations. Bel had been given two keys, led up into the woods by the adjutant. They must have walked for at least half an hour.

When they got there, there was a building, built into the side of the hill. A tunnel, two rooms. Hidden. Camouflaged.

Barrels of water, provisions. Hard tack, dried smoked meat, all wrapped and sealed. Small arms. Dynamite. Enough logistics for her to take on the whole of the third Reich single-handed.

Two weeks; a lifetime.

Her orders were that if it came to it, the first thing to go was the reservoir. The adjutant shook her hand, walked off. He didn't look back. From that moment on she was on her own.

Bel squealed, sucked in a hasty breath, tried to focus her eyes back on the real world. With the photo clutched tight in one hand, Bel dug out her phone, scrolled down to Fox's number, hit call. He answered at the second ring.

'Fox,' the familiar voice snapped.

He didn't sound happy. 'It's me. Bel. I need you to go on-line for me. Find out anything you can about two-oh-two battalion, Home Guard. Did you get that? I think there's some kind of underground building hidden in the grounds of this place, or somewhere nearby. It's got something to do with sabotage, some sort of resistance movement, from the war. I think that's where Emily is.' Bel hit the off button, turned back to Jeremy. 'Did your uncle say anything about this training thing he was on? What it was about?'

'Nothing, I'm afraid. Like I said, his generation didn't talk about anything to do with the war, it wasn't the done thing.'

Bel stared at the photo. There had to be something. The need bit into her soul, gouged a line of pain across her heart. She willed the dog to jump out of the image, to bark, to run, but it refused to do anything even remotely psychic. Bel tilted the picture so that the light coming in at the window played across its surface, hoping that might prompt the dog into action. Nothing. She turned it over to look at the back. There was more writing. Jeremy had missed it, only read the front. Written in a small, neat hand in one corner, "Zeus and I on secret training. We are the only two who know."

Zeus! The dog had a name. This man, this Uncle Edwin knew where the secret bunker was, and so did the dog. Bel could feel that she was so close now, so close she was almost scared to breathe.

'The dog, this dog, Zeus. I need to know all about it. It's important. You've got to tell me everything you know. Please.' Bel was almost shouting at Jeremy.

'I don't know what to tell you. Uncle Eddie always had dogs, loved them all his life. He even had a small graveyard made for them. All his dogs were buried there when they died. He wanted to be buried there himself, but I don't think the authorities would allow it.'

'He had a pet cemetery?'

'It's in a little glade a few hundred yards behind the main house. Of course, it will be completely overgrown now. I don't think anyone's been there since he died, more than thirty years ago.' Jeremy gave a little shrug.

'Can you show me? Can you take me there? Please?'

'Yes, of course. It's up past the maintenance sheds, in a little dip at the back. I'll show you.'

Bel's phone shuddered in her pocket as she pushed open the door, walked swiftly across the entrance lobby and out into the failing light that dusk brought. She paused at the top of the steps, took the call.

'Bel, it's Fox. You were right. Listen to what I found on-line. Two-oh-two battalion Home Guard was part of a secret army set up in nineteen forty to carry out sabotage following the anticipated German military invasion of Britain in that year.' Bel listened intently as Fox continued. 'The men were organised into small groups, some of them working on their own.' Jeremy and Bel hurried down the steps, turned left, started up the slope towards the massive shed and the woods beyond. 'Operating from... shit! Get this,' Fox continued, 'operating from hidden bunkers all across the British Isles, charged with causing maximum disruption to the advancing Nazi forces in the event of invasion.'

Trembling from the increasing adrenalin rush, Bel willed Jeremy to move faster, but his face was already starting to show the strain. She slowed down, linked arms to give him some support. 'Listen, Fox, you've got to get back here. Now! I think I'm on to something. We're going up past the maintenance shed where the vans are kept. Meet me round the back. Hurry!'

Bel and the old man passed the huge corrugated-steel shed, came to the top of the rise. Jeremy pointed over to the right, where the ground sank into a wide hollow, led the way carefully forward. He was right, the glade was completely overgrown.

'What are you looking for?' he asked, breathless.

'I don't know. All I know is that it's something to do with your Uncle Edwin's dog, Zeus.'

'There are gravestones here somewhere, lined up in an arc, to one side,' he replied between hurried breaths. 'I remember from when I was a child, exploring the grounds.' He began to pull at the tangle of ivy that had overgrown everything like a green blanket. Bel followed his lead, started pulling at clumps of vegetation with both hands. 'There's something here,' Jeremy said, as he uncovered the corner of a block of carved stone, about eighteen inches high. It leaned awkwardly to one side. Bel stood next to him, grabbed a hank of twisted vines, pulled. It came away in tiny jerks as each root let go its grip. After a few seconds the stone was clear. Bel hunkered down, scrubbed one hand across the front of the stone. Letters, carved an age ago, frozen in time. She traced a finger across the impressions, visualising the faded letters as her finger moved across the chiselled indentations. 'Brutus. This one was called Brutus. We need to find Zeus. I need to find where Zeus is buried.' She moved sideways across the tiny hollow, half-crouching, swinging her arms in a circle around herself, feeling for the next gravestone. A crack against her knuckles. She shook off the pain, started pulling handfuls of ivy, dragging it to one side. Another name, this one sharper, newer, less worn. 'Groucho. No good. Keep going, don't stop.'

'There's another, here.' Jeremy called, pulling at clumps. After a few seconds he called out again. 'Sam. It's Sam. I remember Sam from when I was a boy. He was a Jack Russell.'

Bel frowned her frustration, took another step forward. A growl rose from somewhere deep in her imagination. Her breath caught in her chest. She twisted round, looking for a gravestone, took a step back, then forward again. There it was again, like a warning growl carried on the wind from another world, thin and low. She looked around. The ground looked too flat for a gravestone, nothing there but a low mound a few inches high. She knelt down, feeling forward with both hands. There *was* something. A long, low slab, unlike the other grave markers, about three feet by eighteen inches. As she put one hand down on it to pull away the undergrowth, Bel heard the growl again. There was no mistaking it this time; a long low sound that vibrated inside her head, filled her whole awareness. She knew without thinking that she was in the right place. She held her breath, stood motionless. 'Zeus. Come on, Zeus, show me.' The words came as a whisper through gritted teeth as Bel pressed her hand flat down on the cold stone slab, closed her eyes, focussed on the image of the dog from the old photo, willed it to come to her.

Long seconds passed. Nothing. Then...

Snuffling among the trees. Sights, sounds, scents. Following my human up through the trees, on patrol, checking the perimeter. Another visit to the other place, making sure, again and again, making ready.

Something punched up from the ground, a spasm of energy that swept around the little hollow like a storm. The hairs on Bel's arms bristled alive as a fire of electricity arced up from the stone slab under her hands, fanned out, earthing itself among the branches of the surrounding trees. A dark cloud twisted as it rose, then dropped, boiling, rolling, until it twisted, settled into a frantic maelstrom on the ground a few feet in front of Bel. The dog stood, head lowered as if ready to fight, looked up at Bel, a low growl shuddering on its sharp-toothed jaw. Bel struggled to catch her breath. 'Zeus. Show me,' she shouted.

The answer was another long, low growl of power, before the dog spun round and leapt towards the edge of the vale. Within a second it was twenty yards away. Bel scrambled after it, leaving Jeremy far behind. She heard heavy steps behind her. She looked back. Fox was off to one side, catching up fast. She pushed on, desperate to keep the phantom in sight, a shimmer of movement more substantial than a shadow, less than real.

'Have you found her? Do you know where she is?' Fox stumbled as he caught up with Bel, his breath rasping in his throat. He looked ready for a fight.

'There's another dog. I'm trying to follow it. Look, there on the brow of the next rise.' Bel pointed towards where she could see the dog hovering, crackling fat sparks on the next ridge.

Fox looked across, then back at Bel, a puzzled frown on his face.

A voice, little more than a broken whisper in Bel's ear.

I'm here. Hurry. Please, hurry.

'It's Emily. I can hear her. We've got to be close.' Bel tried to focus her thoughts, screamed an answer in her head.

Emily, I need you to concentrate like never before. Tell me where you are, Emily. Show me!

Her answer little more than a sob. I'm here, I'm here. Please, hurry.

Where? You need to tell me which way to go. Please.

I don't know. Can't you see me?

Bel could hear a violin begin to play.

Bel had been running too hard, too fast. A bolt of bile rose in her throat. She staggered to a halt, cramp twisting her guts. She bent over and splattered the rhododendrons with a thin grease of bile and coffee. When she could look up again, she could see the phantom dog hovering on the crest of the next rise, little more than a wisp of smoke against the skyline. She wiped the back of her hand across her mouth, spat bits. The dog turned away again, ran down the other side of the hill, out of sight. Bel screamed inside and hurried to follow, made it to the top of the rise just in time to see it run on, down the dip, through the undergrowth, up the other side.

Bel felt as if she didn't have time to breathe anymore, her eyes were blurred with tears of effort. The sun had dropped now to touch the tallest trees, scattering diamonds of light through the canopy. Zeus stood level with the next thicket, tail thumping wildly from side to side, shining with a pulsing energy of not-light.

He gave a yip of joy, turned, ran on through the trees. Bel willed her legs to keep moving. Fox was close behind her now; his breathing heavy, his pounding steps heavier still. Bel didn't say anything, she had no words, no breath to spare. She scrambled over a low wall, ran on up a narrow track into the woods, crested a long ridge.

Her legs were shaking with effort. She needed to stop, catch her breath, but the dog ran in loops and circles just ahead of her, urging her forward again.

Bel had played this game before; another ghost, another dog, another time, leading her to the little clearing in the woods, the place where the other girls were buried.

The girls. Bel took a second, scanned around, trying to get her bearings, but couldn't work out where the little clearing was from here. It could have been miles away, or only a few paces, she'd never know.

The dog yipped, turned again, bounded away. Bel started to run again.

She felt as if her legs weighed about a million tons each. She forced them to keep moving, the muscles to contract, to carry her onwards.

Downhill was a little easier. Her breath was burning in her throat.

She put up an arm to fend off a branch that lashed across her face as she dodged and weaved down the slope, the ghost dog still ahead of her.

She could taste blood, couldn't work out why; the branch, perhaps?

Zeus was running straight at the side of the next hill, seemed to pick up pace, then leapt, vanishing in a silent explosion of soil and brush.

Bel stumbled in surprise, fell forwards, rolled onto her knees, pulled herself up, wincing at the new pains she had bought.

Fox was at her side in seconds. 'Are you okay?' he gasped, his mouth hanging wide.

'The dog. It's gone. It just ran into the side of the hill.'

'I don't understand.'

'Neither do I. It must mean something, though. Come on. Let's see if we can see anything.'

'Where do you want me to go?'

'The dog went in here,' said Bel, pointing at the thicket of undergrowth right in front of them. 'I don't know.'

Fox started kicking at the undergrowth, snagging his foot in a trailing vine. 'I can't see anything. What am I supposed to be looking for?'

'I don't know, but it was right here, right where we are.'

Fox grabbed a skein of ivy, pulled, grunting with effort as the vines popped free from the ground. Bel reached down to grab a handful, began to pull at the twisted sinews.

Fox dropped to his knees; his teeth gritted with effort as he tore at the foliage. 'There's something here.'

'What is it? What have you found?'

'I don't know, hang on.' Fox pulled more clumps away, stopped, moved his hands backwards and forwards across the ground. 'I think I've got something.' He pulled more undergrowth free. 'It's some sort of a barrier, a fence, I think. One of those woven branch things. Look!' He was tearing at vines and bracken now, throwing clumps to either side.

'You're right. Look for an edge.' Bel began to work her hands across the grass and vines, digging in, feeling her way along. Fox moved the other way. 'It's here,' Bel squealed, 'I've got it. Help me pull this free.' Fox almost barged her out of the way, dug his hands into the tangled vines, pulled, crouched to take the strain, pulled again.

It began to move, in inches at first, then buckled, twisted, swung away from the face of the small hill. It was a willow hurdle; big, at least five or six feet long almost as deep. Leaves and tendrils were tightly threaded, the whole thing a living fence. The vines cracked and popped as they tore free. Fox dragged the whole green raft to one side.

'What the hell!' Behind the camouflage panel was a brick arch, dark red in the green, about four feet high, full of shadows. 'This is it. It has to be!' Bel screamed at Fox.

She could hear Emily's voice, loud now in her head. It sounded so close, just out of reach.

Help me, help me, please!

'Emily!' Bel's reply was little more than a sob.

'She's here,' Bel whispered to Fox. 'It's Emily. Emily,' she cupped her hands round her mouth, tried to shout, 'we're coming. We're coming to get you out. Hang on, baby, hang on.' The words tore at Bel's throat as she called out to the trapped girl.

Fox pushed forward, scrambled into the narrow space. 'Come on then, let's get her out.' He was almost bend double, his hands on his knees. He flicked on the light on his phone, began to shuffle along the narrow tunnel. Bel steadied herself against both walls as she shuffled along behind him, switched on her own phone. The concrete floor showed patches of damp. A foisty smell filled her nose. Five feet, ten, twenty, the brittle white light from their phones threw hard shadows that seemed to jolt and thrash against her eyes as they moved forward. A wall of bricks ahead, rusted metal doors to either side, padlocked shut. 'Damn!'

Fox scanned around, saw the two brass keys hanging on hooks halfway up the blank wall. Bel put her hand against the cold, cold metal of the left-hand door.

'Is she there? Can you hear her?' Fox asked. Bel knew the unspoken question: 'Is she still alive?'

'I can't tell. I can't hear her anymore. Hurry, please.'

Fox turned the key in the lock, fumbled free the hasp, pushed open the door.

Bel pushed past as Fox forced the heavy steel door open, scanned the room with a single sweep of her phone. The arched roof dripped cold condensation onto a thin mattress pushed against one wall. Emily was lying on her side, arms wrapped around herself, as if seeking comfort. Her violin a discarded jumble of splintered pieces on the concrete floor. Bel scrambled forward on her hands and knees, hurried to the girl's side. Bel felt the clammy cold of Emily's skin under her fingers as she pressed one hand against her neck, searching for signs of life. She held her breath, concentrated for long seconds, until she finally found the fluttering thready pulse in Emily's throat. 'She's alive!'

'Damn,' Fox cursed. 'There's no signal. I need to phone for an ambulance. Are you going to be okay?' He turned to leave without waiting for Bel's answer.

Bel watched him leave, then cuddled close to Emily, willing her own body heat to somehow transfer into the unconscious girl. 'Emily, we're here. Don't worry, you're safe now. We've come to take you home. Emily, can you hear me?' She was rewarded with the slightest flickering of Emily's eyelids, the merest sigh of breath.

An eternity passed as Bel lay there, rocking Emily in her arms, whispering nothing, anything, until the paramedics arrived. They brought in a helicopter; Fox told her later. They landed on the lawn near the lake, started working on her straight away, got her to hospital in less than an hour.

Bel felt a deep cold of released adrenalin strike through to her bones as she walked back down to the mansion with Fox. The sun was shuttered now by the crowding trees, taking all the heat out of the day. Bel began to cry.

END

Printed in Great Britain
by Amazon

87847806R00149